When Light Breaks

**Center Point
Large Print**

**This Large Print Book carries the
Seal of Approval of N.A.V.H.**

When Light Breaks

PATTI CALLAHAN HENRY

CENTER POINT PUBLISHING
THORNDIKE, MAINE

This Center Point Large Print edition
is published in the year 2006 by arrangement with
New American Library, a division of Penguin Group (USA) Inc.

The text of this Large Print edition is unabridged. In other
aspects, this book may vary from the original edition. Printed in
Thailand. Set in 16-point Times New Roman type.

ISBN: 1-58547-850-4
ISBN 13: 978-1-58547-850-7

Library of Congress Cataloging-in-Publication Data

Henry, Patti Callahan.
    When light breaks / Patti Callahan Henry.--Center Point large print ed.
        p. cm.
    ISBN 1-58547-850-4 (lib. bdg. : alk. paper)
    1. Older women--Fiction. 2. Golfers--Fiction. 3. Reminiscing in old age--Fiction.
    4. Southern States--Fiction. 5. Marriage--Fiction. 6. Large type books. I. Title.

PS3608.E578W46 2006b
813'.6--dc22

2006015903

I dedicate this book to my sweet Meagan.
I thought of you as I wrote every page of this novel,
and I pray that you will always hear
God's still, small whisper in your heart.

ACKNOWLEDGMENTS

I had always hoped that I would bring something of worth to the writing, but I soon discovered that it was the other way around—writing has enriched my world in many ways, and one of the most beautiful of these ways is the heart-expanding friendships I've discovered along this journey of publication. This story is more complete because of many friends, family members and colleagues, and I am indebted to every single one of them.

First I must express my gratitude to those integral in the formation of this novel. Kimberly Whalen is beyond an agent. She is a genius in storytelling and thematic structure; this novel is richer, deeper and cleaner because of her understanding of the story's heart. Ellen Edwards is an editor of such immense patience, acuity and thoughtful, cohesive editing that I express my esteem with a humble heart. I want to thank Laura Zidar of the PGA TOUR for her expertise and kindness while answering my numerous questions about the golf tour; if I have made any mistakes describing the tour, they are my fault alone. I am, as always, grateful to Sandee O for being willing to share her expert knowledge about cameras and photography.

I want to extend my heartfelt gratitude to those who have entered my life through this wonderful world of writing, and therefore enriched my writing with their friendship and insight. To Mary Alice Monroe, lyrical, gentle in spirit and wisdom—I am honored to call you friend; to Marjory Heath Wentworth, South Carolina Poet Laureate, who can light a room with her very presence; to Dorothea Benton Frank, a wild Irish soul whose very words can lift a spirit to greater heights; to Annabelle Robertson, whose wit and genuine warmth has brought raucous laughter to many a dreary day; to Jackie K. Cooper whose generosity and authentic heart know no bounds; to Gracie Bergeron at the Margaret Mitchell House, I am grateful for your joy in life, even in the harder times—you are an example of a courageous woman; to Mary Kay Andrews, who makes me laugh—and what is better than that?; to Haywood Smith who always, above all things, has an awe-inspiring faith. All of you encourage and inspire me.

To those at Penguin Group (USA) and New American Library who support my work, I am continually thankful. To Kara Welsh, Leslie Gelbman, Claire Zion, public relations extraordinaire, Carolyn Birbiglia, and members of the sales, art, and marketing departments who make sure these stories reach readers—although words are not enough, I am extremely thankful.

My family is the solid ground upon which everything else works and I love you with everything I have: Pat, Meagan, Thomas and Rusk, I couldn't do any of this without you. To Anna Henry—your courage has been an inspiration to keep going when the going gets tough.

And, of course, this novel would not exist without the support of the readers, librarians and booksellers who read and believe in my work. I will never know all your names, but please know I am infinitely grateful for your support. To all those who came to signings and readings, to those who threw parties and events, to those who reviewed and wrote articles about the previous books—thank you.

My longtime friends are generous, kind, warm, funny and supportive. What more could a girl want? I wish I could thank every single one of you by name— you keep me sane and I love all of you.

May stillness be upon your thoughts and
silence upon your tongue!
For I tell you a tale that was told at the beginning
. . . the one story worth the telling. . . .

—A TRADITIONAL IRISH STORYTELLER'S OPENING

All the words that I utter
And all the words that I write
Must spread out their wings untiring
And never rest in their flight.

—WILLIAM BUTLER YEATS

I was surrounded by water just as I was surrounded by memories. I was born here in the South Carolina Lowcountry, raised first by both my parents, then by just my daddy. My hometown, Palmetto Pointe, was a place encircled by river, estuary, marsh, and ocean all at once; bodies of water cushioning us like the earth's pillow.

One silver dawn in early March, I stood on the dock overlooking the river shrouded in early-morning mist; the hummocks and spartina blended together in the gray-silver dawn. The oyster shell mounds glowed in the rising sun like pearlized and ragged pieces of earth outlining the river. I'd come earlier than usual for my morning run. The sound of my older sister's crying had come through the bedroom wall of our family home to join my own spinning and twisting thoughts, and sleep was as elusive as the no-see-ums—the almost invisible biting bugs—I swatted at during a summer day.

I'd been able to hear Deirdre cry through the walls since I was nine years old, since Mama died. I don't think she ever understood I could hear her, not even now that she was grown and had come home to escape another too lonely night apart from her husband, Bill, from whom she'd separated. Our family, the Larsons, had learned to hide such emotional displays—they were not for public show like the family portraits or the Waterford Lismore collection. Our feelings were as well hidden as the family silver during the War of Northern Aggression.

I extended my arms over my head, then leaned down to stretch my hamstrings in anticipation of running my usual three miles. A school of menhaden fluttered below the surface of the water like butterflies under silk fabric. The tide was low, yet rushing in from the ocean to cover the mud banks, to give shelter to the crabs scurrying in the morning dawn. The ebb and flow of my memories weren't nearly as reliable as these tides. On some days I was flooded with remembering, and on others I was as empty as the marsh at extreme low tide. But that morning, like the flotsam that rises to the top of the waves and is flung onto the beach after a storm, a very particular day returned to me. The sun broke free from behind a low, flat cloud, and my heart opened to an old memory.

I was thirteen years old.

It had been almost four years since Mama—the angelic Margarite Larson—had died. She'd willingly stopped treatment for her cancer and had left us. She'd chosen death over family.

So I'd run away from home. I'd packed my purple suitcase, walked across the front lawn to the Sullivans' house next door, then stood on the front porch. I set my bag down, knocked on the door with all the assurance a thirteen-year-old could muster on a blistering August afternoon, with sweat dripping down my forehead. Mrs. Sullivan answered the door and smiled at me. "Hey there, Ms. Kara. How are you this summer day?" Her smile lit up the entire front porch like a million fireflies.

I patted my suitcase, lifted my chin. "You're my new family," I said, and nodded for an exclamation point.

Mrs. Sullivan took me in her arms, wrapped me tight and allowed me to believe my proclamation with her pure acceptance. The sharp scent of paint thinner filled my nose, and I knew she'd been working on her oil paintings. She led me into the house, put up her paintbrushes, and cooked me a grilled-cheese sandwich dripping in butter. Then she brushed my hair and sang me a song about a bridge over troubled waters.

"Now, honey, tell me why you would want to run away from your beautiful home."

I turned to her and shook my head. "It's just terrible. Daddy has changed too much. His face is always hard and stern." I scrunched my face up. "Like this."

Mrs. Sullivan laughed, squeezed my cheeks.

"He talks all low and monotone. He doesn't run through the rain with me anymore, or let me get extra sprinkles on my ice cream cone. He won't let me wear shoes in the house or get sand in the cuff of my jeans or even bring home a starfish for my dresser—says they smell. I've been thinking that the real Daddy will come back—that he's not really what everyone calls him, grumpy and moody—but four years seems long enough to wait for my real Daddy to come back. And he hasn't. So—here I am."

The kitchen screen door slammed and we both turned to her son, Jack, who came running through the doorway, sand flying out of the cuffs of his pants, shoes on his feet. "Hey, whatcha doing here?" he said to me as he threw his baseball cap on the kitchen table. I was stunned when no one yelled at him to put his hat in its proper place.

"I ran away," I said, hit my palm on the table for emphasis.

"Oh, you did?" He looked at his mom, then blew a large Bazooka bubble. "Must've taken you a day or two to run this far."

Mrs. Sullivan laughed, and it felt like a betrayal. I wanted to give a smart answer to Jack Sullivan with his dirty face and bubble-gum lips, but tears found their way into my throat, then rose to my nose and finally my eyes. I turned away. I'd known Jack my entire life; our birthdays were three days apart, and he'd never made me cry—except that time he'd thrown me in the river and I'd sliced my heel on the oyster bed.

He lifted his hands in the air. "Oh, I was only joking, Kara. Only joking. You didn't really run away, did you?"

I nodded. "My mama's gone and now Daddy is too."

Jack dropped the baseball glove I hadn't seen in his left hand—it was so much a part of him that I didn't even notice it. "What? Your daddy . . . ," he said.

16

Mrs. Sullivan held up her hand. "No, she just means he's changed."

"At least he's around," Jack said.

I glanced at Mrs. Sullivan. Pain flew across her face like a shooting star I wasn't sure I saw. I flinched as I thought of her husband, who came and went as the alcohol allowed.

"He might be around, Jack Sullivan," I said, "but he's a different man. My real daddy is gone." I straightened in my chair.

Jack sat down at the table with his mother and me, took a bite of my sandwich, then punched my shoulder lightly. "You wanna go help me find a conch shell for my summer project? I have to make a musical instrument out of something in nature."

I jumped up. "Sure." Then I turned to Mrs. Sullivan. "What time do we need to be getting home for dinner?" In my home, punctuality was a god to honor at all costs, and I assumed it was the same here.

Mrs. Sullivan stood, drew me in her embrace again. "Honey, you need to be at your own home by dark."

"No." I didn't yell this or even have a fit, just stated the fact.

She nodded. "This family is a big enough mess without adding kidnapping to its list of charges."

I shook my head. "Well, I'll find somewhere else to live then."

"No, you won't," she said, and pulled me closer. "Because you can come here whenever you want, and because if your Daddy lost one more thing he loved, he'd be destroyed for sure."

And I knew this was true. Guilt washed over me, and it tasted like the time I'd been slammed down by an unexpected wave, biting my tongue and swallowing more seawater than I'd thought possible.

I followed Jack Sullivan out the door and into the pre-twilight evening of summer. This was the time of day when I wondered what had happened to the day, where it had gone. Had I used up the sunlight, guzzled the day like one should during the summer? Had I done everything . . . right?

I caught up to Jack, and skipped next to him; he looked at me and stopped.

"What?" I squinted at him against the fading sun, pink and periwinkle in the edges of the clouds.

"Do you really want to run away from home?" he asked.

"Yes, I do," I said, surer than I'd ever been.

He touched the bottom edges of my dark wavy hair. This was something he'd never done—touched me in a gentle way like I was a fragile shell that would fracture under his hands. He twisted a curl around his finger, and I felt it all the way to the inside of my head, through my scalp—a tingling of a sort I hadn't known existed, like electricity, but deeper and wider and less jolting.

Then he let go, looked at me. "Why would you leave? You have the best family I've ever met."

"Because it's not the same anymore, at all. Mama's gone and now it seems Daddy is too. Deirdre is mad all the time and Brian is too busy with his friends to notice me. So, it's time for me to go."

I thought Jack would laugh, but he didn't. He stared straight ahead, looking at me but not. His eyes were gazing almost through me. "Just because your family changes doesn't mean you can leave them. I wish my dad would change. . . ."

And it was right there, after he touched the edges of my hair, as he spoke of his dad with a color and depth to his brown eyes I'd never seen before, that I knew the need for his touch. Not the touch I'd felt with him wrestling in the ocean or shoving me off the dock into the river, but a different kind that at thirteen years old I could not define. A kind of touch I didn't know how to ask for and didn't know how to give. But I tried.

I held out my left hand; it wavered in the air before I knew what to do with it. Then I reached up and touched his cheek; my palm against his skin, my thumb ran over to his top lip, and stopped there. He stood still, stiller than the snow-white egrets on the marsh, which looked like statues. Then he reached up and put his hand on top of mine. Fear—the kind that makes your stomach loose like you're on a dropping plane—overcame me; fear that he'd remove my hand.

But he didn't; he closed his eyes and let our hands stay there—together. In the next second, he opened his eyes and leaned toward me, dropped his forehead onto mine. Our noses touched, then our lips. It was my first kiss, and more gentle and kind than I had expected after watching spin the bottle at our middle school parties. It lasted only a moment, a split second of time that could repeat itself over and over if I allowed it, like the waves coming one after the other even if you weren't watching.

Neither one of us said a word; we stood back and stared at each other as if we'd just met, as if we'd just discovered something so new and strange that we didn't know what to call it.

We turned together and walked toward the sand dunes, over the footbridge covering the sandburs, which dug themselves into your bare feet and stung worse than a bee. When we reached the beach, we sat and watched the sun disappear in a hundred colors and patterns of light below the horizon.

I lay on my back and he sank down next to me. Instinctively, as we'd done a hundred times, we made silent snow angels in the sand, brushing our arms back and forth, allowing our fingertips to graze against each other. We lay like that in silence, knowing the game we were playing: the first one to see a star in the disappearing day won. I focused on the sky . . . wanting to find it, wanting to wish upon it. Then a small speck rose above me—appearing like it always did, as if it had always been there, but I hadn't paid enough attention. Usually I hollered when I won this game, but this time I whispered. "There it is."

Jack touched my elbow. "I see it."

"Did you see it first?" I whispered.

"Nah. You win. Come on, we best get to dinner or we'll be grounded for sure."

20

And I knew that for the first time he'd let me win the game, and this was the one fact, beyond the kiss or the brush of his fingertips, that let me know he loved me. Yes, he most definitely loved me. And I loved him.

I stood, and he took my hand inside his, and I thought how perfectly it fit, custom-made for me, like one of Daddy's tailored suits from the seamstress on Magnolia Street. Jack glanced at me with a question on his face. I smiled at him and immersed myself in the new openness I felt below my breastbone; maybe, just maybe this emotion would fill some of the empty space where Mama's absence ached.

My definition of love did not, then, extend beyond familial devotion, so when I felt the opening, the possibility of another kind of love—my heart stretched as if it had been taking a thirteen-year nap, and it was just beginning to fully awaken.

I pondered this feeling for weeks and months afterward, wondering why it had changed between this boy and me, this boy from next door whom I'd known ever since I could remember. Had I always loved him or did I just miss my mama and want his?

Even now, at twenty-seven years old, I couldn't answer that question, but thankfully it didn't matter anymore. Jack was gone and had been for a very long time. I now understood true love, lasting love—not just adolescent angst and want, not the kind of love that would leave me like Mama and Jack had. I was now comfortable in my world, one I did not need to run away from.

CHAPTER TWO

I met Maeve Mahoney two months before my wedding. The sweet promise of warm spring days and fragrant evenings followed me through the front door of the Verandah House and down the hall of the upscale nursing care facility, my high heels clicking against the linoleum floor. My tailored linen pantsuit from Tahari fit crisply over my white button-down shirt. I glanced at my watch: I was right on time. I'd been dreading this meeting with Mrs. Mahoney—trying to make conversation with a ninety-six-year-old woman assigned to me for my community work through the Palmetto Pointe Junior Society.

My to-do list had spread onto page two of my Day-Timer, and I barely had time to eat, much less spend an hour at the nursing home. I was smack dab in the middle of the busiest time of my life—the most fulfilling too. I mentally flipped through my schedule: right after this appointment, I needed to rush to my wedding dress fitting.

I pushed open the door to room 7. A tiny white-haired woman sat perched in a tartan-covered chair, a James Joyce novel—*Finnegan's Wake*—open on her lap. Her eyes were closed, her mouth open. Her hair stuck up like the cotton on top of a Q-tip while her head leaned back.

Tarnished silver photo frames lined her dresser and

22

bedside table; faded faces stared at me from behind dusty glass. Lace doilies were spread in uneven patterns around the room. A wooden crucifix hung over the headboard of her single bed; worn wooden rosary beads adorned the chain. An oil painting of a bay full of sailboats at evening hung crooked and low on the wall. I walked toward the painting, touched the splintered wooden frame. Despite the thatched roof houses barely visible in the background, and the rough water of an unknown bay, something about the scene seemed familiar.

The room smelled like the rest of the building: Keri lotion and scrambled eggs, carpet deodorizer—an odd combination. The staff of the Verandah House had done their best to make this facility feel more like a nice hotel than a nursing home. An ice cream store with a red-and-white-striped awning, a movie theater and a chic salon were all situated in the front foyer to give visitors the feeling of a miniature hometown.

I sat next to Maeve Mahoney on the remaining chair—a thin metal chair with a pink-flowered cushion. I attempted not to disturb her as I pulled the wedding files from my satchel and flipped through *Southern Bride* magazine, scouting ideas for my bouquet until I found just what I was looking for: white and pink peonies with a satin bow tied around the bottom, Swarovski crystals on the end of thin silver rods poking out of the flowers like rain. I reached for my tabbed wedding notebook, turned the plastic-sheathed pages to "Flowers" and stuffed the picture inside. I wrote the details on a lined, legal-sized pad of paper.

Forty minutes passed as I worked on my wedding, and Maeve slept, making soft snoring noises. Then her voice cracked. "Is that a wedding magazine you'll be looking at?" There was an Irish lilt to the words.

I startled, glanced up at her. "Yes, it is. Hello, I'm Kara Larson. I've come to sit with you a while . . . maybe read to you or whatever you'd like." I spoke the words the volunteer coordinator had told me to say.

Maeve's wrinkled hands stroked the sides of the chair; she squinted at me and leaned forward, pointed to the magazine. "You getting married?"

"Yes. In about eight weeks. . . ." I nodded.

"To your first love?" She pushed a strand of curly gray hair off her face. Her eyes were the color of green sea glass, the kind that has been washed in the ocean for years, worn clear and smooth.

I laughed. "No, but I love him very much."

Her eyes filled with tears, glistening over the green. "No one ever marries their first love anymore. There is just too much . . . else to do. Too many options. Always looking for the next best thing, when it is usually the first best thing that was the best thing all along." In her Irish accent, her simple words sounded like a poem.

I took a deep breath—what could we talk about now? "Did you marry your first love?" I asked.

24

"Now there is a story," she said. "A beautiful story of love and betrayal, full of truth."

"Tell me," I said, glancing sideways at my watch.

"You first, you first. Who was your first love?"

A twinge of betrayal pinched beneath my chest. I shouldn't even think about my first love, not with my fiancé—Peyton's—four-karat princess-cut diamond perched on my left hand.

"Peyton . . . he's the man I'm marrying." Why was I having this discussion with a woman who still had oatmeal from breakfast on her chin?

"No . . . go back. Before him. Before the first kiss. Before the first time you said you loved him. Back further."

"What?" Yes, she was mad. "Before what?" I asked, groping for some appropriate response.

"Back to the first boy who gave you butterflies. The first boy you wrote about in your diary; the one you loved, really loved. Not the first boy you slept with, but the first boy you dreamed about."

"Slept with? Why, Mrs. Mahoney." I covered my mouth with my palm. Where was she going with this?

"Yes, before him."

I closed my eyes. I didn't have to reach that far back—he lay like the cornerstone of my memories, as if all the others were formed on top of his. His name rolled off my tongue as though I'd said it yesterday. "Jack Sullivan."

"Yes, him. That far back. What happened to him?" Maeve leaned forward in a quick movement.

"I haven't seen him since I was fourteen years old."
I looked at her.

Then a tear dropped from her eye, ran to the top of her cheek and joined the oatmeal on her chin. I reached for a Kleenex on her wooden bedside table and wiped both from her face. A slow wave of something painful and lost long ago overcame me. If I was forced to define it, I'd have called it hopelessness.

"Why not?" she said, or maybe sang.

"What?" I threw the Kleenex in the wicker wastebasket.

"Why haven't you seen him?"

I shrugged. I would not discuss Jack Sullivan.

Mrs. Mahoney took a deep breath. "He lived across the lane. His father and brothers were involved in the 'troubles,' and my mother disapproved. Before he left, he told me he loved me and would come back for me. And I knew he would."

"Did he?" I glanced again at my watch—one minute remaining until I had to leave to meet the dressmaker downtown.

Mrs. Mahoney sighed, picked up the book, then placed it back on her lap. "Did he what?" she asked.

"Come back for you?"

"Who?"

"The boy across the lane," I said, then blew a long breath.

"You need to find him." She lifted both hands in the air, as if in supplication.

"Who?"

26

"The boy across the lane."

"Mrs. Mahoney, I don't know the boy across the lane."

"Not my boy. Your boy." She rolled her eyes, as if I exasperated her and not the other way around.

"He lived next door, not across the lane," I said. We had obviously steered into the land of confusion. "I've got to get going, Mrs. Mahoney. I'll see you tomorrow."

"Ahya," she said, "you be thinking about what I said now, won't you? I don't want to be the only one telling stories around here. We trade stories, you and I. You know, when you start to think about things, talk about them . . . they happen."

"Oh?" I stood.

"You know, dear, everything happens for a reason. You've been sent to me, I do believe. Yes, I do believe that. You look much like me in my younger days— dark waves of hair, green eyes, marrying the right man. Now you be careful what you believe—it is who you are."

"What?" I gathered my satchel, looked down at Maeve.

"You will help me, I know you will."

"Well . . . ," I said, "I will visit you. I promise. I'm not sure how much I can help you, though."

"Oh, we'll get to that in good time. We will. As I tell you the story, we'll get to that. There has to be a way to find him now."

I nodded, not knowing what else to do, and completely unsure who she wanted me to find. She lifted her right hand as though she were giving a benediction. *"An áit a bhfuil do chroí is ann a thabharfas do chosa thú."*

Gibberish, I was sure. So I nodded and smiled at her. "It means, Your feet will bring you to where your heart is." Her eyes slid shut.

A sinking feeling of inadequacy overwhelmed me. I had no idea what language she was speaking, but it wasn't mine.

I left Verandah House and ran out to the car—the Mercedes Daddy had given me when he bought his new Ford F-150 after he decided he was truly a pickup truck kind of man. Which is absolutely not the kind of man he was; a Mercedes was just his style. But what twenty-seven-year-old woman in her right mind tells her daddy she doesn't need a Mercedes, that he looks like a fool driving back and forth to his law office in a four-by-four pickup truck?

I drove through Palmetto Pointe to the dressmaker and thought about Peyton Ellers—the man I would marry. And I smiled.

I once believed love was an elusive emotion—coming and going, leaving and staying whenever it caught a whisper of ocean breeze. The kind of love that stays, that sticks in the chambers of the heart, is the type of love that is only a mere longing or remembering. I believed this because it was all I knew, all I understood.

I loved Mama, but she was gone. I once loved Jack

Sullivan, but he was also gone. I loved Daddy, but he was a changed man, and sometimes I thought I only loved what I knew of him, what I remembered of him from the days before Mama died. I watched couples who professed their true love, and I often, very often, wondered if they really loved each other right then, right at the moment they said it, or only that they had once felt it, experienced it and then convinced themselves it was forever.

I had come to understand that I would never love enough to marry, enough to say, "Okay, yes—let's spend the rest of our lives together." I'd become fond of a couple of men, even forced the word "love" from my lips. But never enough, never quite enough to promise forever. As women can do, I'd spent hours discussing my failure with my best friend, Charlotte. "Why can't I love enough? Well enough?"

Through the years Charlotte had had many theories about why I hadn't fallen for someone. In college she believed I missed my mama too much to let anyone in. Then she believed—on college graduation night, when I had had too much red wine—that I was waiting for someone to make me feel *just* like Jack Sullivan had made me feel. By the time we'd started our careers and moved back to our hometown, she surmised I just hadn't found the right man.

I'd worked at my job as a PGA TOUR manager for five years when I met Peyton. I didn't usually have much contact with the pro golf players or their families—I worked behind the scenes making sure everything was organized for the golf tournaments. Although my job was insanely demanding, it offered me a sincere sense of accomplishment. I did everything from ordering the volunteer uniforms, to picking out the menus for the catered meals, to finding child care for the players' kids. I arranged the trophy ceremony and the pro-am tournament the day before the major, along with handling a thousand other details associated with the tournaments.

My many responsibilities—taking care of the house, my daddy, and my job—ensured that I was constantly busy. It wasn't that Daddy was sick or disabled. As I'd grown up, I had just naturally and slowly taken over Mama's role at home. Sometimes I felt that I missed her less when I was acting in her place. If I stepped directly into her shoes—did the grocery shopping, prepared the meals, washed the dishes and did the laundry—she was somehow still present, still in the house if those chores were done and done well.

We did have a housekeeper who cleaned, the same one since I was born, but I took care of everything else, and wasn't out looking for one more thing to fill my life.

Then on the tenth green of the Palmetto Pointe Golf Club I met Peyton Ellers. I'd escorted a professional photographer onto the golf course during a practice round for a local golf tournament—called a scramble—to take pictures of Peyton. Of course I knew who Peyton Ellers was—everyone in Palmetto Pointe knew who he was. He'd moved to town ten years earlier as a young pro golfer. He'd played on the Georgia Tech Golf Team, then the Nationwide tour until he moved to the PGA TOUR. News of his arrival was in all the papers, stories of how this gorgeous pro golfer had bought his mother a house on the river and himself one on the golf course. To the shock of the golfing community, he'd moved to Palmetto Pointe, South Carolina, instead of to one of the higher-end Florida courses where most of the professionals lived.

At thirty-five years old, he was moving toward the top of the earnings list for the PGA TOUR—and he was single. The press loved him, the PGA TOUR loved him, and the girls loved him.

Peyton's would be the ideal photo on the PGA TOUR's brochure to showcase our new Pete Dye–designed golf course, and announce Palmetto Pointe becoming a new PGA TOUR tournament.

The photographer, Jim, and I walked onto the green as we waited for Peyton to come over the hill. The wind whipped my hair into tangled circles. Jim set up his cameras and asked for my assistance as he filled each one with film and checked the lighting against the river in the background. "Are you using one hundred ASA or higher film speed?" I asked, pushing my hair out of my face.

Jim paused in adjusting his camera. "Both. I wanted to get some of Peyton in action and some of him posing against the water's edge."

"Will you use the digital or your Nikon F3 for the action?" I lifted the black camera. "And are you using color or the reverse Polaroid I've seen you use for some of your portraits."

He smiled at me and lifted his camera. "You want to do this shoot instead of me?"

I laughed. "I wish I knew enough to do it. I love photography."

"I see that." He handed me the Nikon and winked. "Why don't you take a couple of shots from another angle while I get him from the front?"

"Really?" My heart lifted.

"Really," he said, and pointed. "Here they come. My goal is to get Peyton from many angles; I'd love to get the water and oaks in the background."

I nodded. The air thrummed around me and I gripped the Nikon tighter.

Peyton approached and I stared at him through the camera lens; he had a swagger of confidence, the aura of an athletic man who was perfect to photograph. I snapped pictures of him walking down the fairway with his golf club swung over his shoulder, his hat low on his forehead, brown curls poking out from under his cap.

Jim stepped to the side and began to take his own pictures.

Peyton stopped at the side of the hill and lined up to hit the ball. The river behind him glistened like a sage ribbon. I ran to the other side of the green, squatted, and snapped pictures as rapidly as I could.

Jim made a noise in the back of his throat. I stood and turned. "Did I get too carried away?"

He laughed. "No, but you were in another world. I need to move us closer to that side of the trees. Can we walk over there?" He pointed to a roped-off section of fairway.

"Yes, that is just for the crowd control tomorrow." I tilted my head. "Come on, follow me." I handed the camera back to him. "I think I used all the film. Sorry." I scrunched up my face.

He laughed. "He's easy to photograph, huh?"

I blushed. "I guess he is."

Peyton came around the corner then, stopped and held out his hand to me. "Hi, I'm Peyton Ellers."

I took his hand and shook it. "Hi, I'm Kara Larson, the tour manager for the Open next year. Thank you so much for agreeing to have your picture taken for the brochure."

"Nice to meet you," he said. "It's always great to have a face to go with the name of the person I've been working with for months. No one told me you looked like a green-eyed angel."

I couldn't turn away from his stare—something warm and familiar rested there. I took a step back, banged into a dogwood tree in full bloom, then tripped over an azalea bush shedding its red flowers onto the grass. So graceful of me.

Peyton smiled, then turned and introduced himself to Jim, asked him how he wanted him to pose.

Two nights later, at the celebration party for the golfers and their families who had participated in the scramble, Peyton came through the doorway and his arms overflowed with dogwood and azalea blooms he'd stolen from the tenth green. He walked straight up to me, handed them to me, and asked if he could have the honor of seeing me at least one more time.

He stood there with his dark curls wild around his head, a grin dominating his face, and I said that, yes, I'd see him one more time, but that would be all.

He laughed. "It's better than nothing."

Of course it was another year of "one more times," until he got down on one knee and placed that four-karat princess-cut diamond on my left ring finger.

When I said yes, everything changed inside my heart, and I didn't doubt my ability to love. My heart had only been waiting for this—for him. The emptier years of not loving another man had nothing to do with my being unable to love, or missing Mama, or waiting for someone exactly like Jack. They were all about the right man. It was easy falling in love, this open-heart feeling, which made me smile whenever I thought of Peyton, of his touch or his voice.

I didn't care so much about having the big wedding, but because of my family's long history in town—direct descendants of the English duke who founded the seaport of Palmetto Pointe—and Peyton's status as a professional golfer, a huge society wedding was what we would have in less than two months.

I steered the car through streets that were as clean as Disney World when it opened first thing in the morning. Palmetto Pointe might have more ante-bellum homes per square block than any town in

America. The U.S. and South Carolina flags flapped in the wind. The benches in front of the stores were freshly painted. The ash and oak trees had been planted at exact intervals down Main Street, Spanish moss hanging from the branches like a brochure for the Lowcountry.

I let up on the gas and braked at the red light in front of the five-and-dime; Mrs. Harold waved at me from the bench in front. She'd lost her husband five years ago and had slipped into a time and place no one in town contradicted—that it was 1964 and she was waiting for a letter from her husband in Vietnam. I waved back and smiled. Maybe someday this town would smile at me when I went crazy.

Probably not, though. I was Porter Graham Larson's youngest child, and certain things were expected of our family.

I pulled my car in front of the Palmetto Pointe Bridal storefront. Through the plate-glass window I saw Gretchen pacing inside. I slid out of the car and walked toward the shop, satchel in hand. As usual, my day was exactly on schedule.

CHAPTER THREE

T he bridal shop was completely walled in mirrors. Gretchen stood in the middle of the circular room with her hands on her hips, staring down at me from the podium. My daddy had hired a

35

dressmaker from Atlanta—said he wanted the best for his little girl. There was no avoiding my figure from any angle in this space; I noticed how much thinner I'd become over the past few months.

Good stress, Charlotte called it, but it most definitely did not feel good. I couldn't sleep as I envisioned a misplaced name card at the reception dinner, or discovered the bridesmaids' dresses had been shipped to Parague instead of Palmetto Pointe.

I attempted to turn away from my image in the mirrors. "Humph," Gretchen said. "My flight leaves in two hours, we must finish this now."

I nodded like an obedient child and walked back to the dressing room, where my wedding dress hung on a padded hanger. I slid the curtain shut and stripped down to my underwear. I traced my finger along the lace-covered buttons running down the back of the dress and sighed. The dress was exactly as I had sketched it, and suddenly I wanted Mama there to see it. If there was ever a time in a girl's life when she wanted her mama, it was when she was trying on her wedding dress.

I slipped the dress over my head, but left it open in the back for Gretchen to fasten.

Your feet will bring you to where your heart is.

I rolled my eyes. Poor old woman—rambling on about the past and lost love. It had nothing to do with me—so why did the words make me feel sad? I stared at myself in the mirror. Without the veil, makeup, and flowers, I looked like a little girl playing dress up. I cinched the dress in at the waist and stood on my tippy-toes. A little better.

Peyton had had only one request about the dress: "Please don't let it look like a prom dress with whipped cream on it," he'd said. "*Golf USA* magazine will be there with photographers." I'd told him that surely, by now, he knew I had better taste than that. He'd kissed me and told me that I'd picked him, so surely I had absolutely perfect taste.

My gaze slid down to the skirt, covered in the thinnest silk made, as light and transparent as angels' wings. I hadn't known they made a silk so sheer—but Daddy had said he'd pay for it.

I lifted the dress higher from the waist, avoided touching the skirt, and slipped on the white pumps provided in the dressing room. I hadn't bought my shoes yet. One of the many unfinished tasks that kept me up at night was choosing whether to hand sew water pearls onto the shoes or leave them plain.

I stepped out of the dressing room and walked up onto the podium in the center of the room. Gretchen stood in front of me, pins sticking out of her mouth, two deep parallel lines furrowed between her eyebrows. "If you keep losing weight, we will have to alter this dress every month. My God, child, eat something . . . anything."

"I am," I said, and bit my lower lip.

"And your hair," she said. "You must get some highlights. The cream in the dress does your brown hair no good. No good at all." She yanked at the back of the dress and began inserting pins.

A pin poked my hip. "Ow." I jumped.

"Stand still, Kara." Then she mumbled something incoherent about brides and decisions and the South— a bad combination altogether.

"What?" I glanced down at her.

"Stand still."

"Hmmm," I said, and cracked my neck to the left. I should have taken a nap instead of fulfilling my hour's duty at the nursing home. But I was six hours behind on my volunteer quota, and I'd be placed on suspension soon if I didn't catch up.

I groaned; a twenty-seven-year-old woman on suspension. It sounded ridiculous. But being a member of the league was part of my pact with Palmetto Pointe— a covenant all young women with deep roots in town adhered to. Grandma and Mama had both been members—who was I to break the chain? Charlotte and I talked of quitting, but hadn't. Maybe now would be a good time to do so.

Where *was* Charlotte? She was supposed to meet me for this fitting.

"Damn," I mumbled.

"What now?" Gretchen stood from her crouched position and stretched her back.

"Oh, I'm sorry, I didn't realize I'd spoken out loud. My friend Charlotte was supposed to meet me here. I wanted to see how she likes the dress."

"Ugh . . . young women are always needing reassurance. You're twenty-seven years old. It only matters if you love the dress. You do, don't you?"

"Yes, yes." My hands flew through the air as they tended to do when I spoke emphatically. My brother and sister always said I looked like I was trying to fly when I was only attempting to make a very strong point.

"Put your hands down," Gretchen said through clenched teeth.

"Sorry. It's not that I don't love the dress. I do. I really do. I just wanted to know what Charlotte thinks. Jack doesn't want the skirt to look . . . oh, forget it." I rubbed at my eyes—one of the many reasons I didn't like to wear makeup, as my mascara came off on my fingers.

"And who is Jack?"

My head snapped around; a pain shot through the cramped muscles in my neck. "What?"

"You said Jack."

"No, I didn't."

"Yes, you did."

Sunlight shattered into the room as though someone had thrown broken glass. Warm coastal air filled the air-conditioned space and Charlotte burst through the doorway—all light, all energy. Her blond curls seemed to need a minute to catch up to the rest of her as she came to an abrupt halt in front of the podium.

She placed her hands on either side of her face, covered her dimpled cheeks. "Oh. My. God." Tears filled her eyes. "That is the most beautiful, amazing dress I have ever seen. And except for those dark circles under your eyes, you look absolutely, freaking amazing in it."

"Really?"

"Like a dream, a dream about an angel." She winked at me, and I rolled my eyes. She knew I'd had dreams about angels since I was a young child, since Mama died.

Gretchen snorted. "She's worried Jack won't like it."

Charlotte raised her eyebrows, then dropped her chin as her tongue curled out into the corner of her mouth. "What?"

"She"—Gretchen waved her hand at me—"needed—"

I held up my hands. "Whoa, everyone. Gretchen . . . this is my best friend, Charlotte." I nodded toward Charlotte. "Charlotte, this is Gretchen. She made this amazing creation from my sketch."

Charlotte held out her hand and shook Gretchen's.

"Nice to meet you," Gretchen said. "Now, who is Jack?"

I groaned. "Long story."

Charlotte looked up at me on the podium. "Please tell me you're not talking about Jack Sullivan."

"Can we please talk about this later?" I nodded toward Gretchen.

"No, we cannot," Charlotte said.

Gretchen laughed and poked more pins into the dress.

"It's not a big deal," I said. "The Irish woman at

Verandah House asked me about my first boyfriend and . . ." I stood as still as possible beneath Gretchen's pins.

"The woman the league assigned you?"

I nodded. Gretchen finished and glanced at her watch. "Girls"—she clapped her hands together—"Enough. I have a schedule to keep."

Charlotte and I looked at each other and stifled a laugh. Then she mouthed, "Jack?"

I shrugged my shoulders and stood taller, shook my head. "It's nothing, really."

Charlotte took two steps backward, sat down on the cream velvet couch and crossed her legs, then shook her finger at me like one does at a child caught with her hand in the cookie jar.

But I hadn't gone into anyone's cookie jar. Not at all.

I left Charlotte and Gretchen and returned home, parked the car in the drive and glanced at the red numbers on the dashboard clock: 11:45 a.m. I had exactly fifteen minutes to grab a snack and the papers I'd left printing on my home computer, then get to the PGA TOUR offices by noon, as promised.

Our family's white plantation-style house sat on a slight hill, an incline you might only perceive if you were mowing the lawn and had to push up, like I had to when I was a teenager. Evenly spaced oaks lined the driveway and the edge of the lawn. There was one gaping hole, like a missing tooth, on the left edge of the house, next to Jack Sullivan's old house, where a tropical storm had torn the tree from its roots, leaving all the other oaks untouched.

Yes, Jack's old house was next door. You'd think that would make me think of him all the time. But I'd gotten so used to its being there, and it had changed hands so many times that I hardly noticed it at all— like a scar on someone's face that you can't ignore at first, but you stop seeing once it's familiar to you. If someone mentions it, you say, "Oh, yeah, I don't even notice that scar anymore." Five families had lived there since Jack had left, and each family had repainted, added to or subtracted from the structure.

A long time ago, I would stare at the Sullivan house and imagine a million ways in which Jack would come back, come find me. He'd stand on my front porch with a thousand peonies, or find me reading a book on the beach, or just show up and sit next to me on the dock, take my hand like he'd taken it the first time. And nothing would have changed, he wouldn't have left. But those were the immature dreams of a girl who hadn't yet grown up. Even if Jack walked up to me today, his smile eager, his strides long, he'd be a different person.

I deliberately turned away from the Sullivan house and walked to my front porch. I opened the door to the muffled sounds of someone on the phone: Deirdre. I groaned. I needed to get in and out as quickly as possible, not become caught up in a discussion with my sister.

I took a left out of the foyer into the library and grabbed the papers off the printer, then moved toward the kitchen, almost tiptoeing to be quiet.

"Hey, Kara. What are you doing home?" Deirdre's voice came from behind me.

I turned. "Hey, back at you. I had to grab a couple quick things before I head for the office."

"Where were you?" She lifted her eyebrows.

"I had to visit a woman at the nursing home, and then I went to a fitting."

Deirdre rolled her eyes; her voice followed me into the kitchen. "The wedding, the wedding, the wedding. Can you possibly think about anything else?"

I would've slammed the kitchen door on her words, but it was a swinging door and emitted an ineffectual swooshing noise. She stepped into the kitchen.

"Really, Kara. Is there anything else going on in your life?"

"Deirdre, I don't have time for this—I'm late for work. What are you doing here anyway?"

"I have the day off and I thought I'd meet Daddy for lunch, and in case you forgot—it's family dinner night."

"I've never forgotten, Deirdre." I found a protein bar in the pantry, slipped it into my purse.

She leaned against the kitchen table; the circles under her eyes looked as though a child had drawn them with blue crayon.

While separated from her husband, Bill, Deirdre was working at a local boutique for a family friend.

My oldest sibling had been angry for so long that I barely remembered her any other way. Daddy had once told me that her hostility started when Mama died. But I'd loved Deirdre since the day she woke me in the middle of the night, took my hand and led me down to the ocean's edge under a full moon. She told me to hush as we watched baby turtles crack open their shells, which looked like iridescent Ping-Pong balls, leave their sand nest and crawl through the sand toward the ocean.

I don't know how old I was, but it was before Mama died, and my heart could barely tolerate the knowledge that the mama turtle had left these eggs behind, hoping, maybe not even hoping but assuming, that they would hatch and make it to the water. How could any mama leave her child? At that age I believe I already knew Mama would leave us. But memory is a cloudy, disjointed thing—like disconnected dreams with images scattered and thrown to settle where they please. There is no filing system for memories, no place to slot them by year or name or category. They are either wispy and soft as twilight dancing on the water or hard as the jagged edge of the oyster bed slicing your feet to shreds before you know you've been cut.

I've held on to that memory of Deirdre and the baby turtles, knowing her heart is full and good and her hands soft and firm. I just haven't seen that piece of her since. She married a man named William Garner Barrett IV. You must always say "the Fourth" when you say his name. They'd been separated for a year now

44

and Deirdre lived by herself in their two-bedroom home, but often came to our childhood home to spend the night in her old bedroom.

My heart softened with this memory of the beach. I reached across the space between us and hugged her. "I've got to go, Deirdre. We'll talk later."

"Yeah," she said with a vain attempt at returning my hug. "When you're done planning the social event of the year."

When I arrived at the office, all chaos broke loose like an unexpected hurricane. I plugged my left ear with my index finger, and held the phone receiver to my right ear as I attempted to hear the manager of the Upswing Band. Caroline, my new intern, and Frieda, my boss, were both talking at once as I held up one finger to let them know I couldn't hear them. My cell phone buzzed on the desktop just as the computer rang with more incoming e-mail. An overwhelming need to scream washed over me.

"What do you mean you can't play the benefit?" I spoke into the phone through clenched teeth. "You committed to this event six months ago."

The manager's voice sounded scratched, as if he'd been smoking since he was eight years old. "There was an internal miscommunication and we are double-booked that weekend."

"No," I said. "Something better than a benefit for tuberous sclerosis came along and you thought you'd grab it, yes?"

"No." He seemed to speak through closed lips. "We are very sorry for the inconvenience and hope you'll think of us for your next event."

I closed my eyes and took a deep breath, then glanced over at Caroline and Frieda, both wide-eyed and waiting for me to finish. "Yes, thank you," I said, and slammed the phone down.

Frieda leaned against my desk, palms flat on its surface, and stared at me. "What just happened?"

"The band for the benefit canceled."

"The tournament is in four weeks, Kara. Four weeks. Where are you going to find a band in that time?"

"Don't worry about it. I will take care of it."

Caroline shuffled her feet, as though she wanted to leave the room.

"Well, you better figure it out very, very quickly," Frieda said. "Since you seem to have your wedding, which is a full two months away, completely and utterly organized, why don't we use that band?"

I took a sharp breath. "What do you mean?"

"I mean"—Frieda stood straight and looked down at me—"if you spent nearly as much time working on this tournament as you do on that wedding, we wouldn't be scrambling now."

"That is not true." I stood up. "I have worked incredibly hard on this benefit. I can handle it, Frieda."

She held up her hand. "No excuses, just a band. And now."

I nodded, then sat back down as Frieda turned on her

heels and walked out of my office. I motioned to Caroline to close the door. My office was as organized as the rest of my life: the mahogany desktop uncluttered, with files in separate slots, and a picture of Peyton in a silver frame. Wingbacked chairs in matching pink and green fabric were arranged in front.

Our PGA TOUR office was located in an old wood-slat house across the street from the Palmetto Pointe Golf Club's tenth green and iron front gates. The older woman who'd previously lived in the house had not appreciated the golf course taking the place of the wild nature once spread before her window, so she'd gladly sold the house to the PGA TOUR. The pink-and-brown bathroom stayed, but I'd had the walls in the other rooms painted and the green shag carpets yanked up, revealing antique heart-of-pine floors.

My office was located in a back corner in what had been the woman's bedroom. A large window overlooked the front lawn, with a sweeping panorama toward the golf course. I loved my view—it was the green where I'd met Peyton, where my new life had started. Over the past six years, I'd done well enough at my job to be put in charge of the first ever Palmetto Pointe Open—a huge honor and responsibility that had, unfortunately, coincided with planning my wedding.

When the door clicked shut, I glanced up at Caroline. She twisted her watch around her wrist. "Kara, what are we gonna do?"

"We'll find a band. It's not that hard, Caroline. Let's

go over the checklists, make sure everything else is in order, then we'll figure out the band situation."

Caroline pulled up a side chair, sat down and tilted her head sideways to glance at the papers on my desk.

"Okay . . . did you line up the table rentals?" I tapped on the folder.

Caroline nodded. "Yes, and the caterer is confirmed, but she needs you to decide among the menus." She stood and walked toward the filing cabinets. "I put them in here."

I nodded and scribbled a reminder on my desk blotter just as a knock resonated on the office door. I didn't look up until Peyton's voice said, "Hello, can I come in and get a kiss from my girl?"

I was thrilled it was Peyton and not Frieda at the entranceway. His curls were wild from a day on the golf course, his shirt clinging to him in all the right places. I jumped up and went around the desk, hugged him and gave him a quick kiss. He pulled me to him; I motioned toward Caroline. "We're working here." I lifted my eyebrows at him.

He glanced at her. "Oh . . . I didn't see you."

She nodded, but didn't answer.

"It's okay," I said. "What's up?"

"Nothing . . . just coming in from a practice round."

I nodded. "You feel ready to take this tournament in a few weeks?" I smiled at him.

He grinned. "I hope so." He backed toward the door. "You remember today is the day I shoot that commercial for the tournament. You'll come, right?"

"I wouldn't miss it. See you there."

"Perfect," he said, nodded, and left the room.

I took my seat at the desk and glanced at Caroline. "Okay, back to the menus."

She lifted her pen in the air and waved toward the golf course through the window. "They're filming a commercial today?"

I nodded. "Yeah, Palmetto Pointe GMC just signed on as one of the tournament sponsors and Peyton is in the commercial."

She lifted her eyebrows. "I'm sure he loves that. . . ."

"What do you mean?" I stared across the desk at her.

"I just mean it's a big honor. . . ."

"Okay," I said, "back to work."

We spent hours making sure every element was in place for the inaugural Palmetto Pointe Open. Nothing, absolutely nothing could go wrong. We'd prove to the PGA TOUR that they hadn't made a mistake in giving us this tournament. We'd added a benefit for tuberous sclerosis on the last night: an event to raise money for charity, meet the players, and party with the winners.

I rubbed my eyes with my fingers; smudges of mascara came off. "Okay, Caroline . . . it looks like everything is in order." I handed her a folder. "I'll go hunting for a band if you'll talk to Palmetto Pointe General Motors about which truck they'll donate for the hole-in-one contest."

She nodded. "I've got it under control."

"Yeah, just wait until advance week—the week before the tournament—when there's no such thing as 'under control.'"

Caroline laughed, stood and stretched. "Great, I can't wait."

"There's no way to explain it . . . just experience it."

I looked at the e-mails that had poured in over the three hours Caroline and I had met. I groaned. Caroline glanced over her shoulder before she left the room. "Kara."

"Yes?"

She stared back for a moment, as if she could read my thoughts. "Nothing," she said, then nodded. "I'll see you tomorrow."

I turned back to my computer. I had exactly two hours to return phone calls and e-mails before I headed to the golf course and made sure I stood at the edge of the eighteenth green as Peyton filmed his first national TV commercial.

The Pointe River moved behind me in a slow ebb toward the Atlantic Ocean, the wind pushing in the opposite direction. A white egret stood on the top of the dock's pillar watching Peyton hit his fifteen-foot putt. I clapped when the ball fell with a clink into the hole. Peyton turned, found me on the sidelines, and winked. I nodded at him and blew a kiss. The cameras caught the wink, and a crewman hollered, "Perfect. The wink was perfection. I think that's a wrap."

From my bag I lifted my brand-new Nikon N80,

which I'd bought with my Christmas bonus, and snapped pictures of the scene. Later Peyton and I would be thrilled I'd photographed these times, then glued the pictures into a scrapbook. "That was the first commercial you were in," I'd say after time had passed, when there'd been lots of other ads featuring Peyton Ellers.

I ran my finger over the black surface of the camera. Photos were my memory-stapler. With each picture I took, with each click of the camera, I was stapling the moments in my memory so I wouldn't forget. I'd hoarded all the pictures of Mama that I could find, but they were never enough. Now I took photos wherever I went, of whatever I did, so I'd never forget, never be caught on the other side of remembering.

A cluster of girls on the far side of the green called Peyton's name, and they motioned for him to come over. He moved toward them with that saunter I'd noticed the first time I met him, a walk of such assurance that he appeared to be headed into a gunfight knowing he was the fastest draw.

The crowd of girls smiled, swung their hair over their shoulders and bent over the rope toward him. He reached them and signed the various objects they held out: hats, paper, T-shirts. Then a blonde scooted under the rope and pulled her button-down blouse to the right, exposing just enough skin for him to sign his name in a bright blue Sharpie.

I took in a sharp breath and felt a forceful punch from below my ribs. I'd seen this kind of behavior before while working these tournaments, but I'd never seen anyone do it to Peyton, my fiancé. Had I believed he was immune to such blatant flirtation because he was engaged, that other women wouldn't run after him? Seized by primal ownership, I walked around the green, placed my hand on the small of his back. He turned to me, wrapped his arm around my waist, nodded at the fans, and walked with me toward the locker room.

"What was that?" I whispered as we approached the clubhouse.

He shrugged. "A fan with nothing better to do."

"You didn't have to sign her . . . skin."

Peyton stopped, stared at me. "Kara, it's nothing. I didn't . . ."

I held up my hand; a cool breeze lifted my hair off my shoulders, and I wasn't sure if the chill that ran down my body came from seeing this woman, or from the leftover winter air just exiting our Lowcountry.

"I know," I said, "I know it's nothing. But it's gross nonetheless."

Peyton smiled and kissed me. "It's only you, only you I love."

I let the chill pass, but released his hand as I headed toward the clubhouse.

"Hey," he called. "Where you going?"

I looked over my shoulder. "I cannot be late for dinner. You know how Daddy gets when any of us is late."

Peyton rolled his eyes. "I swear, that man has an

internal alarm clock. I have never met anyone so anal about being late . . . about doing everything exactly so."

I stopped, turned and walked back to Peyton. "What?"

"Kara, you've got to admit it, he's a little more . . . uptight about things than most."

An up-and-coming young golfer whose name I could never remember came from behind Peyton, punched the side of his arm. "Keep making those putts and you're a shoo-in next month."

Peyton turned away from me and shook the young man's hand. "Yeah, but I'm watching you carefully . . . you're coming up behind me way too fast."

The golfer smiled, hiked his bag up over his shoulder. "See you tonight?"

Peyton glanced at me, then back at him. "Yeah, sure. . . ."

The man walked off, and Peyton pulled me into a long kiss. "I'm sorry. I wasn't trying to be cruel about your dad, really. I have just truly never seen anything like it."

"It's his way of . . . keeping some control over his life. Ever since Mama . . . left us." A wounded piece of me attempted to rise behind my chest with tears; I pushed it down and touched Peyton's arm. "Where are you going tonight that you have to miss family dinner?"

"They're every week. We won't be able to go every week after we're married. . . . You know that, right?"

"No, I don't know that. Family dinner is very important to us. It keeps us . . . I don't know . . . together, I guess."

"But when we're married"—He snuggled up to my neck with his lips, then whispered in my ear, "we'll have our own family dinners."

A smile spread across my face, and a tingle reached beyond my neck to my stomach.

"Well," I said, "where will you be tonight?"

"Ah, big party for Lee Pennington's birthday."

"Oh?" I raised my eyebrows. I'd been working for the tour long enough to know where Lee Pennington liked to celebrate. "Nice, Peyton. Great way to spend a night without your fiancée."

"It's not a big deal, just a party."

"Probably at a strip club," I said between clenched teeth. I felt repulsion toward him I didn't want to experience, negativity I wanted to deny. I'd loved him since the first moment he'd told me he loved me, and I wanted to feel jealous, not repelled. I closed my eyes and found that place of adoring him, then opened my eyes. "Don't go," I said.

He kissed me. "Why don't I meet you later tonight?"

"Babe, you'll be out so late," I said, unable to hide the barbs that had entered and attached themselves to my words like sand spurs to the cuff of my jeans.

"I'll try and call." He had reached for my hand, when three men came from the side and grabbed him. "Come on, buddy . . . let's get outta here."

Peyton turned to me, mouthed, "I love you," and

sauntered in his adorable way toward the locker room with his golf bag over his shoulder. A green grass stain ran along the side of his khakis.

I turned away and blew a long exhale through pursed lips. My stomach gripped in a fist. I wasn't sure why, but I felt off-kilter. There was something I should be looking at, but I didn't know where to find it. I rubbed my eyes. I was letting the chaos and being overextended affect my feelings, then was placing them smack on top of Peyton. I loved this kind man who'd wrapped his arms and his life around me.

I sat down at a wrought iron table on the round stone patio at the back of the clubhouse, propped my chin in my palm, and dug my elbow into the tiny holes of the iron.

I'd been watching these pro players for years. I knew about their long hours on the road, their late nights with the guys. Right now, with my stomach in a tight lump, my throat constricted, I couldn't thread the positive feelings through my insides to where love resided. Then I remembered all the things I loved about Peyton: the way he walked, talked, touched me, loved me. I dwelt on the way he made me feel the minute he came in a room—how he filled my heart.

I stood, stretched, and headed home to family dinner—one of the mainstays of life I cherished.

CHAPTER FOUR

T he following morning I rose early and finished my three-mile run before the sun met the horizon. I stood on what felt like the edge of the world, but was merely the community dock. This was the only quiet time I would have all day. My breath came quick, and I felt as though I were the only human alive in the gentle morning with the whirring cicadas and chirping frogs.

The sun shimmered below a sliver of pink cloud, then burst into flame at the borders. I lifted a hand to shield my eyes, leaned into a lunge. My breath slowed. I stood and then bent forward at the waist, stretched my hamstrings to the groaning point, then hung there, viewing the coastal world from upside down.

The palmetto branches waved at me in reverse patterns; firmament and pavement switched places as a running shoe appeared in the asphalt sky. I jumped upright and smiled at Charlotte.

"You went without me."

"I did. I'm sorry." I grimaced. "My day is so insane and I wanted to get started. . . . I couldn't sleep anyway. But," I sighed, "I could now. . . ." I sat on a bleached-wood bench and dropped my hands onto my knees.

"Girlfriend, you've got two more months of this

wedding stuff. You better learn to pace yourself a little better."

I glanced up at my friend. "Oh, it's not the wedding. Now would be a very good time to have Mama."

Charlotte squeezed me tighter. "I know. But I promise I'm here to do whatever you need."

"I know," I said and sighed. "Hey, you don't have any of those old boyfriends you've stayed just friends with in a band, do you?"

"No, why?"

"I need a band."

"Can't help you there." She stood and stretched. "I guess I'll run without you this morning, unless you're up for another three miles or so."

"No way. I have to be at Verandah House by eight a.m., then I have two tour meetings, and I'm seeing your mom about the flowers at three and . . ."

"I'll catch up with you there," she said. "And don't forget the shower your future mother-in-law is holding in your honor is at seven tonight."

I groaned. "That is tonight, isn't it?"

"You looking forward to it?"

"Not so much," I said. "It's our fifth shower. Peyton and I stand there grinning like complete fools oohing and aahing over gifts—it's so arcane and embarrassing."

"At least you called him Peyton this time."

I scrunched up my face. "Very funny. That was a completely honest mistake. Maeve asked me about him—"

57

"Okay, then." She pulled her tank top down over her stomach and started to run in place. "Meet you at Mom's shop at three today. . . ." She reached her arms over her head and went off running, waving over her shoulder.

I waved back and then stared out over the river. I had placed Maeve's story in the back of my mind. There was too much to do to let my thoughts wander aimlessly down the path of her past losses. But staring at the water, I thought of her oil painting of boats on a bay and smiled, warmth filling my chest.

The motor operating the head and foot of Maeve's bed would surely burn out any moment now. Up, down it went, halfway up, all the way down, head, foot. My nerves were raw and the whirring rubbed like a nail file on the edges of my skin. She'd been playing with the bed controls and ignoring me since I'd walked in the door half an hour earlier.

"Stop," I said, my teeth grinding against each other.

She jerked her head up from the fascinating vantage point of her feet and glanced at me with a dead stare. "Who are you?"

I took a deep breath. I shouldn't have snapped at her like that. I softened my voice. "I'm Kara Larson. I came to sit with you again today. Would you like to play cards? Or I can read to you, if you'd like."

"How about poker?" She laughed.

I grinned. "Okay."

"You know," she said in a broken voice, "I've been

58

waiting for you to come back."

"I've been here for thirty minutes." I patted the bed rail.

"Well, dear, why haven't you said anything?" She moved her eyebrows together.

"I have—" I stopped. "Why don't I get some cards so we can play for the last thirty minutes I'm here."

"Are you on such a tight schedule?" She lifted her hands as a question. Her voice was soft, melodic, almost like a lullaby I'd heard once and then forgotten.

"I do have a crazy day," I said.

"You are exhausted and frail. You must not let life eat at you this way, must not let it take your energy from you. Life can either nourish or drain you."

"I'm fine," I said.

"Well, before we continue with my story, dear, tell me a little bit more about yourself, your mum and da and, of course, your Jack."

"My mama left us when I was nine years old. Jack left when I was fourteen. That's really all there is to it. So . . ."

"That's never all there is to it. You poor dear—your mum left the family?"

I shook my head. "No, she died. . . ." I turned away with the sting of withheld tears behind my eyes; I would not cry in front of a stranger.

"Oh . . . but there is a difference, no?"

"Not in this case, there isn't. So, tell me about what brought you here to South Carolina."

"Ah, so you don't want to talk about you."

"I don't." I fiddled with the side of her bedcover, spread the fringe in an even pattern across the sheet.

"Well, then. Where was I in my story?" She gazed upward. "When his hooker—"

"His hooker?" I took a sharp breath and suppressed a laugh, held my palm over my mouth.

She glanced at me. "A hooker, my dear, is a sailboat in our Galway Bay. It is a sailboat so distinct there is no other like it in the world. It has three brown sails, and is bowed like a water creature flying over the sea. This boat has carried and nourished our Claddagh village for hundreds of years, bringing in the herring and cod." She pointed to the oil painting on the wall.

"I see," I said, glancing at the sailboats moored to a foreign dock.

"Trawlers have replaced these boats—but Richard fished with nets from his hooker even when they were telling us we needed to use trawlers, that we would be lost to the modern world."

I pointed to the painting. "Is that Galway Bay?"

She smiled. "Ah, yes, it is." Maeve stared off at the ceiling and continued. "When his brown sails flew back to the bay, I was filled, not emptied. There was nothing more I could do, but it overflowed my heart, spilled into my soul for all of my life. The simple sight . . ."

I took a deep breath. "What?" Her story had wound around to so many places, I was uncertain where we were in this timeline of leaving and returning, of lost and found. Her eyes came back to mine from the far-off place she'd gone. "There are certain people, certain events that will fill you up, and others that will drain you. And whatever is in your life is taking life from you. I can see it."

Her words caused an ache, like an old bruise, to rise in the middle of my belly—the ache for Mama. Her words were something a mama, my mama, would have said. A warm swelling rose to the base of my throat. I placed my hand there, tried to swallow.

"I've upset you," Maeve said in her singsong way.

"No." I shook my head. "I'm tired."

"That is what I'm trying to say to you—no need for that." She glanced around the room as if she expected someone else. Then she leaned forward and patted her hair. "Did you find him?"

"Find who?" I asked.

"Jack," she said.

"Of course not. I'm not looking for him."

"I looked for him everywhere I could—for months, then years I waited."

"Tell me." I felt I was on the edge of a new day, a new discovery.

"My parents, they didn't like him at all. He lived across the lane, you understand?"

I nodded.

Then Maeve slipped into the place of story, the place where she must have lived and understood back then.

"Spruce trees hang low and cast shadows between us. Long whispers of leaves and wind carry our words

61

back and forth. The houses are lime-washed, and the roads are mud in some places, cobblestone in others. When it rains, the houses are splattered with mud, making Claddagh appear as though we don't take care of our clachans built in jagged rows. But we are neat, clean, and we love our land. From my home at the edge of the sea I look up to St. Mary's on the Hill and down the path to the bay and Nimmo's pier. I think how strange this is—how we worship God and nature at the same time."

She stopped, her mouth open.

I touched her hand. "It sounds like a beautiful place." And I meant it; I wanted to go see this magical village.

"You have never seen nor will you ever see anything more beautiful than the simple, exquisite Claddagh village. Rocks are strewn at the side of the road; peat moss grows at the edges. Behind our homes there is the Big Grass, where we play hopscotch and tag and the boys hurl rocks. We dive for coppers—coins—for the tourists and play hide-and-seek by the water. The wind off the bay is often harsh, but never too much for us. Never. The wind tastes and smells of freedom and life and sailboats. . . ." She stared off toward the ceiling. "The sky is blue—so deep and wide and changing by the minute. It is the year 1918, the year I am nine years old, that I know I love him. He has dark hair, the same color as the sky before night—when the sun is gone, but the light has not fully escaped. His eyes . . ." Maeve looked at me, squinted as if she'd forgotten I was there.

I nodded for her to continue.

"Where was I?" she asked.

"His eyes, Maeve."

"No, not his eyes. The morning . . . the morning he left."

"Yes, the morning he left."

"It is 1922. I am thirteen years old when I understand that he loves me as much as I love him. I'd known I loved him since I was nine years old, but ahya, my mam told me no one knows who they love at nine years old. But, Kara . . ." She looked at me, leaned forward. "It doesn't matter the age, only the knowing. Mam told me I didn't even know what I wanted for dinner, much less who I loved, but I told her that I knew who I loved and what I wanted for dinner."

Maeve said this last sentence with a voice and a face so young that I laughed before I could stop myself.

Her mouth formed a round O as she blew out a long breath. "You know, Mam wanted me to marry the boy down the lane—always had. It was decided when I was born. But I loved Richard, I did. But soon— you've got to know—soon, our families' expectations influence what we believe, who we love."

"Yes?" I asked, eager for more.

"Oh, yes, dear. This is the thing we must guard against: that others' expectations, especially our families', do not become our own."

Then in a song of story, Maeve described her home

63

and her love for the boy across the lane.

"The morning arrives cold and empty—I feel it when I wake between my two sisters. I shiver, and pull the quilt to my chin. The previous day was the most beautiful day of my life—we had a procession to carry Our Lady of Galway statue to St. Mary's on the Hill. She'd returned from Dublin after being cleaned, she did. He and I had marched together in the procession, brushing our fingertips against each other, singing the hymns, holding our rosary beads. All in our village, even our houses, were dressed in finery. But the next morning an unfamiliar sound rises in the predawn light—gravel crunching, low voices.

"I crawl from between my sisters, put my feet into the lambskin slippers made from sheep on the green hills. I slip down to the front door, past my brother's room, past my parents' room. The fireplace is full of ashes. I open the front door a crack, enough that a blast of frigid air sucks the breath from my lungs. I become even shorter of breath as I spy the dark cart, as black and gaping open as an evil monster, in front of Richard's home. We have no streetlights, so only the full moon reveals the road.

"I draw my shawl around me, open the door wider. I pray to the statue we had carried up the hill just the day before. Oh, Our Lady of Galway, please don't let anything be wrong with Richard. I'll be a nun, I'll sacrifice . . . just not him. I reach up and touch the Siera tile over our doorway that signals our dedication to Jesus. These are the selfish words I pray—to help me, not Richard's family, but only me. Maybe what happened afterward was my punishment . . . like the color of the sky—gray and shadowed with the brown sails of the Claddagh fishermen—" Maeve stopped, stared at me, lost as though she'd wandered down this lane where Richard lived, and found only me on the whitewashed stoop.

"Go on, Maeve. The black cart . . ."

Her face lit from within. "Yes, yes. Please, not Richard, I begged." Maeve grabbed my hand. "Have you ever been that desperate? Begging, begging . . ."

She didn't wait for an answer; I had none. She stared up at the ceiling as if watching the story on a screen.

"My wild black curls fly around my head in the cold, my thin, transparent skin turns red in an instant. I step out onto the stoop, open my mouth to call or scream for Richard, but only hollow sounds come from my throat. I see no one; emptiness as wide as the world from end to end rises within me. I remember then an ancient proverb I'd been told—what fills the eye fills the heart. Then footsteps come from behind and I turn to Da. I scream at him."

Maeve stopped talking, her hands flailed through the air. "Da, Da . . . Da!" She sat up with a jerk.

I grabbed her arm. "Maeve, it's Kara. . . ."

She stopped, looked at me. "I know you're Kara. I'm not daft, dear one. Let me tell my story. Then my da grabs my elbow, pulls me into the house, tells me that the problem across the lane is none of our concern. I holler that what is across the street is not a problem, but a family, a boy I love. He tells me, 'Maeve, don't let your mother hear you scream. You are already the wildflower in our family.' Da pulls me toward him. I push him away, ask if Richard is dead, when Mam's rose fragrance washes over me; I lift my head to hear her tell me, 'It is as I've told you, Maeve. That family is trouble. Always was. Now look what they have brought to the lane—fear and death.'

"Mam's hands hold rosary beads, and she rolls them between her fingers: one by one. Her lips move in the familiar cadence of the Hail Marys that surely my mouth memorized even when I didn't know what I was saying. 'God rest their souls,' my mam says. I grab her. 'What do you mean, their souls?' I lunge forward. My shawl falls to the wood floor; the fringe lands in the fireplace. My voice lifts higher and higher until I am screeching at Mam. 'What do you mean *their souls?*'

"My mam closes her eyes and tells me: Richard's parents have passed on. My legs crumble beneath me. I fall to the wooden floor. Pain spikes through my knees as I ask what happened.

"My da places his hand on top of my head, and anyone who saw us might have thought he was a priest who had come to bless the child. He tells me, 'They were caught up in the trouble at the pub in Galway. Someone recognized their eldest son who was with them." I calculate backward from Richard, the youngest, to the fifth and oldest child, who was in

66

his twenties and widely known to have been involved in the Easter Rising.

"I stumble to stand. 'Where's Richard?' I ask, and move toward the door. Mam grabs my wrist, hisses, 'Don't you dare go out there and let the neighbors think you are . . . part of this, that you are involved with the family. The Garda Siochana—the Irish police—will come question us, involve us. Stay in the house.'

" 'What will they do with Richard?' I cry when Mam steps forward, places her palm on the side of my face. 'Maeve, you know we have Industrial Schools.'

"I push at Mam's hand, run for the front door, shove it open and spring across the street faster than I believed I knew how to run. The cart sits flat and cold, angry and black underneath my hand as I run into it, stop myself with an open palm. The cart rocks against my weight.

"A garda emerges from the other side of the hearse, his club raised high, his face angry and red, splotched and faded around his nose. When he looks at me, he lowers his club, then leans down to me. 'Child, go back to your home. This you do not need to see.' I straighten my shoulders. 'Where is their youngest son? I need to see him.'

"The garda nods toward another long cart, wet and glistening like the humpback of a whale just rising from the sea, one that had blended into the waves until someone pointed it out. 'All the sons are taken care of—don't you worry about that. He will be safe. Much safer than he was with his ma and da.' But I don't believe this man. I run toward Richard's house. The garda grabs my arm and pulls me back toward him. 'No, child.'

"I pry myself loose from this man as Da comes from behind. 'Maeve . . . no.' Da wraps his arms around me as the chaos increases. Neighbors come out as the sun ascends. Women scream, run toward the home of their friend. Men come up behind them, hollering at their women and children to go back into their homes.

"I push free of Da—for the first time ever—and wind my way, low and crouched, through the crowds to Richard's house. One small thirteen-year-old girl is inconsequential as they try to push back the others.

"I shove Richard's door open with a forward momentum that carries me across the room to land by the fireplace hearth. I stumble and fall in a heap in front of the dead ashes. The ashes sadden me with the knowledge that no one was there, or would ever be there, to light the fire, to keep it going so these boys would wake to a warm house as we did.

"I struggle to stand, choke on my tears at the sight of the barren hearth. Richard stands erect, his back to the wall, a fifteen-year-old boy staunch as a man."

Maeve paused in the middle of her story. Her eyes glazed over, perhaps from medication, or perhaps once again she'd returned to the land of the lost love. But she turned to me, and it was only pain and sorrow, not confusion, that lay in a fine mist over her eyes.

"He is the most beautiful child. He is more beautiful than any man I have seen before or since, even in the ninety-six years I have been on this earth." She tilted her head against the pillow. "And you will help me find him. You will."

"What?"

"You will help me find him."

"How can I possibly help you find him?" Maybe Maeve thought it was 1922 again, or maybe she believed I was someone else. "I don't even know his last name, Maeve."

"You can't help me until I get to the end of the story . . . until I tell you everything."

I grasped her hand. "What then? What happened to him?"

She pressed her lips together, then spoke. "All anyone ever wants to do is get to the end of the story, find out what happened, what happened, as if that answers any questions at all. It is not about how it ends; it is about the journey. The full story. You have to know the full story to care about or know the ending."

I nodded. "Okay, then what happened next?"

Maeve smiled, then looked over my shoulder as if she could see him. "He has dark curls." Maeve lifted her fingers as if she felt his hair. "Soft like a baby lamb in the back fields. He has freckles over his cheeks and a row across his nose. His skin darkens in the few months of summer when he goes out on his hooker to fish, but it is translucent the remainder of

69

the year. You would not know it darkened as it does, but when he found me again—when the sails returned him over the sea, when the edges drew nearer . . . he was darker. . . ." Maeve's voice stuttered now, like the end of a scratched CD.

"The edges?" I whispered.

"Edges of the ocean. The water is what ties us together, yes? You at one edge, me at the other, but the same ocean, the same water. He was on a different edge and I couldn't get to him. . . ."

I squinted. "And?" I wanted to get lost in the story, in the unhinged feeling of floating into another life.

Then she continued. "But at that moment he stands against the wall. His brothers slouch in chairs around the room. Their expressions are blank, their eyes are dead as the ashes in the fireplace, but not Richard's. He looks at me and I see laughter he will not allow escape—laughter at the way I'd burst into the room wearing my nightclothes, my hair wild from the cold and wind.

"I run over to him and throw my arms around him—this boy whom I have known since birth and loved almost as long, but have never touched except in games of tag, or diving for the coppers or to pass the communion cup. I hold to him as if I am drowning, but I know, as only children can, that he is gone. I fall against his shoulder. 'No,' I cry into him. Then he holds me as if there is nothing else to hold on to in that world. And for us, there isn't."

Maeve sighed, then closed her eyes. A smile as

70

faded and wrinkled as the linen gown she wore crossed her mouth.

"Then?" I asked. "Then what? Did they take him? Where did he go? What happened?" I grasped her hand. My heart beat faster than when I had run the three miles that very morning; my limbs were alive. I wanted to sprint from here and find this boy for her.

Beneath Maeve's eyelids, the rapid eye movement of the dreamer flickered. Then a tear, one small, oblong tear, leaked out beneath her left eyelashes, ran below the wrinkles of her eye and settled in the nest of her facial creases.

I reached for a Kleenex to wipe the tear away, and then thought better of it. For some reason it seemed appropriate to leave it alone, leave it for what it stood for: lost love. I sat quietly, anxious for more. After a moment, I squeezed her hand. "Then what?"

Maeve opened her eyes and stared at me. "You know, the oatmeal was cold again this morning and the—" She glanced at me. "Are you going to fix this or not?"

"Fix what?" I asked, my heart heavy.

"The incompetence. Bloody incompetence." She rolled onto her right side, and the soft sound of sleep came through her lips.

I stood and rubbed my forehead, my eyes, then glanced up at the round, black-numbered clock across the room. Our time wasn't up, but Maeve was gone into sleep. I sighed, wanting more of her story.

I started the car and leaned back on the seat, glancing at the clock: 8:45. No time for food—the tour meeting was in fifteen minutes. I turned the car out of the driveway and onto Main Street.

The light turned red as I pulled into the intersection; I reached for my BlackBerry, chewed on the side of my nail, then typed "Jack Sullivan" into the Internet search engine.

Neuroscientist and school principal were the first two results. I laughed; this was ridiculous. One does not punch in a name and find an address for a lost neighbor.

My fingers flew over the miniature keys as I scrolled farther down to the third listing and read: "The Unknown Souls Band with songwriter Jack Sullivan will be the opening act on March 4th at Chastain Amphitheater in Atlanta, Georgia—"

On the four-inch screen I stared at Jack and Jimmy Sullivan. Time slipped away like a river running backward, years reversed, and I was fourteen, desperate for the lost love from Mama, then Jack. I was waiting with an everlasting ache in the middle of my body.

I stared down at the picture of the Unknown Souls. A band stood with Jack and Jimmy, grinning in a grainy black-and-white photograph. Instruments and microphones were scattered across a bridge over a train track.

My breath caught deep in my lungs and stayed there—refusing to release in an exhale. My chest was gripped by the memory of his face, his hands, the way they splayed across the top of the bridge.

Suddenly a long, obnoxious horn blared behind me. I jumped in my seat, looked up to a green light.

My cell phone rang, and I grabbed it as I gunned the car through the light. "I'm going, I'm going," I hollered to the truck behind me, whose occupant couldn't hear me, but surely saw my waving hands.

"Pardon?" the voice on the other end of the phone said.

"Charlotte?"

"Yep, who are you yelling at?"

"Some impatient truck driver didn't like how I hesitated for half a second when the light turned green."

The truck came up next to me; the dark-haired woman in the driver's seat flicked an obscene gesture with her middle finger and gunned the truck in front of my car. I slammed on the brakes to avoid hitting her. The leftover morning Starbucks, my purse and a pile of folders in the passenger's seat flew toward the front of the car in a scattered array. I reached over in a futile attempt to grab at the flying objects and skidded to the right until my tires ran against the curb.

I jerked the steering wheel to the left, moving the car into the next lane. The gut-gripping sound of metal on metal filled my ears. I veered back toward the right and slammed on the brakes, stopping the car on the shoulder of the two-lane road and dropping my head onto the steering wheel.

A moment later, I looked up at a man who stood at

my passenger-side window, his hand over his eyebrow below a scratch. He knocked on the window; without thinking, I shoved the door open, hitting him in the groin. He bent down as I stepped from the car.

"Oh, oh . . . are you okay? Oh . . ." Fatigue and frustration swamped me.

He laughed. "I'm fine." He stood up; he was at least two feet taller than me. "I was checking on you. I thought you'd passed out on the steering wheel."

I reached up as if to touch his face, the scratch above his eye. "You're the one who's hurt."

"Shit, my fault. I wasn't wearing a seat belt." He glanced inside my car. "Looks like you got yourself quite a mess there, little lady." He then ran his hand over my front left bumper; it was crushed and distorted, digging into the front tire.

I groaned. "Not now."

"No convenient time for a fender bender, huh?" he asked.

His eyes were so brown they combined with his pupils, and his curls were the same color as his eyes, as if they'd been blended together in the same dye lot. "I'm so sorry I swerved into your lane." I glanced over at his truck. "How bad is it?"

"Driver's-side door dented. Not bad."

"Can we avoid the whole police thing here?" I attempted to smile.

He grinned; one side of his mouth turned up more than the other side. "Who will pay for my fancy truck?"

74

I noted his sarcasm as he glanced at my Mercedes, then back at his faded blue pickup truck.

"I will," I said. "I promise." I glanced at my watch: 8:58.

"You running late somewhere?"

"Yes, but that doesn't matter. What matters is that you're okay and . . . oh, let me just call and tell them I can't be there." I released a shaky breath, leaned into the car and yanked the cell phone from the floor. Warped sounds of a voice came through the speaker.

Charlotte . . . she was still on my cell. I lifted the phone to my ear. "Charlotte?"

"Are you okay? You okay?" Her voice came fast.

"Yes . . . I sideswiped this nice man. I'm going to miss my meeting. I haven't even found a band and . . . oh, forget it. I'll call you back." I said good-bye and pushed END, then punched in Frieda's number.

The man reached over, placed his hand on my arm. "Stop."

"What? I just need to tell my boss I'm late." I choked on the last word.

"Damn, I could never resist a damsel in distress. Come on . . . I'll take you to your meeting, get your information, call a tow truck."

"No, really. I know how to take care of myself." I stood taller, wiped madly at an escaped tear.

"I can tell." He smiled, and there was no malice in his words.

"Okay, I know it doesn't look like it right now . . . but I can and I do. Just having a very, very bad day."

"There's worse to be had, trust me on that."

I looked up at this man, his face older than my father's, but younger in the eyes and mouth, as if they'd always carried a smile and wouldn't age with the rest of his face. I held out my hand. "I'm Kara Larson."

"I'd be Luke Mulligan."

"So sorry about this, Mr. Mulligan."

"Come on. I don't need to be in Beaufort until five. I'll take you to your meetin'. Get in the truck."

I hesitated, glanced back at my car. Getting in a truck with a stranger was probably not the best way to top off this hellacious morning. "If we pull the metal back, I bet I can drive my car," I said.

"You might be right." He walked over, pulled at the fender, and yanked his hand away as blood leaked from his palm.

"Oh, oh . . . you're bleeding again because of me."

"No big deal. But I'll be followin' you to make sure you get there."

I reached into my car and gathered the contents of my wallet, which were scattered on the floorboards. "Here, let me give you all my information so you can send me your bill, and I promise I'll pay it . . . anything you need to do to get it fixed."

Luke waved his hand in the air. "I don't need you being fired from your job and not able to pay my bill." He smiled. "So, get on the road and I'll take down your information when we get there."

I nodded, exhaustion threatening the backs of my eyelids. I swallowed; a burning pain shot through my

76

throat. No, I couldn't be getting sick, not now. I touched my palm to my neck: hot. My skin prickled like tiny jellyfish stings across my body.

I climbed behind the wheel and glanced back toward Mr. Mulligan, who jumped into his front seat and turned his truck around to drive behind me. I waved out the window and indicated that I'd turn left at the stoplight.

Mr. Mulligan followed me in my dented car until I pulled up in front of our small brick offices at 9:10 a.m. I parked, jumped out of the car, and held out a business card with my name, address, and phone number as I moved toward Mr. Mulligan.

He honked and drove off.

"Wait . . . ," I hollered after the truck, waving my card like a flag of defeat.

A hand came out the driver's-side window and waved. My hand dropped to my side.

"Kara Larson."

I whipped around. Frieda stood on the front steps. "You coming or trying to pick up cowboys in the parking lot?"

"I'm coming." I stiffened my shoulders, gathered a pile of folders and attempted to ignore my desire to climb back in my car and drive in the opposite direction from Frieda, my job, this meeting.

I followed my boss, mentally flipped through the agenda for the meeting, and attempted to ignore my curiosity about lost love that tapped its persistent finger on my mind.

CHAPTER FIVE

I pushed open the door to the Flower Emporium on Second Street and the scent of fragrant flowers washed over me, loosening the knotted muscles in my neck. I could only identify the gardenia, but there were others in the mix, heavy in the air. Charlotte and the store owner, her mother, Mrs. Carrington, glanced up from the counter, where they sat on bright pink bar stools. Flowers and plants surrounded them in baskets and vases, as though they sat in the middle of a jungle of potted wildlife.

"Well, thanks for joining us." Charlotte stood and touched her watch, but a smile covered her face, as it always did.

"Don't start with me," I said. "What a day. Do you have any food?"

Mrs. Carrington squinted at me. "When *was* the last time you ate? You look like a waif."

"Oh, it's this black outfit. . . ." I ran a hand across my abdomen and black cotton shirt.

Mrs. Carrington, who'd known me since birth, rolled her eyes. "Yeah, and it's this white sweater that makes me look chubby." She reached under the counter and pulled out a Zone bar, then threw it to me. "Eat, child. We have decisions to make."

I nodded and sat on the stool next to Charlotte. "Have you been waiting long?"

"About a half hour. But we made all the decisions for you." She winked.

"I am so sorry. I've been looking forward to this all day—seeing you two."

"Bad day?" Charlotte asked.

"I have an idea." I sat up. "Let's run down to Bay Street, grab a couple oyster sandwiches and do the flowers another time."

Charlotte balanced her elbow on the countertop, leaned into her palm. "Let's get this over with." She looked at her mom. "She had a little fender bender today."

"Oh, dear."

"The weirdest thing happened afterward, though," I said. "He followed me to work to make sure I got there okay, then he took off without my name or number, so I can't pay to have his car fixed."

"I bet he got your license plate or something."

"I don't know. It was very strange."

"Well, you're the one who always believes in angels." Charlotte smiled with that sideways grin she has when she is right and I am wrong. "Maybe he was an angel reminding you to slow down."

"I don't think an old man driving a pickup truck qualifies as an angel with messages," I said.

"How do you know what qualifies?" Mrs. Carrington sat down, plopped a book of bouquet photos in front of me. "Now, let's get these flowers decided. You said you wanted white peonies, and if you want them in May, we have to order them now from Israel or we'll be paying premium price and be lucky to get remainders."

"Peonies were my Mama's favorite."

Mrs. Carrington patted my shoulder. "I know . . . so let's get them ordered."

I lifted my Tiffany-blue satchel, yanked out the pink wedding binder and flipped to "Flowers." I found the picture I'd torn out the day I'd met Maeve, and handed it to Mrs. Carrington. "Can we duplicate this? I love the Swarovski crystals coming out of the flowers."

"Absolutely." She pulled a pad out from below the counter.

"Really?"

Mrs. Carrington sketched and made notes, taking over the designing in one fell swoop. I turned to Charlotte.

"I've got to find another band."

"Flowers, Kara, flowers. Focus."

"Okay . . . okay."

Unknown Souls.

I touched Charlotte's arm. "You ever hear of the Unknown Souls Band?"

"No." She tossed her curls behind her shoulder and pointed to the sketchpad. "Flowers." Charlotte put her hand on my leg. "You okay?"

"I think I'm getting sick . . . or something. I don't feel all that great. Everything—like how much I love both of you—is making me want to cry."

Mrs. Carrington stuck her charcoal pencil behind her ear, pulled her bifocals down on her nose and looked at me. "You worried about this bouquet? You know I've done your baptism, your sister's wedding, your mama's funeral, and I won't mess up your wedding."

"I know." I hugged her. "This might be the one thing I'm not worried about." I leaned over to glance at the sketches. "Perfect. That's exactly what I want—except with white satin ribbon around the stems for the bridesmaids. Thank you so much," I said. "You're like family to me."

Mrs. Carrington nodded. "Tell your daddy that."

Charlotte laughed, then looked at me. "She has a big old crush on your daddy."

"You do?" I raised my eyebrows at Mrs. Carrington.

"Oh, Charlotte, you are so inappropriate . . . I swear, sometimes I'm not sure who raised you." Mrs. Carrington nodded toward the sketches. "Now let's talk about what we came here to talk about."

"Well, more importantly," Charlotte said, "what are you going to wear tonight?"

"Tonight?" I unclenched my fist, raised my palms up in a question.

"Your shower."

I plopped my forehead down on the counter. "Oh . . . I'm so not in the mood."

"Only you would not be in the mood to get gifts." Charlotte laughed and rubbed my shoulders.

My home was quiet save for the creaks and settling of the old house—a private conversation it had with itself daily. I entered the library off the front hall and sat down at the computer. I glanced at my watch—fifteen minutes before Peyton would pick me up for the shower at his mother's house. I sat down on the antique rolling chair and flashed to the Unknown Souls Web site. Large on the flat screen, Jack Sullivan's face appeared.

I would have known him even without the *"Jack Sullivan—songwriter"* written in jagged letters underneath his picture. It was only a head shot, but his hair was still dark and curly, almost shoulder length. A small goatee covered his chin. The last time I saw him, he'd had some fuzz on his upper lip—I remembered the way it felt when he kissed me.

I shook my head.

I clicked on Jack's face and enlarged the picture. He wore a half smile—"a half-ass grin" Daddy used to call that expression. Daddy hadn't liked Jack "one little bit"—trouble, nothing but trouble, he'd said. Mama had just rolled her eyes at Daddy. "That's what they said about you, Porter, and look at you now— aren't you the fine upstanding husband and father." And then they'd kiss and I'd leave the room knowing Mama would eventually talk Daddy into liking Jack. But she'd died before she could do so.

"Be careful what you believe—it is who you are."

Maeve's words rolled across my mind, and I shook them off with a toss of my head. I knew exactly who I loved *and* why.

I clicked on the "About the Band" icon.

82

The Unknown Souls Band was formed after a performance at a benefit for the Mended Hearts Orphanage in Texas. The public response to their music and onstage presence has been overwhelming; requests for performances continue to pour in. The band was started by the two Sullivan brothers: Jimmy, the lead singer and guitarist, and Jack, the songwriter. Five years later, the band has grown in popularity and notoriety. They have just signed their first recording deal, and their first CD was released in February with twelve original songs written by Jack Sullivan. Their unique combination of mellow rock, Celtic and blues is blowing through the music industry like a breath of fresh air.

"Trouble, yeah, right," I mumbled underneath my breath. "Helping orphanages and writing songs is very, very big trouble, Daddy." I leaned back in my seat and released a long breath. A quick flash of something that resembled nostalgia, of being thirteen and full of hope, washed over me, attempted to open a place behind my heart.

I shut my eyes and ignored the memory of Jack's good-bye in the predawn light of that summer morning so long ago. There was a time when I'd known every detail of the scene—reliving it over and over until vividness faded, emotion drained. I'd called upon the memory until it was all used up, until it was poured out, emptied.

There were two events in my life that produced an emotion so specific, so whole that I could not duplicate it with anyone or anything else. One was the loss of my mama. The other was Jack's first touch. Seeing Jack's face, I felt it—a sudden yearning for something unnamed that no one else brought to me.

I closed my eyes. "Jack," I whispered.

"Kara?" Peyton's voice startled me.

I jumped to my feet, tripped on the edge of the Oriental carpet, and kept from falling by grabbing on to the corner of the desk. "Hi, honey . . . hey. What're doing?" I hugged him.

"Umm . . . picking you up. I rang the doorbell four times. You asleep in here?"

"I must've been . . . it's been a very long day. Sorry." I screwed my face up into a pout, then kissed him on the lips.

Peyton kissed me back. "You know, if you make that face and say sorry, I can never stay mad. I have a feeling you'll be using that on me for all time."

The way he said "for all time" sounded so sweet and full of forever—the opposite of loss and leaving and abandonment—that I smiled.

Then he glanced down at the screen. "What're looking at?"

My fingers fumbled to exit the Internet. "Nothing. . . ."

He squinted at the screen. "The Unknown Souls. I heard them a couple years ago in Atlanta. They were awesome."

84

"Really?" I tilted my head.

"Yeah, but I doubt you can get them now . . . they've gotten too big for that kind of stuff."

"What do you mean?" I looked into Peyton's eyes.

"Well, aren't you looking for a band for the tournament benefit?"

"Yes," I said, my voice sounding more like a question than a statement.

"Don't get mad . . . you know I don't intrude on your job. Rick just told me what a mess it all was at the meeting today."

"I'm so thrilled that you have spies who can tell you how I'm doing at my job."

"Now don't get all huffy. If it weren't for your job, I would never have met you. Then where would I be?"

"Not going to this shower." I slouched against the desk, supported myself with my palms.

Peyton threw his head back and laughed. "Don't you dare let my mother hear you say that. She thinks this is an absolute stroke of genius on her part. With her child an only son, she never thought she'd get to do any of this wedding stuff. A bar shower in the room she had designed to look just like an English pub— brilliant, huh?"

"Absolutely brilliant." I grabbed Peyton's hand. "Oh, by the way—how was the birthday party last night?" I poked him in the ribs.

"Boring and stupid. Truly. Those guys act like they're still eighteen and just got their first fake ID."

He nuzzled my neck and kissed me. "I would have much rather been with you."

"Me too."

"I'm sure we have plenty of family dinners ahead of us." The words sounded synonymous with "forever," and they soothed me.

"Come on, let's get this over with." I pulled him to the front door.

"You're ready?"

"Why wouldn't I be?" I asked.

"Because you don't have shoes on and your sweater is inside out . . . babe."

I groaned. "Give me a minute." I turned and ran up the front stairs to my bedroom.

I stood in front of the full-length mirror Mama had given me for my eighth birthday, and stared at my face. "Get it together," I whispered, then yanked my baby-blue cashmere sweater over my head, flipped it right-side out and pulled it back down. The sleeve caught on my hair clip; I jerked it down to a grotesque ripping sound.

"Damn." I yanked the sweater off and stared at a gaping hole in the right sleeve.

I walked to the closet and stared at my clothes. All I wanted to do was slip into my silk pajamas, crawl into bed with a cup of hot lemon tea and read the last chapter of *Beach Music*, discover if love was truly everlasting.

The only sweater still in its dry-cleaning bag was the black one with the beaded trim: guaranteed to be clean. I slipped it on and grabbed my black Gucci boots—the ones that killed my toes, but ones I'd wear until they fell apart because of what I'd paid for them, with my first real paycheck.

I came to the top of the stairs and looked down at Peyton. He stood at the front door with his back to me. He fidgeted back and forth on his feet while he fingered the walking cane collection at the front door, then lifted one that Daddy had bought in Charleston. He twirled it, put it back in the holder. He let out a long sigh and called my name as he turned.

"I'm right here, Mr. Patient," I said, walking down the steps.

"You changed," he said.

"Is that okay?"

"Yes . . . just noticing." He opened the front door and made a sweeping gesture with his hand.

"Sorry . . . I'm just tired."

"You do look a little . . . pale."

I came up next to him, grabbed his hand and placed it on my forehead. "Do I feel hot?"

"No, but you look hot." He pulled me toward him. "God, I cannot wait until we are in the same house and I can see you and hold you whenever I want. This living with Daddy thing is not working out well for me."

Warmth ran over my body, and I immediately thought how to slip away that night before returning home—how to spend a few hours allowing his love to quiet the flurry of thoughts and feelings running through me. With all the craziness in our lives, it had been two or more weeks since we'd been together. I kissed his cheek. "Let's go. I don't want to face your mother if we're even one minute late."

"Good point," he said and clasped my hand. "Very good point."

The large pub room located off the garden terrace of Mrs. Ellers's spacious home was overcrowded and stifling hot. Looking around, I was reminded that Peyton had bought this home for his mother, the fulfillment of a promise he'd made when he was six years old, when his father had walked out on them, to always take care of her. His protectiveness toward her was one of the many qualities in him that I adored. I stood behind the bar, which was piled high with wrapped gifts, and squeezed his hand.

"It is so hot in here," I said.

"It is?" He took a long swallow of beer from a frosted mug with *Ellers Pub* etched in the glass.

This was a moment I should have savored. But I often found that when I should be most "in the moment," I became an observer instead of a participant, as if I were watching my life through the lens of a camera—filtering it through the convex lens, the images distinct but distant. This habit of observing my life had started at Mama's bedside the night before she died, and it hadn't quit yet. I reached for my camera at one side of the bar, lifted it to capture this moment I might be able to fully enjoy later, while looking at the pictures.

There was Daddy talking to Mrs. Carrington at the far end of the room, near the door that opened to a deck. Mrs. Carrington motioned for them to walk outside, but Daddy shook his head and smiled. My heart hurt for him, as I knew how he felt—Mama was still in our hearts even if she wasn't standing next to us. Someone can die, or leave, but the feeling of attachment doesn't leave with them. Oh, if only it did—if only desire for them left when they did.

Scattered throughout the crowd were friends of mine who went all the way back to preschool. They talked loudly, yet all I heard was an overwhelming roar without words.

A handmade wine-cork backsplash covered the wall behind the bar. I was sure that my soon-to-be mother-in-law had drunk every single one of the bottles of wine from which those corks had come.

My kind brother, Brian, stood at the end of the bar flirting with Charlotte. No use in that—Charlotte had been avoiding his loving puppy-dog looks since she was nine years old. I smiled. He was persistent and adorable with his head full of blond curls and his quick blue eyes. He was probably trying to talk Charlotte into going to the most delicious place I knew in Palmetto Pointe—his shack behind a bluff on Silver Creek.

I leaned against the bar as Peyton's mother, Sylvia, moved next to me. She tapped her red fingernails on the polished mahogany bar. "You having fun?" She leaned toward me, vaguely unsteady on her feet even this early in the evening.

"Absolutely." I set my camera on the bar.

"Great. Just great." She glanced up and down at my outfit, squinted. "Isn't that the sweater you wore to the Every-Room-in-the-House shower?"

"What?" I asked, and glanced over at Peyton. Why wasn't anyone else sweating?

"Your sweater." Sylvia pulled on the sleeve. "You wore that to your last shower."

"I did, didn't I?" I rubbed my forehead with my fingertips; Sylvia wavered, miragelike in her too-tight leather skirt and red sweater.

Peyton's voice came from behind me. "Mom, please. Who cares what she wore?"

I reached for Peyton, but never found his arm as the room spun before me. The last thing I saw as I slid to the floor was Sylvia's open mouth. The last words I heard were: "Oh, dear God, is she pregnant?" And it wasn't a question asked with excitement.

CHAPTER SIX

The whitecaps are high and crazed, then suddenly calm as if someone commanded the sea to be still. Daddy is building a sandcastle with Deirdre, and Mama is standing over them with an ancient black Nikon, snapping pictures, laughing. Her hair is flying in the wind—brown, sun-licked curls lifting to the sky. A tunnel of white light comes from the cloud above her, settles around her.

Daddy looks up to her, and there is so much love on his face, around his eyes and mouth, that my heart overflows. The light stretches toward him; Mama touches his cheek, drops her camera on the sand and places both her hands on either side of his face, and kisses him.

Deirdre squeals and pulls Daddy toward her. "Oh, gross. Stop that."

Mama laughs and picks small Deirdre up into the air, into the white light, and kisses her. Daddy plucks a sand dollar and places it at the front door of their gray-white sandcastle. Brian runs toward them, lifts his foot as if to knock the castle down, then falls to the sand, laughing so hard the sound echoes against my chest.

Deirdre screams at him, but she is laughing.

I step toward them, but I can't move, my feet disobedient to the command to walk to my family. I am so hot, waves of fire move across me, through me.

A boat comes into view behind Mama; three brown sails and a bowed front stern sail across the water.

A vortex of whirling panic overcomes me; I scream for my family, but they can't hear me, can't answer me. They are laughing and loving with such intensity that they do not know what is coming.

I burst through the immobility, moist sweat covering me. I get to Mama first, throw my arms around her.

She turns to me, looks at me, but Maeve's eyes stare back at me.

I try to scream again, but find emptiness inside me.

I turn to beg for help from Daddy, but instead find Peyton walking across an eighteenth green waving good-bye to me over his shoulder, his golf club swinging at his side.

I grope through the sand and heat to find that love again, to find Mama kissing Daddy and laughing, to find Deirdre and Brian. The back of my throat fills with sand and I am parched.

They've all left now. I am alone.

I curl into the shell-encrusted edge of the waterline and wait for the water to take me to the other side of the sea, where I will find them, find all of those who left me.

A sob rips upward; pain shoots through my throat, and I open my eyes with searing pain. Deirdre stood over me—a different sister from the one left behind on the beach. She held a cup of tea, a plate of buttered toast.

"Kara, you need to eat something, drink something. . . ."

In the recesses of my mind I knew I'd been dreaming, understood that the place I'd just left was imaginary, yet it was as real and solid and whole as the bed beneath me, as the ache running along my back. I'd seen Mama kiss Daddy that way hundreds of times, seen the love on his face, heard Deirdre laugh so hard she hiccuped and bent over. All those things were true; they'd happened.

Abandonment overwhelmed me and I couldn't speak. I stared at Deirdre, scooted up in the bed. Sunlight danced across the room with the shadows of the coming evening, and I believed that if I could stand and walk to the window I would see a row of clachan houses, a cobblestone street. I closed my eyes, leaned back.

Deirdre sat down next to me; the mattress sank under her weight. "You were crying in your sleep." She touched my arm; I opened my eyes. "Are you okay?"

"Do you remember when Daddy and Mama used to take us to the beach on the weekends?" My voice cracked.

She averted her gaze.

"Everyone . . . all of us." I wiped at my face. "We were such different people. What happened between youth and today? What happened to us, Deirdre? Where are those people, those children, that daddy?"

"You're feverish, Kara. You've had a hundred and three temperature; you're not making any sense at all. Please drink something. I promised Daddy I'd make sure you ate and drank today."

I reached for the tea, let it saturate my throat.

"It wasn't only Mama who left—we all left, we all disappeared," I said.

"Kara, you're scaring me—you had a bad dream, that's all."

"You're right, just a bad dream." I reached for the

93

toast, took a bite, stretched my neck to the left, then the right, and pulled my thoughts into the room. "Deirdre, you've got to tell me what happened at that party."

"Let's just get you better first. Doc Chandler said you had the real-deal flu. You need rest, fluids, blah blah blah."

"Deirdre, tell me about the party. Now."

"Sylvia absolutely freaked out."

"She was worried about me or the party?"

"First she screamed that you were pregnant."

"Yeah . . . that's the last thing I heard."

"Then she went absolutely nuts, claimed that you had ruined her party—the only one she'd been able to give her son, what with his busy, famous career."

"I ruined her party?"

"Yeah. The arrival of the ambulance marked the pinnacle of her fit. She didn't want them on her newly pressure-cleaned driveway."

I threw my head back and laughed. "You have got to be kidding me."

"Nope." Deirdre put her hand on my forehead. "You do know you have to live with this woman for the rest of your . . . married life."

"No, I'll be living with Peyton."

"You get everyone in the family."

I closed my eyes. "Then what happened?"

"They took you off in the ambulance, and you know the rest. You woke up then."

"It's all kinda fuzzy—the hospital, and then just sleep and weird dreams. How's Daddy?"

"He's all right. You know how he gets when he has no control over things. He's irritable."

"You know, we're going to have to find someone to help him after I leave. Just little things like groceries, laundry, and cooking."

Deirdre turned away from me. "I was thinking I'd move back in after you go and . . . do all that."

"Really?"

"It's not exactly a pleasure being in my little home alone. Just because Bill left me the damn, empty house doesn't mean I want it."

I stretched my back and shifted in the bed, and through the fog of half sleep and fever asked my sister the question I'd never asked before: "What happened between you two? You seemed so . . . in love."

She stared at me for a long moment. Her gaze traveled over my nose, my cheeks, then rested above my head. "He doesn't believe I love him."

"What?"

"Shit, forget it," she said.

I let a long time pass in silence, hoping to hear more from her, but she had shut down.

I sank back on my pillows. "I think I'll try and get up now . . . thanks for all you've done in the past few days . . . checking on me, checking on Daddy. I appreciate you taking care of me." I leaned forward and hugged my sister, a rare show of affection.

I thought of work and the thank-you notes I'd have to write for presents I still hadn't opened. I also wanted to stop by Verandah House to visit Mrs.

Mahoney. Her stories and admonitions had been ebbing and flowing with my fever. Whether the flu or something far different caused my preoccupation, I knew for sure that I wanted to see her, hear more of her story.

Spring moved deeply into Palmetto Pointe with the blooming of azaleas and camellias, the daffodils lifting their faces to the sun. The sweetgrass along the sandy paths swayed as if in a dance to the arrival of warm weather. I hurried along the sidewalk, cursing the lack of parking along Palmetto Drive leading to Verandah House. I passed Marshall's Garden and Antique Store, and glanced in the front window. Mrs. Marshall had owned the store for generations, and the family name was written in curved, gold letters that had been there for seventy-two years. The *s* winked at me, missing its middle section. I smiled—the *s* had been like that for as long as I could remember. I turned my head when a statue caught my eye.

I stopped, walked toward the window and stared at the miniature statue. It was two feet tall at most: a concrete garden angel, aged and cracked. The wing I could see was spread wide, her face tilted upward as if waiting for a kiss or for someone to tell her something—expectant either way. There was something about the angel that touched that spot inside me that always searched for Mama. I leaned closer—the angel knelt. I pushed the door open, and a small bell announced my arrival.

Mrs. Marshall looked up from where she stood behind the glass display case, holding a magnifying glass. "Well, lookee here. It's Kara Larson. My, my, what brings you through my door on this beautiful day?"

I smiled. "Good morning, Mrs. Marshall."

"I heard you were sick . . . fainted right there at a party, did you?"

"Not one of my finer moments. But yes, I did."

"I heard you scared your mother-in-law to death, making her think you were pregnant and all?"

I lifted my eyes to the ceiling. "Nothing secret in this town? Nope, not pregnant. Just the flu."

"Did you come to check on those urns and trees you rented for the wedding? They're all taken care of—ordered and confirmed."

I nodded toward the front of the store. "No, I was wondering about that angel in the front window."

"The concrete angel? Oh, she's just for show. No one wants her—her wing is missing."

"It is?" I tilted my head and walked toward the front of the store. "I didn't notice that."

"That's because I have the marble birdbath placed just so."

"Where did you get her?" I stopped and turned toward Mrs. Marshall.

"My junker found her in Savannah. No one wants an angel with a broken wing. I believe she came from a garden."

"Well, I want her. How much is she?"

97

"Now why would you be wanting a broken angel?"

I reached into the display and lifted the angel, held her up to the light. "She's beautiful. Something . . . I don't know."

"I agree with you, but she's broken. I couldn't sell her to you."

"How much do you want for her?"

Mrs. Marshall rolled her eyes. "You can have her."

"Thank you." I hugged her.

The concrete angel wrapped and stuffed under my coat, I headed down the block to Verandah House.

CHAPTER SEVEN

Hello?" I leaned over the front desk and called into the space behind it. Silence met me. I walked out into the hall to the high-pitched calls of nurses and doctors barking orders. I recognized the tone and the words—there was a code red occurring down the hall; they were attempting to revive a resident.

I moved in slow motion toward the noise, toward Mrs. Mahoney's room.

Lab coats flapped up and down the hall—unwelcome and menacing in their import.

"No," I whispered. A nurse scurried by, her face somber and tight, a clipboard held against her chest. She looked up and stopped when she saw me. "May I help you?"

I motioned down the hall. "Did she . . . ?"

The nurse pressed her lips together. "Are you a relative?"

I shook my head in quick motions, which made me dizzy again. I pulled the concrete angel closer. "What happened to her?"

The nurse looked left, then right. "If you're not family . . . I can't."

I nodded. "Okay." Now I'd never find out what happened to Richard on the other side of the sea, to his brothers. I'd never discover where their love had . . . gone. I groaned and watched the nurse round the corner. Why did it matter what happened to an unknown man from 1920s Ireland with a woman I barely knew? But for some reason it did matter and, in fact, seemed desperately important.

I went down the hall toward the front desk, where a cluster of people in white coats stood talking in hushed, urgent voices.

The chaotic whirlwind of noise from inside my thoughts stilled now as surely as the eye of a storm. Inside this quiet was a hum, a white noise. My heart calmed, my eyes closed. Even in my sickness the last two days, as my body screamed *Stop!*, my mind had continued thinking in a flurry about all the things I needed to do and do and do again. I'd thought about all those balls I'd dropped, all those people who wouldn't approve of my "down time" to get better.

Now even those thoughts stilled, and I heard only the sounds of the nurses and secretary making necessary arrangements. No one even noticed me as I sat on the bench facing the desk. I had the sensation I'd shrunk to a child's size.

What had drawn me here when it wasn't my day to visit? I didn't understand my own motivation beyond the need to know the end of the story, to understand the truth it contained. Something about real love. A lump rose in my throat. Yes, love. Maeve had seemed to know it, and the need to understand grew within me, to find out what she knew about love that I didn't.

The lump dissolved and tears fell.

I opened my eyes. Four people were staring at me: a man with nose hairs, a woman whose lip liner covered only the left half of her mouth, and two nurses whose brows were scrunched together in concern.

A nurse with red hair squatted in front of me. "Are you okay?"

I nodded; my heart beat faster.

"Did you know our mother?" the man said, and took a step toward me.

I jumped up. "You're her son?"

He nodded, his double chin jiggling and catching in the top button of his shirt.

Words tumbled out. "I'm Kara Larson. I've been visiting her . . . talking to her. I really wanted . . . I brought her . . ." I stopped.

"Mother never mentioned you." He wrinkled his nose at me.

The nurse touched my arm and motioned for me to follow her. I nodded at the man. I had so many questions to ask him. Was Richard his father? Did they end up together? Did Maeve really want me to find him?

I followed the nurse around the corner to an empty hall. She pinched her lips together in a thin line: a woman's face of disapproval. Growing up with only a father, this was not a look I was accustomed to, and it was one I would have liked to think Mama would never have used. Daddy scrunched his eyebrows together and tilted his head down, or just turned away in reprimand.

I had obviously done something wrong, so I mumbled the words, "I'm sorry," although I had no idea what I was sorry for. There were immediately many things I felt sorry *about:* that I hadn't heard more of Maeve's story, that I'd been too busy to notice any emotion beyond urgency in months. I was sorry that I'd lost touch with Jack Sullivan.

I noticed the nurse was talking. "Pardon?" I looked up from the checkered linoleum floor.

She spoke low. "Mrs. Harbinger's family does not know who you are and they are in deep grief. I suggest you—"

"Mrs. Harbinger?" I focused my attention fully on the nurse now. "It's Mahoney."

Then the nurse's tight lips separated into a wide smile; her middle left tooth was turned to the side. "Oh, dear." Her face softened; the lines around her eyes diminished. "Mrs. Mahoney isn't . . . she's not the one. It was the woman next door. Maeve is still with us."

101

I grabbed her arm, hope rushing up at me like small, fragile bubbles.

"Maeve is . . ."

The nurse nodded. "But I wouldn't suggest you go in and see her just now. It's kind of chaotic. A lot of noise and people confuse our residents sometimes."

I nodded, but just as I had as a child, I did the complete opposite of what I'd been told. I turned with my angel tucked under my coat and walked down the hall, and pushed opened the door to Maeve's room.

She sat up in bed, her hair splayed out on the pillow, her head back, with snores coming from her open mouth.

I stood next to her bed, and her eyes popped open in a wide-eyed stare. She spoke before I could. "Why did you stop braiding my hair? Bloody hell, you took my hair down." She pulled at either side of her tangled tresses. "And then left because? Because?" She waved her hands in the air.

Confusion clouded her face. Such innocent confusion on an old face—a juxtaposition that gave me the briefest splinter glimpse of the tenacious thread between newborns and older patients. I sat in the chair next to her bed, pushed her water glass to the side, and took her hand. I wanted to take care of her, but in the inadequacy of my knowledge, all I knew to do was hold her hand. "The woman in the room next door . . . passed on. I guess everyone got quite busy."

Maeve turned her face away. "That is why they send us here, is it not? This is what waits for me? That is why I want you to find him before . . ."

"You have to tell me who he is before I can find him, Maeve."

"Oh, I will. I will." Her eyes opened wider. "They took him, they did."

"Who took him?"

She leaned back against her pillow and closed her eyes, yet they flickered back and forth beneath her eyelids. It was like watching the schools of minnow beneath the calm sound between the tides.

"The garda took him because he was the youngest— the only one who needed a home. Oh, but I looked for him. Souls bound together can't be forever torn apart by distance and neither by death. The sea may separate us in body, but not in soul. The edge of the sea is where happiness lives, where we feel and know things. Soon we'd be on opposite edges. . . ." She opened her eyes and stared at me.

She whispered now, "Our souls do fuse, combine, you know. But I know you know that, dear. I can see below the pale blur of your green eyes. You do know that. Circumstances, distance, busyness nowadays with you young. It is the busyness. As if you can prove how worthy your life is by how busy it is."

Maeve spoke in the singsong voice of a younger woman. " 'I'm so busy. I'm so overwhelmed. I've got so much going on. I don't have time . . . I don't have time.' I hear it from my grandbabies, from all of you running through these halls. You young wear it like a badge of honor, like soldiers of the IRA wore their scars from fighting in the Easter Rising. Foolish. All foolish—it is only a way to avoid feeling."

I squeezed her hand, then changed the subject. "Who took him? How did you find him? Did you marry him?"

She released a long breath. "There you go—rushing and rushing and rushing like the dumb sheep running through the open gate on the fair green meadows only because someone opened it and the dog circled. There is so much before the end of the story, so much before I found him or even lost him. No one wants to take that journey *through* the story. Only directly *to* the story." She released my hand, patted the angel still in my hands. "What is that?"

I lifted it up. "A garden angel. She was in the window at my favorite antique shop."

Maeve touched the intact wing, then traced across the chest to the other side, where she ran her forefinger along the broken edges, slowly, deliberately, as if feeling for the bones and sinew of a live person. I held my breath as she did this.

A small tear fell from her left eye. "A broken wing."

I nodded. "But I still think she is beautiful."

"She is," Maeve said, her voice cracked but still melodic. "And that is how I felt when they took him. One wing. Who can fly with one wing?"

"I can let her sit at your bedside if you'd like."

But Maeve didn't hear me. She was gone into the land of story, to the place I longed to be.

"They take him so fast I can't react. Keening

women, dirt in the road, cold on my feet, wool against my face. His older brothers, four of them, attempt to pull him from the police, but they hit those boys with their clubs."

Maeve stopped, stared at me, then past me. She ran her finger once again along the broken wing, the tattered edge of concrete.

"After they come into the house and take him, Richard stands at the back of the cart. His hand rises to stop me from pushing against the police. The rain is on his hair, slick and dripping onto his face, onto a pain I have never seen on his features, yet I instinctually know it is a pain of a size I would now understand. All those thirteen years I thought pain was merely frustration or desire or delay, or even a cold hearth when Da came home drunk or . . . well, none of that was real pain in any way. Only now do I understand, and at that moment, in a darker, sharper world, I fall to the ground. The cobblestones are cold against my body, but not uncomfortable. I know where they will take him—to an Industrial School, the worst place for a young boy in Ireland—and they won't tell me which one, they won't tell me. . . ."

Maeve's eyes drifted upward, her hand fluttered in the air. I took her fingers, feeling I should say something, but I didn't. There was a deeper need, hers or mine—I wasn't sure, but it wasn't about saying more; it was about saying less, about hearing more keenly.

She squeezed my hand. "He comes to me and lifts me from the ground. His beautiful wide hands, which

I touched only in dreams or saw chop the wood, now touch me. After all my years of waiting, of lying in my upper loft and imagining his touch, what his hands would feel like on my face, on my arms, now I know. This caress is more, so much more than I'd imagined. This is now and forever—the moment everyone must have, the moment that encompasses all other moments; now and before, now and after: all time.

"He pulls me to stand and holds my face between his hands. 'Maeve, I will find you,' he says. The garda pull him backward, but in that moment, separate and true of time and space, they have no power.

"He kisses me. Everything around us disappears: sight, sound, rain, pavement, cold. None of them exist as his hands hold my face and his lips touch mine . . . then the world rushes back in. Like a great sucking vacuum, the world and all its evil rush in. They grab me, pull me backward. Pain and noise don't return in small pieces, but large: a bombardment. My mam screams, garda holler, his brothers shout obscenities in Gaelic, neighbors beg for respect for the dead.

"Richard reaches down to the ground at the side of our lane, where we lived across from each other all our lives, the one with our clachan of homes, our thatched roofs and lime-washed homes, and pulls a mountain aven flower—white and pure with a yellow center—from the side of the road. It is a sole flower, which had forced its way through the broken cobblestones. These flowers usually grow in clusters, but only one grows at our feet that morning. He places it in my hands as they pull him away. He says again, 'I will find you.'"

Maeve stopped and closed her eyes. I patted her forearm. "Did he? Did he find you?"

"For a long time," Maeve said, "I saw him everywhere: in the waves, in the mountain aven, in the three brown sails of the hookers on Galway Bay. Everywhere. But he was gone."

I held my breath; she stared at me and spoke. "What happened to your Jack? Did you even bother to look for him, find him, or he you?"

"This is your story. Mine is simpler. Next-door neighbor moved away. I'm in love now—getting married to the most wonderful man."

"Oh, but this *is* your story. The truth of a story is what the storyteller aims for. You just haven't seen it. We live our stories over and over in every generation, at the edge of every sea. And the mistakes go on and on."

"What do you mean?"

"Finding what we long for and being brave enough and wise enough to build our lives around that, without considering what others expect of us or what we *should do* and who we *should* be."

I sighed. "Are we still on the same subject, Maeve?"

"What, do you think me daft? Of course we're on the same subject. Are you brave enough?"

"Maeve, now this isn't like it was with you and Richard. These are different times."

"And the same."

"No," I said.

"Yes, it is the same. Just tell me how you said good-bye. Tell me what happened."

"His family moved away very abruptly when his father . . . . it's all quite sordid and sad. I don't remember all of it."

"You do remember."

I leaned back in the chair. "I want to hear what happened with Richard."

She grinned with only one side of her dainty mouth, as if winking at me with her smile. "I will tell you the rest of the story after you tell me about saying good-bye to Jack. How old were you?"

"Fourteen, almost fifteen."

"Hmmm."

"Ooh, I don't want to tell this story. It's old and irrelevant now."

"Then don't." She closed her eyes, and in less than a breath, she was asleep, like a child collapsing after Christmas morning. I slumped back in the chair—so weary. Weary of my work, of being sick, of the knot in my neck, of the wedding plans.

I rose from the chair and placed the concrete angel on Maeve's dresser, on top of one of the many lace doilies. I walked over to the oil painting, ran my finger along the bottom metal label on the frame: GALWAY BAY: CLADDAGH.

"What are you doing with Grandmama's painting?" a voice said from behind me.

I jumped, turned to a woman standing in the

108

doorway, her hands on her hips, her mouth straight and bloodless. Her auburn hair was pulled back in a clip, yet curls sprang from all directions, as if fighting the hold.

"Nothing . . . nothing," I said. "I was visiting her today . . . and she just fell asleep. I left my angel for her. . . ." I pointed at the statue. "And I was getting ready to leave."

"With her painting?"

"No," I shook my head. "I've been her assigned companion."

She turned toward the door, waved at it. "Let's talk out there, please." She nodded toward the hall.

I followed this woman through the door. When we reached a sitting room, she guided us toward an empty corner, where we sat opposite each other in floral armchairs. "What do you need with my grandmama?"

"I don't want or need anything from her. I care about her. I've been visiting her for a couple weeks. I just sit and talk to her . . . that's all. I don't want anything from her."

The woman rubbed a trembling hand over her forehead. "This just sucks. Like I don't feel guilty enough already, now I have a stranger making me feel worse because you see her more than I do."

"I've only met with her twice before. I'm not trying to make you feel guilty."

She looked up. "I know, I'm doing that all by myself." Her features softened as she removed her suit jacket, leaned back in the chair. "Grandmama came over to the States for a visit, and then she got too feeble to live with us, and we've all been so damn busy . . . and now Mom is sick too and I'm just tired of it all. I can't take care of everyone. I have a six-year-old too. . . ."

"I'm sorry you're going through all that. Really I am. I don't want anything from Maeve. I've just grown . . . fond of her. I've wanted to meet the family."

"Why do you want to know about us?" Her face closed in again; she turned her wedding ring around and around without looking down. I glanced at her hand: a Claddagh ring with a large emerald encircled her left ring finger.

"A Claddagh ring," I said.

"Yes. You haven't answered me. Why do you need to know about our family?"

I sighed. "Listen, I'm not trying to find out about your family. Just Maeve. You see, she's been telling me the most beautiful story, a love story really, and she never gets to the end, and I want to know how it ends . . . if she married . . ." I bit my lip.

"Let me guess . . . a young man and his true love are separated by the sea when he is taken away. The young maiden waits and waits and he returns with a gift—the skill of knowing how to make a Claddagh ring." She held her hand in the air, pointed to her ring—a crown over a heart held by two hands. "This is what they look like. They stand for love." She pointed to the heart. "Loyalty"—she pointed to the

110

crown—"and friendship." She ran her finger around the hands.

"I know," I said, a memory bumping the surface of my consciousness. "I have one."

"Well, anyway—the Richard Joyce she talks about gives his lover this ring and they live happily ever after."

"Is that how it ends?"

"What do you mean?"

"She only got as far as Richard being taken . . . how the sea will separate them and how she doesn't know where he is."

"What did you say your name is?"

"I didn't; you didn't ask. It's Kara Larson. And yours?"

"Caitlin Morgan. Listen . . . Kara, I hate to burst any bubble you might have about my grandmama, but that story is an ancient Irish legend about the Claddagh ring. A man named Richard Joyce from Galway—the Claddagh village where she lived—was on a merchant ship headed to the West Indies in the 1600s. He was captured by Algerian privateers and sold into slavery to a Turkish goldsmith who trained him for over fifteen years. All during that time his lover believed in his faithfulness and waited for his return."

I stood up and began to pace the room. "Maeve didn't say this man was kidnapped . . . she said he was taken by the garda."

Caitlin nodded. "Yes—she gets her stories confused now."

"Okay—did he return to her? He said he'd find her no matter what. . . ." At least I could discover if that part were true.

"Yes. When William the Third ascended the throne, he freed all the slaves in Algeria. The goldsmith valued Richard, since by then he had become an expert designer, so he offered Richard money and his firstborn daughter in marriage. But Richard returned to Claddagh, to his true love. There he designed and made the Claddagh ring—for her."

"Oh . . . and this is a legend?" I stopped in front of Caitlin's chair, my voice broke.

"It depends on who you talk to. Some believe it is true, others don't. Richard Joyce is known to have made the first Claddagh ring, but whether the story is true? Who knows? It doesn't really matter—the point is that it is Grandmama's favorite. She's told it over and over to us until I have it memorized. We all wear the ring; we all know the story and what the ring stands for: love, loyalty, and friendship."

I stared out the tinted nursing home window. "Wow. I thought she was telling a story about her life. She didn't change his name. She said his name was Richard."

"Richard Joyce. Grandmama is a bard—a storyteller in Ireland. She loves to tell stories. She believes they guide and define our lives."

"But she changed the names and even some of the places."

"Galway Bay?"

"No, she didn't change that, but here's the weirdest part—she asked me to find him."

"Find him?" Caitlin Morgan twisted her Claddagh ring again. "She must be even more confused than usual."

"Or maybe she wanted me to find . . ." I stopped, reached for my own engagement ring and held the top of the diamond with my thumb and forefinger.

"Find what?"

"Nothing," I said, waving my hand. "She did tell me he was taken into an Industrial School—some kind of horrible foster home in Ireland."

"Oh . . . I get it. Well, that makes me even sadder . . . she's mixing up her stories. Grandmama was a huge advocate in the reformation of Industrial Schools, where she believed children were neglected. She was instrumental in exposing the maltreatment and horrible facilities. She is very well known in Ireland for her devotion to this cause. She just got her two stories mixed up. Bloody hell, she's ninety-six years old. Of course she got her stories mixed up. She calls me by my cousin's name sometimes."

I sighed. "Well, it was a pleasure to hear the story anyway." I turned to walk away, slinging my purse farther up on my shoulder. I lifted my chin. "It was nice to meet you." My feet were leaden, my heart as well.

"You too."

I walked away, my soul opening in the wrong places—the sad places where Mama's absence

113

throbbed, where hurt and disillusionment lived. Maeve's story was just a legend—her own concoction of truth and myth, fiction and nonfiction.

I left Verandah House and walked down the block toward my car, then changed my mind and my direction and ended at the community dock on Bay Street. I sat and took my shoes off, let my feet dangle above the water. When high tide rolled in, I'd be able to just touch the surface of the water. Low tide. High tide. They rolled in and out twice a day, a continuous movement of the earth's oceans. If only my memories were as reliable. If I told the story of Jack Sullivan, of his leaving, would I, more than thirteen years later, now confuse the truth in the telling? Would I mix the facts up like Maeve had?

Well, maybe Maeve knew exactly what she was doing—maybe only the myths were worth recounting. A true story: Jack Sullivan. Now there was a very true story.

CHAPTER EIGHT

Some of those days with Jack were blurred around the edges and couldn't be brought into focus, even with the magnifying glass of pure concentration. But I did remember crab trap buoys bobbing on the surface of sharp winter whitecaps, barefoot races over the dunes, sea oats dancing in a storm, the wind warm and moist on my face, a corner of yellow sailboat—snapshots someone forgot to label with place and time.

Our street had been thick with oaks, planted so closely together that their branches and roots intertwined to form a wall, but within those roots Jack and I found caverns, private hiding places for when the dinner bell rang or Jack's dad came screaming drunk to the front porch.

If we hid long enough, dinner would pass or Jack's father's anger would subside, and we'd emerge. Sometimes it was just Jack and me, but many other times my brother, Brian, or Jack's brother, Jimmy, joined us. We were pirates or explorers—anything other than ourselves. Deirdre never came. She was older and behaved more appropriately than I did. And I knew this because I was told so numerous times a day by Aunt Martha-Lynn, who lived with us in the days before Mama died and for a while afterward.

Mama died on a winter day when I was nine years old, and I don't remember a time of not knowing she would die. I don't remember finding out or being told that she would let illness take her, I just understood it. Someone must have told me she was sick, because she didn't get the ovarian cancer until I was seven years old. But even in the days before I was five years old, in the fragmented memories of toddlerhood, I knew she'd leave us. This can't be true, but demonstrates how memory is a cloudy and upside-down thing, shifting like the topography of the earth after a quake, tectonic plates of memory and imagination re-formed.

This was one of the reasons I took pictures now—to keep the memories in order.

After Mama died, Jack knew I craved more than ever those moments of solitude in the cavernous root system of our trees. In this hidden place, our friendship grew with each season and became separate from what we had with his brother, and my family. Eventually it was a bond of just Jack and me: one single tree.

Our friendship then flowed to the estuary, which ran sideways past our houses, to the river, the marsh, the beach. We spent all our free time together when he was not playing a sport, and I wasn't reading or studying.

I don't believe we would have defined our relationship then as boyfriend and girlfriend—our constant companionship was not planned or discussed. Boyfriends and girlfriends asked each other out. Our coming together was a natural outgrowth of something planted in the caves of the live oaks, in the solitary moments of grief and confusion.

One morning, a humid August morning, with few precious days remaining until high school began, I curled into my sheets, turned my face toward the fan in the corner of my room. The morning light whispered across my windowsill, but had not fully arrived. I had been in the same bedroom in the east corner of our home since the day I was born, since the day Mama brought me home from the hospital wrapped in a white lace blanket crocheted by Aunt Martha-Lynn.

I saw the coming day—every day—before anyone

else in my family, and there was something amiss with this particular morning, something my half-asleep brain defined as wrong. I walked to the window and lifted the Battenburg lace curtain. Sun sifted through the lace holes like honey poured onto the floor, my arm, my cotton nightgown.

I heard the sound before I saw the truck: a grinding, damaged sound not meant to exist in the dawn. Gas odor joined the morning fog, which still lay between our homes, not having yet rolled back toward the water. The truck was visible over the trees: a large moving van in the Sullivans' driveway.

I turned from the window and never hesitated as I ran from my room, down the side stairs, through the kitchen and out the back door. My feet were bare; the ground was warm and sticky like chocolate. I ran across our wide front yard, then through the trees and hedges to the Sullivans' yard.

I ran smack into a large man carrying a box. "Whoa, missy, watch where you're going." He shoved the box into the back of the truck, its interior already filled with containers and furniture stacked against each other in odd-shaped patterns of morphed monsters.

"Whose stuff is that?" I squinted against a spotlight, which shone into the rear of the truck.

The man wiped his forehead with a handkerchief, waved at the Sullivans' house. "Excuse me, we're in a major rush here. You best get out of the way before you get hurt. The missus wants to leave before sunrise."

He pointed to the horizon, to the sliver of dawn on the marsh beyond our creek that seemed to be waiting for permission from this man before it burst forth.

I pushed past him and ran to the front door, where Mrs. Sullivan sat on the stoop, her head in her hands.

I stopped short. I had never seen her in any position but standing tall, smiling with her hand holding a dripping paintbrush or molding a wet lump of clay. She was an artist, something Aunt Martha-Lynn often said with a smirk, or an acid tone to her voice. "You know how artists are, always flighty and—"

No, I didn't know how artists were, but if they were all like Mrs. Sullivan, I thought they must be pretty cool people. Her house was always a bit messy with interesting things, like a birds' nest on the kitchen counter (Aunt Martha-Lynn would've had a heart attack), or a clay pot drying in the sun, or a half-finished oil painting on driftwood. Pieces of Mrs. Sullivan's art were piled in corners and on tables.

Often at night she had friends over, friends who wore long beads and beards, who smoked cigarettes that were thin and simmered sweet and heady compared to Daddy's pipe.

Daddy often forbade me from going into Jack's house, which Aunt Martha-Lynn called a den of iniquity, whatever that was. But I had enough friends, including Charlotte on the next street, for Daddy not to know where I was all the time.

I reached down and touched the back of Mrs. Sullivan's head. She looked up at me. A ripe bruise, like an apple tossed on the road, covered the left side of her face, distorting her features. Her eye was swollen shut.

I'd seen other bruises on Mrs. Sullivan before: her arm, cheek, calf. She always told me the marks were from horseback riding, or a fall or clumsy motion on her part.

I gasped. "A horse again?"

"No," she whispered, "there never was a horse. It was and always will be from Mr. Sullivan." She stood and placed her hand on the side of my face. "Precious Kara, so sweet, so innocent. I'm sorry."

"For?" A fear rose, a fear I had never felt before, one of unexpected abandonment. It was tinged with the fear I'd felt when Mama was gone, but that had been planned for, expected.

In my experience, people you loved were not allowed to leave unannounced before dawn's light with a bruise covering one eye. Mrs. Sullivan wrapped her arms around me, pulled me into her patchwork shawl. "We are leaving today, Kara. I am taking my boys and we are leaving with what we can before Mr. Sullivan returns."

"No!" I screamed and pushed her away.

"Dear child, I was hoping you would not awaken, but you are here, and of course you would be. Your sensitive spirit felt Jack leaving."

"Where are you going?" I whispered.

"I don't know." She looked away.

"Yes, you do," I said, because I saw it was true, in

her eyes, in her glance toward Jack.

"Please try to understand," she said without meeting my gaze.

Jack came up next to his mother. We had danced around our growing relationship all summer, touched hands and cheeks and legs more than was necessary on the beach, in the water, on the boat. The sensations and promise they held were too enormous to talk about. We'd been approaching our growing love quietly, like coming near a scared baby osprey in the nest without its mama. Gentle now, slow now . . .

There would be no more waiting. Jack stood behind his mother and I loved him, enormously, fiercely, openly, and desperately. Of course I did—I had for my entire young life. But there had been time then, huge swaths of time, in which to discover our feelings, to let them grow. Or maybe we love so profoundly when we know love is about to leave us, empty and alone.

Now Mrs. Sullivan had ripped time away—nothing remained but mere moments.

The sun rose. Its light landed on his face, revealed an age and a weariness I had never seen before. A cry grew behind my heart. Jack opened his arms and I went into them, buried my face in his shirt. He smelled like sweat and sleep combined. He'd been packing and loading the truck with his brother.

I'd dreamt about Jack's touch during that summer, that summer of waiting. Now I knew the rush and release of all I'd held in some locked place in my middle. I have since come to believe this was why I had no patience in my adult life—the patient waiting I'd done for Jack when I believed I had all the time in the world was wasted.

The moving man slammed the rear door of the van, then backed out of the driveway. I held fast to Jack. "Where are you going?" I asked, the words mumbled into his shirt. He didn't answer, but stroked the back of my head, ran his fingers around and through my sleep-tangled hair.

"Mama won't tell us." His voice came choked, full of pain.

"What?" I pulled back from him, looked up at his face.

"Kara, Father hit her for the last time. . . . I know we've never talked about what he does. Yesterday was a very bad day. She's done with it and so are we. He's gone, but we don't know for how long. Mama packed everything she could. We're leaving . . . now."

"Why didn't you . . . tell me?"

"I didn't know until last night . . . when Mama started making us all pack up."

"You weren't going to tell me?" A sob tore its way up my throat.

"I knew you'd hear us in the morning. I knew you'd come. You always come at the right time. If you'd come before now you'd have made it . . . worse than it already is."

"You can stay. You can stay here with us . . . your mama and Jimmy can leave. You can stay. You can." I

121

grabbed on to his arm, squeezed as though that would keep him there.

"You know I can't leave her. There is no way. But I will call you as soon as I know where we are . . . as soon as I can. I promise I'll come find you. . . ."

"If you don't, I'll find you," I said, small and fading.

"I know you will. I know." He touched my face, leaned in and kissed me. All the yearning was mixed with the pain of his leaving, with the dread of farewells. His lips touched mine and I understood the word "one."

A screeching of tires erupted down the road, a ripping sound. Mr. Sullivan's car careened into the driveway. Jack released me. "One more minute, we only needed one more minute," he muttered.

Jack ran to his mother, who was shutting the trunk of the car, and stood in front of her as Mr. Sullivan staggered toward them.

Time and space stood still, like in the Bible story where God tilted the earth and paused time for a moment.

"Son." Mr. Sullivan grabbed Jack's shoulders, his voice level and low. "Get out of my way now. This ain't none of your business."

"Don't touch her, Dad. Don't touch her again." Jack's voice was older, deeper, not the voice of the boy I knew: a man.

"You have no idea who you're messing with, son. You think you're protecting your precious mother, don't you? Do you know who she's been sleeping with? Who she's been messing around with while she pretends it's all about the art, the painting?"

"Stop," Jack said.

"You want me to stop? Maybe you should've told your mother that when she was—"

Now it was my turn. "Stop!" I hollered, and ran toward them. "Stop." Then I turned toward my house and, using all that was left within me, screamed as loud as I knew how. "Daddy, Daddy!" My voice and face were raised to my home next door.

Mr. Sullivan reached his hand into the air, opened his mouth and released a gnarled sound of anger. The thick smell of bourbon came from deep within him, where it must live. I thought to duck, bend down away from his hand, but my astonishment at what he was about to do stopped me—a paralyzing disbelief.

When his hand came down and across my face, I was still screaming for Daddy. The sting of pain was shrouded by incredulity, shock. I fell to the ground, not from the pain, which I barely felt, but from the force. My knees buckled and my palms stopped my fall. I felt the sting of pavement more than the slap that had forced me to the ground.

Jack's howl was animalistic, raw against my open heart. He lunged toward his father and pummeled his face with clenched fists just as my daddy came running full speed toward us. His feet were bare, his striped pajama bottoms tied at the waist, his mouth moving with words I had never heard him say, ones I did not know were within his cultured expressions.

Daddy pulled Jack from his dazed father, who was now on the ground. I jumped up, ran toward the confusion, toward Daddy and Jack. Jack lifted his left foot, reached it back and kicked his father in the ribs. A loud crunching sound made nausea rise to the back of my throat, just as the pain from the slap ascended to my face, to my cheek. I turned and bent over.

Jack grabbed me, pulled me to him, and the sting of the slap, the emptiness waiting just past me with a vortex of loneliness, faded. He reached into his pocket, withdrew his hand in a fist, then held his hand out to me and opened it. On his palm lay a round gold ring—one I distinctly knew was a Claddagh ring. "I meant to give this to you for your birthday next week, but now is as good a time as any. Not the way I meant it to be."

Mr. Sullivan groaned behind us, words garbled and empty of meaning. Jack looked down at him. "Not the way I meant it to be at all."

I lifted the ring—words gone, emotions churning. Jack took the ring from me, then slipped it onto my right ring finger. "I'll call you when we get . . . somewhere."

Then I heard Mrs. Sullivan screaming, "Get in the car. Get in the car. Get in the car." It sounded like a mantra from a deranged lunatic.

Mr. Sullivan stood up then, his fists clenched at his side, blood leaking from his mouth. "You son of a bitch, I'm going to kill you." He lunged toward my daddy, who sidestepped him. Mr. Sullivan fell to the ground with the momentum of his delirious anger.

Sirens screeched across the road. Flashing lights joined the rising sun, and dizziness enveloped me as I heard my daddy tell Mrs. Sullivan to get in the car and go, go now, he'd take care of the rest.

Jack turned from me, then back again. He touched my cheek, kissed me one more time, a long, beautiful kiss.

"I'll find you," I said as the dizziness became complete and I let go—released the control to stand.

When I awoke, I was in my bed with Aunt Martha-Lynn standing over me, clucking, holding ice to my cheek. I looked up at her, swiped at the ice pack, which hurt more than the leftover ache of the slap.

"Are they gone?" I meant to say, but no sound, no voice came out.

"Shhh. Shhh. You're fine." She leaned toward me, a tear falling down her cheek. "You've lost your voice from screaming for your daddy. He probably saved poor Mrs. Sullivan's life."

I shook my head. "Jack did." I mouthed the words.

"Yes, child, so did Jack. You both did. Now Mr. Sullivan is in jail . . . and they're gone."

"Gone," I mouthed again, then rolled over and let the sleep take me where I needed to go: oblivion.

In those young years I doubted if anyone else had ever experienced such an amazing memory of joy mixed with such staggering pain. How could both be present in the same moment, exist together in the same space and time? I wrote about it: poems and letters. When Mama had died there had been grief without joy. But when Jack had kissed me good-bye, there'd been both.

I still didn't understand it, but I didn't know anyone who did. And, truly, I'd stopped thinking about it.

I swung my feet over the dock, and water licked my toes. The tide had come in during my remembering. It was incredible to me that I could still, after all these years of forgetting, bring up details. Or maybe I had changed some of them, colored over parts. I didn't know. The only way to know would be to ask Jack.

No. I cracked my neck, stood. This was insanity. I needed to stop by the florists and double-check the flower order, call the dressmaker and check on the progress of the bridesmaids' dresses, call in the menus for the golf event, and, of course, find a band.

A band: the Unknown Souls.

CHAPTER NINE

I avoided all thoughts of Maeve's myth of the Claddagh ring, of a good-bye on a dawn Low-country morning, and plowed through my work for the remainder of the day. When I settled into the library that night to read over the list of things left to do for the tournament, the bruised fatigue of the flu pulled at my eyelids. I lay my head back on the leather chair, took a deep breath of Daddy's pipe tobacco.

The warm, yearning feeling for Jack that had once

sat directly in my middle awakened. Sweet Jack. He, his mother, and Jimmy went to Arizona. He finally sent me a letter, which arrived a month after he left. This was an interminable length of time for a girl in love, twisting her Claddagh ring around and around until a raw spot appeared on her finger.

Eventually high school started, but my heart didn't. We wrote back and forth, back and forth until life sped up, until high school and dates and dances and cheerleading filled the emptier moments of missing Jack, and the picture of our good-bye became tattered and faded.

Mr. Sullivan eventually disappeared into a pit of alcoholism and unemployment. The last I heard of him was when I was in tenth grade, and he was found asleep on Main Street. He'd lost his house, his wife, and his family. Although people murmured clucks of regret and said, "Poor Mr. Sullivan, his cheating wife up and left him with nothing," I had no sympathy for him. I felt nothing but contempt for the man who took Jack away from me and slapped me to the ground.

Daddy didn't let us talk about what had happened that early morning, and there began the slow process of denial. He'd deemed the Sullivan family trashy and was relieved when they'd left.

A thump startled me as my files fell to the floor. I opened my eyes. "Shit," I said, and leaned down to pick up the papers, then lifted my gaze to see Charlotte standing in the library doorway.

"Hello, girlfriend," she said. "You look like hell."

"Thanks." I threw a pillow at her and sat up.

"No, really, you do. Not just like you've been sick, but like you've . . . been really sick."

"Very long day."

"Thought the doc told you to take it easy."

I shrugged. "I tried. I went to see Mrs. Mahoney today, and I've got to get through these files tonight."

"Oh, that's just what you needed to be doing—visiting Mrs. Mahoney."

"I just sort of . . . ended up there."

"Well, you never ended up at Mom's and she asked me to drop these drawings off for you."

I groaned. "Oh . . . I remembered, and then I guess I forgot."

"What in the world are you so preoccupied with?" Charlotte sat on the edge of the ottoman in front of my chair.

"If you don't remember, I've been in bed, sick for days on end."

"I just came by to check on you. Every time I've come the last few days you've been sound asleep."

"Hey . . ." I hesitated, then continued, "do you remember when Jack left?"

Charlotte rolled her eyes, then lay all the way back on the ottoman, her legs dangling off the end. She stared at the plaster ceiling, where a cut-glass chandelier had hung since before I was born. "How could I not? Terrible day . . . and you didn't snap out of it for what? A year, maybe two? Thought I'd lost you forever."

128

"Hmmm."

Charlotte leaned across the chair and grabbed my hand. "You're getting married in a few weeks. Now is absolutely not the time to wonder what happened to Jack Sullivan. Things work out the way they should. He's probably married with seven children and living in Seattle."

"No," I said, and swung my legs to the floor and stood.

"What do you mean?"

"Follow me." I motioned for her to come to the computer, clicked open the Internet and pulled up the Unknown Souls Band.

Charlotte took a deep breath as I clicked on Jack's face and biography. "You Googled him?" she asked. "You have just opened up an entire can of . . . problems if you don't leave this alone. But now that we're here . . . what's he doing?"

"Best I can tell, he and his brother, Jimmy, formed a band, Unknown Souls. They did it at first to raise money for an orphanage, but they had such a great response, they kept on playing. Now they're getting popular and actually have a recording contract. Peyton's heard of them."

"You asked Peyton about Jack?"

"No." I punched the side of her arm. "He found me looking at the Internet."

"And . . ."

"He thought I was looking for a band for the golf tournament. He told me they've gotten too big to play benefits, but that he heard them play a couple years ago and they were really good. They somehow combine Celtic, rock and bluegrass, or something like that."

"Wow. Wouldn't you just love to hear them?" Charlotte tapped the computer screen.

I nodded.

She leaned down. "Probably not a very good idea."

"Just to make this all a little crazier . . . I'm thinking of asking them if they'd play the tournament fundraiser."

"I love crazier." Charlotte leaned back on her heels.

"I've been hanging out with you for way too long if I'm even considering contacting them."

"No way," she said. "You're not blaming me. I will take no responsibility for what comes after this. But"—she grinned—"I will participate in any way you wish—only at your urging, of course."

"Okay—enough. I've got to get some sleep." I pushed print on the tour dates. "I'm wiped. Thanks for checking on me. I'm going to sleep and maybe, just maybe tomorrow I'll be back on top of my game. Please apologize to your mom and thank her for sending the drawings."

"She's worried about you."

"She's been worried about me since Mama died."

"True, but she is more so now. Says you've got too much on your plate."

I nodded. "Tell her I'm fine. I'll stop by tomorrow, okay?"

Charlotte hugged me. "I actually have a date tonight. I'm off."

"Who?"

"This guy I met at your shower . . . some friend of Peyton's. Tom Schneider—you know him?"

I shook my head. "Golfer?"

"Yep. And I guess they leave for a tournament tomorrow . . . so we're going out tonight."

"Peyton already left for the tournament—some PR thing this evening."

Charlotte hugged me and left. When I opened the door to my bedroom, I faced over three days' worth of dirty laundry, papers, and strewn clothing. I wanted Mama. I wanted to curl up in her lap, let her pick up the clothes, let her stroke my forehead. This need didn't come from a recollection of her ever having done such things for me—or maybe it did. My memories were mixed up and scattered now.

I walked over to my dresser, pulled out the top drawer. I'd lived in this room for my entire life, except for the four years at college. I knew where everything was stashed. I pulled out the white marble jewelry box Aunt Martha-Lynn had given me the Christmas after Mama died. A row of padded ring holders was on the left side, a compartment for earrings and necklaces on the right.

I opened the top and stared inside at a tarnished chain with a dolphin pendant; a leather bracelet with *Kara* engraved on the flat side, braided at the edges; a mood ring permanently stuck on black; and a

Claddagh ring slanted sideways in the frayed lavender silk. I lifted the ring from the box and slipped it on my pinkie finger.

I closed my eyes. Tomorrow I would do everything I could to get Maeve to tell me the end of her story—even if it was a legend. I could not afford to be patient; I would not waste time, because I never knew, as with Jack at dawn, when I'd run out of it.

CHAPTER TEN

A week came and went; the moon rose full, and the tides reached higher than normal, running over the seawalls at the end of Palmetto Pointe. Maeve wasn't lucid enough during this time to even know I was present at her bedside, much less to resume a story she hadn't finished. I continued to leave my wingless angel in her room in the hope that she'd remember what she'd begun.

I had researched the legend of the Claddagh ring and found that there were a couple of theories regarding its design and appearance on the shores of Galway Bay, and that yes, Richard Joyce's was one of those legends. This meant that I did know the end of the story. I did know what happened to him and to their love. So why did I keep returning, hoping and waiting for Maeve to reveal the ending?

Was it because I didn't have the ending to Jack's story? I didn't really know what had happened to him?

I sat in my car at a red light with my window open to breathe in the scent everyone else said you couldn't smell, but I swore I could: high tide. I reached into my briefcase for the list of Unknown Souls tour dates. They were playing in Savannah the next night. I'd known this for a week and had watched and waited—not for an excuse to go, but for an excuse *not* to go: an event, party, or appointment. But tomorrow loomed with empty spaces on my Palm Pilot, and Savannah was only an hour and a half away.

A honk pulled me from my reverie, and I turned left onto my street and then into my driveway, where Peyton's Jaguar was parked. He was leaning against the hood talking on his cell phone. I jumped from the car and gave him a silent hug as he continued his conversation. He hugged me back and patted my bottom, held up his finger, and mouthed, "Hold on."

"Yes, Mom. No problem. See you in a few." He dropped the phone into his back pocket and hugged me again. "Hey, darling."

"What are you doing here? I thought your tournament went until tomorrow...."

"Yeah, it does if you qualified."

"What happened?" The last time Peyton hadn't qualified for the final round, I'd had to half carry him out of a bar in Boston back to his hotel room, then listen to him throw up for hours. The start of a beautiful relationship, indeed.

"I had a lousy day. Couldn't find the damn green no matter what I did. It absolutely sucked. Chad scumbag

133

Scarborough qualified. He's never beat me, ever, in ten years."

"I'm sorry." I scrunched my face into a scowl. "Really I am. And I'm even sorrier I wasn't there."

He scooped me into his arms. "Me too. I probably would've done a lot better if you had been. But it was a smaller tournament."

I nodded. "How did Caroline do?" I had sent her to help with this tournament, a chance for her to gain experience for the Palmetto Pointe Open.

"Kara, I have no idea. I don't keep up with the event planners."

I held up my hand. "Whoa, sorry."

"No, I'm sorry. Just in a foul mood. Everything seemed to be going smoothly . . . I'm sure she's doing a great job. I was just a little focused on the course, not the parties."

"Well, that would be a first." I laughed.

"I just wanted to come give my beautiful fiancée a kiss . . . I promised Mom I'd go straight to her house."

"What?"

He shrugged. "Something about needing my help in the garage apartment."

"Oh . . . okay. See you tonight?"

"Well, I promised Ray I'd meet him to discuss this investment idea he has. . . ."

"Tomorrow?" I pouted.

He wrinkled his nose. "Kara, I'm sorry. I've got to fly to Miami to check out this new golf course the tour wants to use. I'm on that committee."

"I know, I know. . . ." I leaned against his chest. "When will I see you?"

"Saturday. Promise. You didn't think you'd see me until then anyway. We'll hide away all weekend. Deal?"

"Perfect. It's been . . . weeks since we've been alone." I kissed him, touched the side of his face. He reached up and took my hand.

"Where did you get that?" He touched the ring on my small finger.

"I found it in an old jewelry box. It's a Claddagh ring."

"I know what it is." He tapped his finger on top of my engagement ring. "Can't touch this, though, can it?"

"No, it can't." I kissed him. "An old friend gave it to me—God, all the way back in middle school," I said.

"Wishing you were back in middle school?"

"No." I lifted my hand to the sun. "Just found it and thought it was . . . nice."

"Isn't it supposed to be like the Irish wedding ring?"

"Yes, but it can be given friend to friend, sister to sister, mother to daughter. . . ." I lifted it up. "It means love, loyalty and friendship."

"It's dented." He touched the side of the ring.

"I know. That's where Deirdre slammed my finger in the car door." I hadn't even realized I remembered that.

"You know what? It is weird the things you remember." He kissed me before he drove off.

"Yes," I whispered to the empty driveway. "It is weird the things I remember."

Peyton's car turned the corner. I couldn't say other women on the tour hadn't warned me—it was terrible being married to or in love with these players who traveled all the time. I pulled out my cell phone and dialed Charlotte's number as I climbed the front stairs, then sat down on the porch swing.

"Hey . . ." She sounded winded.

"You in the mood for a road trip tomorrow?" I could barely believe I was asking.

"Why?"

"Thought I'd check out a band for the tournament." I pushed my feet against the floorboards to set the swing in motion, as if trying to convince myself that this was a perfectly normal day, a perfectly normal request.

"Kara? Are you sure?"

"Ah, forget it. . . . Where are you?"

"The gym," Charlotte said. "Let me call you back, okay?"

"Okay." I hung up the phone, leaned back in the swing, then clicked the phone to off.

The rain awakened me—soft and light, but the air full of humidity, as if it were pregnant and overdue. My head was heavy and I wanted to roll over and go back to sleep. And, as I did every morning, I mentally scanned what I had to do that day. I had a PGA TOUR meeting at eight a.m., where I would, once again, have to admit I didn't have a band. Then there was a full blank space—Savannah. Of course I hadn't typed it in, barely admitting to myself that if the day opened up, I would go.

Peyton was in Miami, and Charlotte had a full day, since her freelance article for the local paper was late. And I did need a band, didn't I? I got out of bed, stretched and stared at myself in the full-length mirror across the room. Had I changed much since I was fourteen years old? Since the last time I saw Jack? Completely. Where a scrawny girl once stood, with scabs on her arms and legs from believing she could keep up with the boys while running or riding her bike, now there was a woman with long wavy chestnut hair, rounded knees and elbows, a manicure and pedicure: all the rough edges smoothed.

I walked to the closet and stared at my outfits until I chose a pair of wide-leg, black Donna Karan pants with a fitted white linen button-down top. I'd wear my full-length black toile coat if the weather turned. I slipped the Claddagh ring off my pinkie finger and tucked it back into the jewelry box.

Before I walked out the door I stood in front of the computer with an overwhelming need to see, clearly see, what 1920 Galway Bay would've looked like, what Maeve once saw. I searched the Internet until I found an antique postcard on eBay with the inscription *The Claddagh, Galway* etched on the bottom. It was an old black-and-white photo that had been hand colored. The whitewashed houses with thatched roofs squatted behind a bay wall that was full to over-flowing with hookers. The boats had been painted green and red, the sails folded down like children tucked in for the night.

I tried to imagine Maeve living in one of those houses at the edge of the sea, watching out the window for Richard, waiting and waiting. I looked at the postcard again and then clicked on "bid now." I upped the bid by five dollars, closed down the computer and grabbed a Tiffany-blue cashmere scarf and tossed it around my neck.

By the time I'd left my PGA TOUR meeting, my plans for Savannah were confirmed. When the planning committee had asked me what I'd done about securing a band, I'd told them I was on my way to Savannah to follow up with the Unknown Souls. The committee had been relieved.

Rain hit the windshield in intermittent bursts. I popped the Unknown Souls CD into the player, and sped south on I-95 toward Savannah. The information inside the cover stated that all twelve songs were orig-inal. The music coming out of my speakers was haunting, conveying a lovely but lonely ache through both the music and words. The lyrics were written by a man who knew sadness, who understood want.

A raucous, fun song called "Without You" came toward the end of the CD, yet even this song, with its primal drumbeat and guitar solo, offered an exquisite sadness in its comedic take on all the things the singer could do without his lover. I attempted to remember this voice, Jimmy's voice, in song—but I had never heard him sing. What I did remember about Jimmy was his laughter.

Jack's lyrics spoke of dreaming and flying, of loss and love. My breath caught in the edges of my chest; tears rose. These beautiful songs were written by this beautiful boy I had once known and loved. An hour and a half later, I pulled off the exit to River Street, hit the REPLAY button, and parked in a metered spot to hear the song "Flying" one more time. I closed my eyes and leaned my head back on the headrest. A pan flute played in the background with a lyrical sound as delicate as engraved crystal.

When the song was over, the rain had dissipated. I reached behind the seat and grabbed my purse, tossed it over my shoulder. There were three hours remaining until the concert, and the headache forming around my temples was hunger's signal.

My boots clicked in a staccato sound down the cobblestone sidewalk of River Street. I rounded the corner to an antique garden store, walked in and found myself asking about garden angels—did they have any?

A sweet woman, as round and red as a strawberry, escorted me to the back area, where garden statues of every variety stood at odd angles, reminding me of every bad movie I'd seen where children who were hoping to be adopted stood in a room with pleading eyes, facing prospective parents. There wasn't a small angel in sight. I turned away and walked back into the store, browsing the garden accessories.

"Where would I find the closest café?" I asked the shop owner.

"Two doors down to the right." She waved out the door. "Best brie and apple sandwich I've ever eaten. And trust me"—she patted her abdomen—"I've eaten in a lot of places." She smiled and I smiled back at her.

Outside I glanced at the sky. A thin veil resembling a screen ripped from a porch door advanced toward me: a wall of rain. The café was two doors up, the car two blocks down. I ducked my head just as the downpour hit me with its full force. I ran toward the café, my scarf pulled up in a futile attempt to shield my hair.

I burst through the door of the café and wiped the dripping rain from my eyes. Several faces in the room turned to me and smiled. It was a French-style café, with open sides and covered roof, where the tables were set far enough back to stay dry. A girl wearing all black, who appeared to be no more than eighteen, walked toward me. She had an earring in her nose and at least six in each earlobe. I smiled and attempted to wipe the hair off my face.

She laughed. "Wet out there?"

"Just a little, not so much." I shook water off my hands.

She laughed loudly, and more patrons turned to us. There was a table directly in front of us seating six people: four men, two women. I turned away, as I'd been taught better than to stare.

The girl lifted a menu. "Only one at your table?"

"Yes." I held my purse with both hands over my chest. "Only one."

She motioned for me to follow her and I did, but I couldn't help glancing toward that table of six. They all had large, dark beers with heads at least an inch thick. All of them were laughing. Their table looked like a fun, safe place to be. I sighed and caught a glimpse of myself in the passing mirror. My hair was stuck in wet strands against my face, and mascara had pooled under my eyes. I looked away. I was such a fool for leaving my umbrella in the car, and I hadn't brought a change of clothes or more makeup.

As we scooted past the table, I wiped mascara from below my eyes. One of the men seated there, his eyes dark and gold, glanced at me. His hair hung in thick waves, stubble on his chin and cheeks. My chest opened as if someone had blown a breath of luxurious coastal air into me; my stomach sank.

I meant to turn away from his stare, but couldn't. He raised his hand to push the hair out of his eyes. A leather bracelet encircled his wrist, braided and intricate in a Celtic design. I noted each detail: his hair, his goatee, his eyes, his bracelet. It wasn't until I turned away and saw his reflection behind me in the mirror that I could see the whole of him, not just the pieces.

Jack Sullivan.

Surely I was imagining him. Maeve had said something about thinking of things and they come, they happen; about following your feet to your heart. I

141

stopped, turned. The whole table came into focus: three other men, an older woman, another woman—beautiful, exotic, with her arm draped over Jack's shoulders, a beer raised in her other hand.

Jack mouthed my name, "Kara?" in a question.

I stood transfixed, motionless on the outside while everything inside moved or quivered. My throat constricted, my heart quickened, my held breath escaped.

"Jack?" My voice shook.

He nodded and stood from the table, and the other five people stopped talking. The girl watched him, her arm in the air as if his shoulder were still there. He came next to me, and his mouth broke open into a familiar smile.

"Hi, there," I said, my arms wanting to move to hug him, yet stuck at my sides. The hostess tapped my shoulder, pointed to a single table in the corner. "There's your table when you're ready."

"Thank you. . . ."

"Kara Larson. My God." He touched the tips of my hair.

I reached up to my hair, my face. "I'm soaked, aren't I?"

"Yes, you are." He laughed, and the sound was resonant with memories of innocence and childhood.

I tried to smile. My white linen shirt was see-through, my bra clearly visible. I looked up at Jack, crossed my arms over my body. He smiled and pulled me into a hug.

He released me just enough that I was still against

his chest, and I looked into his face.

"What are you doing here? Do you live here?" He pushed a strand of wet hair off my cheek. I shivered.

"No . . . no. I'm here on business and . . . got caught in the rain. I still live in Palmetto Pointe."

Jack glanced over his shoulder, nodded at his friends. "Join us. I only have a million questions to ask you. How have you been? How is your family? The old house? And how's Charlotte?"

I laughed. "All well. All good. You?"

"Now that is a much longer story. Sit, please sit with us."

I backed away. "No, no, I wouldn't want to interrupt, and I have a table and . . ."

"Nice table." He pointed to the corner. "Should be some good conversation over there." He grinned that grin Daddy hated.

I pulled my shirt away from my skin. "Funny, Jack Sullivan."

"Come on, come meet everyone."

"The band?" The words slipped from my mouth.

"Yes." He smiled. "The band. You know about them?"

"A little," I said. "I read about them. . . ."

He pulled a chair from a neighboring table, set it between his seat and another man's, put his arm around my damp shoulder and walked me to the table. "Hey, guys, I want you to meet an old friend. She used to live next door."

The man across the table stood. He wasn't as tall as

143

Jack, but broader, his hair short with curls moving in all directions. He had the appearance—with his softer, half-mast eyes and tousled hair—of having just woken up. "Mary and Joseph, is that you, Kara Larson?"

Jack's older brother, Jimmy. I walked around the table. He met me halfway, hugged me, picked me up off the ground. "We wonder about you . . . don't we, Jacky? We say—I wonder what happened to that adorable Kara Larson? And lookee here—you're past adorable and into gorgeous."

I blushed; I felt it all the way to my wet roots. "Oh . . . I'm soaking wet."

"And quite sexy, I might add." Jimmy threw his head back. He was the same as I remembered him at seventeen—he filled the room with his boisterous laughter.

His spirit had always seemed to shine just a little bit brighter and louder than anyone around him. Jimmy pulled me to his side with one arm. "So what has happened to you?"

"I never left Palmetto Pointe . . . I'm still there, same house and all." It sounded so boring, so mundane that I had the urge to tell him everything in between. But he had already lifted my left hand into the air. "My God, woman, I could skate on that diamond. . . . Who'd you marry?"

"I'm . . . not married. Well, not yet. I'm engaged. . . ."

"Well, that's nice." Jimmy squeezed me. "Since my brother seems too stunned to speak, I'll introduce you.

144

This here"—he slapped the head of the man in front of us with an open palm; the man turned, looked up at me over his shoulder and smiled—"is Harry Makin, our drummer. Over here"—he waved at a tall, thin man slumped in his chair, who looked like he should have a cigarette dangling from his mouth—"that there is Bobby, he's our bass guitar."

Jimmy loosened his hold. "And these two gorgeous dolls"—he waved his hand toward the two women—"are Isabelle and Anna. They're our backup singers and lifesavers."

The blonde he had called Anna threw a wadded-up napkin toward him. "You call me doll again, you'll be singing my soprano part."

Isabelle, the woman who had had her arm draped over Jack, waved with one finger. She looked like an Isabelle: dark and intimidating. Her cheekbones appeared to have been carved from plaster, her features so chiseled that I had to force myself not to stare.

"Hi, nice to meet all of you. I'm so sorry to interrupt your meal." I scooted out from under Jimmy's arm. I did not belong here with these fun-loving and obviously very close people. What had I been thinking?

"Sit down now." Jimmy laughed and steered me by my shoulders to take the chair between Jack and Harry. I sat; my knee brushed up against Jack's, and he looked at me, smiled.

And then it happened. I was fourteen—almost fifteen, thankyouverymuch—and I was waiting, waiting, waiting for Jack, for his touch, for his kiss.

He tousled my wet hair. "So good to see you. You'll have to tell us everything you've been doing."

I nodded and looked around the table. What would it possibly be like to belong to such a group of people? I felt as though I was in the wrong boutique store, trying on the wrong style clothes for my personality and body type. "You've had a much more interesting life . . . you first," I said.

"Interesting is one word for it." Jimmy took a long swallow of his dark beer, slammed the glass down and laughed.

The waitress approached the table. "You don't need your table?" She pointed to the small round table in the corner.

I looked directly at Jack.

"No, she'll stay with us," Jimmy said. "And could you please bring her one of these?"

"You want a Guinness?" Jack tapped the side of his glass.

"Absolutely," I said, although I'd never had one.

Jack unrolled the napkin-wrapped silverware. "You still talk the same. Still. . . ." All five people around the table raised their eyebrows, as if waiting for him to finish his thought. When he lifted his beer, conversation flowed again.

The two women discussed a song with confusing lyrics. Jimmy and Harry argued over whether to get the guitar fixed in a town they didn't know well or wait until Charleston, where they knew someone.

The food arrived on large pottery plates, and I

146

remembered a time when I was a child, probably seven or eight years old, and I was caught in a riptide, pulled out to sea as though a rope were tied to my body. Panicked, I scrabbled toward the surface, fought and clawed my way through the water, unable to find air, banging against the sand and shells on the bottom. Then I had remembered—Daddy said that if I ever got caught in a riptide, I was to let the current take me into calmer waters, where I could reach the surface, then swim parallel to shore—away from the pull. I'd stopped fighting, closed my eyes, and let the current carry me to the stiller waters, where I'd burst to the surface to gasp for air and swim—away from the danger. In the few moments of peace out there, I had understood the absolute calm of letting go.

And, here, at the table with these people, I did the same. I wasn't an observer—but a participant. Soon I would need to swim sideways, but right then I drank my Guinness, bitter and warm, laughed and talked with Jack and his friends. Soon I was past the undertow, floating in their conversation.

I wanted to stay there for a very long time, with Jack's knee brushing up against mine, his hand touching my arm every time he made a point, his eyes—the very same ones with the gold flecks inside the darker brown—looking at me when he spoke. But it ended. The waitress brought the bill, and Jimmy paid it, not allowing me to pick my purse up from the ground. Before they all stood from the table, I grabbed my camera from my bag.

"Wait, don't move. Let me get a picture. . . ." I stood and backed away from the table. This was a single slice of time I wouldn't need a picture to remember, but I wanted one anyway, something to hold. They all scooted together and I held the camera, counted, "one, two, three," and snapped the image of them at the table surrounded by finished beers and empty plates.

As we walked out of the restaurant, I was floating, free. I excused myself to the bathroom to avoid good-byes and awkward reactions to being in their group when they had other places to go, other things to do that absolutely did not include me. I locked the door behind me and leaned into the mirror. My face was flushed, my eyes bright and wide. My brown hair hung around my face in tangled curls. There was no makeup left on my face. I reached into my purse and swiped some pale pink lip gloss across my mouth. Childish games would now be set aside. It was nice remembering how I enjoyed Jack and Jimmy, how I was once a young girl who lived next door to this energy. But it was now time to return to real life.

When I left the bathroom, Jack still stood at the front doorway of the restaurant, leaning against the door frame, a grin on his face. He didn't see me until I came up next to him. "Whatcha grinning about?" I asked.

He wrapped his arm around my shoulder. "Finding you in a restaurant in Savannah, Georgia. All the places I've been . . . and here you are."

"Oh . . ."

"And I thought you promised to find me." He squeezed me tighter.

I did find you.

"Did I?" I shifted my purse higher on my shoulder.

"Oh, how easily we forget." He laughed, then pointed to his group standing around a tour bus. "You probably have to get back to work."

"Work?"

His eyebrows came together. "Thought you said you were here on business."

"I am . . . I was. I'm . . ."

"Well, if you're done, you want to hang with us? We have to get to the auditorium and set up, do the sound check and all that. Come on. . . ." He nodded toward the others.

"I don't know, Jack. I don't want to interrupt your work, and I need to drive back to Palmetto Pointe."

Jimmy hollered toward us. "Come on, we're gonna be late. Come with us, Kara. You'll love it."

Jack grabbed my hand and pulled me toward the bus. "Come with us."

The current took me, and once again I let go and nodded, followed Jack with a rushing sound filling my head like I was underwater. Large block letters ran along the side of the bus: UNKNOWN SOULS. A Celtic design filled the inner letters and wound its way along the length of the bus.

I had so many questions, but they sank, for now, to the floor and the currents of the sea. I sat back on the nubby cushion of the bus seat and watched, in fascination, this world I didn't know existed, a world far from my own.

The six of them talked of instruments and lyrics, of lighting and sound, and I was once again an observer. Arguments turned to laughter, and they lightly punched, touched, and handled each other with familiarity.

My face felt stuck in a permanent grin. As the bus approached the auditorium, Jack came next to me and sat down, placed his hand on my knee. This simple action caused much more than a simple response, as everything in me remembered his kiss, his touch.

"You okay? You look a little shell-shocked," he said.

"This is not a world I'm used to . . . but please don't make me leave yet," I said.

He stared directly at me. "It is so damn good to see you."

I glanced up at a motion above me; Isabelle stood over us, her frown deep. "Jack."

"Yes?" He lifted his hand from my knee.

"Mark"—she nodded toward the bus driver— "needs you. Something about security at the gate."

"Coming," Jack yelled toward Mark, then looked at me. "Just wait here . . . we'll get you into the concert."

"That would be great." I was sure my grin looked goofy next to Isabelle's sly smile. She sat next to me as Jack walked toward the front of the bus. "Now, how do you know Jack and Jimmy?" She flung one long leg over the other.

"I used to live next door to them a long time ago," I said.

"And when was the last time you saw them?"

When their father slapped me to the ground, when their mama took them from me, when my heart stopped beating.

"Oh, when they moved away from Palmetto Pointe, back in the late eighties."

"Hmmm. . . ."

"How do you know them?" My curiosity was more intense than my manners now.

"I've lived with them since high school. Been with them ever since."

I nodded and vaguely wondered what "with them" meant.

The bus came to a stop and Jimmy hollered, "Let's rock and roll!" And everyone stood up, grabbed a bag or instrument, jumped out of the bus.

I stepped down, and Jack came up beside me. "I need your driver's license for the security pass."

"Okay." I opened my purse and reached for my wallet. In slow motion, the Unknown Souls ticket I'd bought from Ticketmaster fluttered to the wet pavement.

Jack looked down at it, then up at me with the cutest thirteen-year-old grin. "Oh, you've already got a seat."

I closed my eyes, wished whatever current I'd been riding would take me under.

He placed his hand on top of my head, heavy and

151

warm. I opened my eyes and he stared at me. "Business, huh?"

I nodded. "Sort of. I need a band for this golf tournament benefit I'm planning . . . and well, sort of."

He leaned down and picked up the ticket, handed it to me. "I'll get you a better seat than this."

"I'm sure you will." I slapped both hands over my face, then peeked between my fingers at him.

He bent down and separated my fingers wide so we were eye to eye, as if we were under the roots of our old tree. "Why didn't you say anything?"

I shrugged. "Embarrassed. But not nearly as much as right now."

Isabelle hollered from a few yards away, "Let's go, Jack."

"Hold on," he shouted back, but didn't turn to her. "You still want to go?"

"Absolutely," I said, feeling fourteen years old and ready to follow him anywhere.

He grinned, put his arm around my shoulder and pulled me toward the back doors of the coliseum.

CHAPTER ELEVEN

The chaos inside the building was far greater than anything I'd ever seen, and it stole my breath, as does a stunningly beautiful painting or sculpture that you don't expect to be as exquisite as it is.

I sat in a metal chair on the far side of the stage and watched in amazement. Jack and Jimmy threw a football with the crew while Isabelle and Anna called to them to get their asses back to work. Harry tuned the guitars, and soon Jack walked toward me with an older man. I stood.

"Kara, this is our band manager and security guru, Luke Mulligan. There isn't a job he hasn't done—some he can't even talk about." He ducked a punch from Luke. "But he'll make sure you get a good seat and aren't left to the wolves around here."

I looked up at the older man: screeching tires, metal grinding. I wanted to cry, but instead a laugh bubbled up. "I do believe I know Mr. Mulligan, and I think I owe you something, sir."

He laughed, hooked his thumbs in his jeans pockets. "Well, well, life does have a funny way about it, don't it?"

"What?" Jack looked back and forth between us.

"Why did you take off like that?" I asked Luke.

"I just believe that every once in a while everyone deserves a mulligan—you know, like in golf."

I laughed. "Absolutely, like in golf."

"And you looked like you could use a mulligan that day more than anyone I'd seen in a very long time. No?"

"Yes, but I don't need one now, so let me know how much it cost."

Jack pressed his hand on his chest. "You want to catch me up?"

Luke slapped him on the back. "Can't stand to be on the outs, can you?"

"Very funny. Story, please."

"Jack here"—Luke nodded toward him—"loves a good story."

"This is *not* a good story," I said, my hands in the air. "I hit your kind band manager's truck with my car, and he drove off without letting me give him my contact information. It was a very, very bad day and not a good story in any way whatsoever." I offered Luke a small curtsy. "Thank you. It was a much-needed mulligan—but I actually got really sick with the flu after that. I'm so sorry, but I can pay you now. Really." I reached for my purse.

"No." He held up his hand.

"What were you doing in Palmetto Pointe?" I searched the bottom of my purse for my checkbook.

"The band had a show nearby—at the Historic Festival in Beaufort." Luke placed his hand on my arm. "Stop looking for money. I won't let you pay."

"Oh?" I glanced at Jack, who turned away. "You were in Palmetto Pointe?"

Luke nodded. "Yeah, but just for the day before we headed to Beaufort—great show. You see it?"

"No, I didn't know. . . ." Trembles ran through my heart, like I'd just been slammed to the floor of the sea after trusting the current. Jack had been in Palmetto Pointe and not called me. Now here I was looking like I'd chased him down in Savannah. I wanted to groan. I didn't.

"You know," I said to Luke, "I'm really glad to see you. I was starting to believe you were an angel of some sort."

"Not an angel." He lifted his arms. "No wings."

"No wings." I smiled.

He tapped my shoulder. "But you look like you could have some buried somewhere. If anyone looks like an angel, it's you."

"With a broken wing," I said and tried to laugh.

"Listen," Luke said, "I have to get back to set up. Let me know if you need anything at all."

I nodded, but Luke didn't see me as he walked off.

Jack gestured toward the back door. "Let's get out of here for an hour or so before I have to help Jimmy warm up."

I glanced around. "They won't be looking for you?"

"Nope, I always sneak off by myself—to get my head together before the show."

"Well, then surely you don't need me messing up your quiet time."

"Do you want to go for a walk or not?" He squeezed my elbow.

I looked over my shoulder, shrugged. If he hadn't even said hello to me in Palmetto Pointe, would I follow him now?

"Come on." He lifted his palms up, and then slapped them together in a prayer pose. "Please?"

I fiddled with the latch on my purse, gazed at the floor, then up at him. "All right."

We strolled in silence along the river, moist air surrounding us after the rain. I slowed down, fell behind him for a minute. "You walk the same," I said.

"Oh, yeah?" He looked over his shoulder. "Does my arse look the same?"

I threw my head back and laughed. "No, it is much, much larger."

He reached behind and grabbed me, picked me up, squeezed me with a tickle under my ribs.

"In a good way, in a good way." I attempted to twist away, laughing.

"I'm sure." He set me down on the ground.

I stood still for a moment and watched him walk. He turned. "You coming?"

I nodded, wanting to tell him to pick me up again, laugh again . . . kiss me. But of course I didn't say any of those things. I twisted my diamond ring and smiled.

We reached a bridge over the river and leaned against the rail without speaking, gazing at the water below. The river moved in its furious and unending surge toward the ocean. It didn't matter who stood and watched this water, who swam in it or fished in it or dumped trash in it, it just kept moving—like time. I could do and do some more, make my to-do list the most important and organized list ever, and time would just flow past me, over me, through me, just like this river. And if I needed any proof of this theory, Jack Sullivan stood next to me as a grown man.

In all my memories of him he had remained the same: just like my photographs always would. But this was no memory, he was flesh and bone. I couldn't make him into who he was, who we were, any more than I could force the river to flow in the opposite direction.

"I did try and see you in Palmetto Pointe," he said in a low voice.

"Oh?" I looked up at him.

"Yep, I drove past our old houses."

"That's looking for me?" I poked his side.

"Yes, it is. You stood on the front porch with some guy—I'm assuming your fiancé—and I didn't want to . . . interrupt. I called the next day, after the concert, but whoever answered said you were sick in bed and couldn't come to the phone. And I just kinda let it go at that. It didn't seem like the right time to . . . track you down or anything."

"I got sick the same day I hit Luke. Not in my list of top-ten days."

Then the silence, which had been comfortable, became awkward and full of unsaid words, until we spoke over each other.

"So, tell me about your fiancé."

"So, where have you been living—tell me . . ."

I smiled. "Fiancé? His name is Peyton Ellers—he's a—"

Jack's laugh interrupted my words. "I know who he is. Wow, that's great, Kara. When's the wedding?"

"It's coming up so fast, end of May. But surely you don't want to hear about it—my life is boring compared to this." I swept my hand back toward the coliseum.

"You, old friend, don't know how to be boring. Okay, when did you last know where I was?"

"It was 1992—September. You wrote from Chicago. That was the last I heard from you. You told me that you'd moved there from Arizona . . . that your mom was doing well, that you . . . missed me." I spoke too fast. Knowing exactly, to the month, when I'd last heard from him . . . I turned away to hide my rising blush.

"I'm sorry, Kara."

"For what?"

"Losing touch."

I waved my hand in the air. "Ah, don't be. Life moves on, you know? I'm sure you were very busy and so was I. Life moves on. . . ."

"Yeah, you said that." He grinned and pulled me next to him. "Very philosophical—life moving on and all that."

"Don't you dare make fun of me."

"Well, it wasn't because I didn't wonder how you were. I just got sucked up into the band and moving around and . . . some bad stuff happened with the family."

"What bad stuff?" My hand automatically lifted, touched my own cheek as though I still felt the slap from his father. "Your dad never found you, did he?"

"No, nothing like that." He looked up to the sky. "We moved a lot, Kara. Mom just couldn't find her peace in one place. When we ended up in Chicago, slowly easing our way across the country, she got

158

involved with some . . . bad people, started getting a little more into the drugs until she got arrested one night, and Jimmy and I ended up in foster care for a brief time."

I instinctually threw my arms around Jack. "No."

He hugged back and didn't let go. It felt good, and I stayed against his chest as he finished the story. He was shorter than Peyton, and my head fit right onto the cleft of his chest, comfortable as the words vibrated below my head and filled my ears. I had the thought that this was what babies must feel like when they lay against their parents, the words felt as much as heard. I didn't even try and move as he told me where he'd been.

"It wasn't that long in foster care." He ran his fingers through my hair, pulling apart the rain-induced tangles. "We were there for a month—it's where we met Isabelle. When Mom finally had her hearing and was released, and we vowed to all pull it together, she took Isabelle also. We packed—again—and headed as far south as we could before we ran out of money. When we hit Houston, Mom got a job at a diner and we finished high school. She was really happy there. She found this group of artists and began to paint again. It was like painting kept her out of trouble. It was when she wasn't doing her art that life disintegrated. So, although we lived in a crappy apartment over someone's garage—Jimmy and I in one room, Isabelle in the living room with cardboard doors, and Mom in a cramped room meant to be a walk-in closet—those were some of the better years. And, just like Mom had, Jimmy and I found our outlet—music. I'm sorry you and I lost touch—surviving took all our effort at that time."

He was silent for a few moments and I thought maybe he wanted me to say something, lift my head from his chest, but then he placed his hand on top of my head and kept it there.

"We started playing for the school and local parties, until there was this large fund-raiser for foster kids. We knew we had to play it, so we did. Isabelle sang backup. And the rest, as they say, is history."

Now he lifted my chin. "See? Boring."

I shook my head. "No, beautiful. You made something of . . . nothing. It's beautiful. Where did you get the name of the band?"

"Well, we didn't mean for it to stick. We called that first concert Unknown Souls for the kids who had been forgotten, like Isabelle, and then it just stuck."

"Now it's scrawled across your very own tour bus. Overnight success."

"Yeah, five years until overnight success."

I smiled, settled into the current again. Now was probably a very good time to escape, to swim parallel to shore.

I touched the side of Jack's face. "I'm so sorry you went through so much bad stuff. I just figured you'd moved on with your life and totally forgotten about . . ."

"I never forgot." His voice came hoarse.

I thought of the Claddagh ring at home. I wished I could raise my hand and show it to him, and we'd laugh about it. "How about a girlfriend, wife, fiancée?"

"It's hard when all I do is . . . leave. We don't stay in one place for very long—like that country song, 'Lot of Leaving Left to Do.' "

"Leave," I said, and tasted the word, its meaning. "Isabelle?"

He shrugged his shoulders. "We've tried." He leaned over the railing, tossed a rock into the water. "It's easier, and it's also harder than it used to be. But . . . really, you don't want to hear about it."

"I guess you need to get back to the concert. . . . Doesn't it start"—I looked at my watch—"in less than an hour?"

"Yes . . . but I need to hear about you. Where have you been? What's shaped your life until now? And how in the hell did you end up in a café in Savannah?" He leaned toward me. "And did you find me or did I find you?"

"Neither . . . just coincidence. Well, sort of." I felt an inner quiver, as if I'd had too much caffeine. "Part of my job at the PGA TOUR is to plan a benefit event after the tournament."

"You work for the tour?"

I nodded. "Yes, and I thought that maybe, just maybe I could talk you and your band into playing at the benefit. So I did come to Savannah to hear your concert . . . and I've just had a lot of weird things

161

happen that pointed to you." I said it, then turned away, shook my head. "We've got to get you back to work, right?"

He placed his hands on my shoulders, twirled me around.

"Nice blow-off there. Okay, let's go."

There was so much about him that was familiar: the same grin and tilt of his head, the golden specks in his eyes in the exact same pattern—like small internal bursts of light. His shoulders had remained broad: a restful place. He still had his walk, a relaxed gait with long strides that reminded me of a Southern drawl . . . easy, slow, and yet you get there in the same amount of time.

Yet there was also unfamiliarity now: his long wavy hair, his partial beard, muscles that had only been hinted at back then. His voice was deeper now, fuller, as if it hid secrets.

We were walking toward the auditorium when I stopped, touched his elbow. "I do need a band for my event. . . . I know you guys are way too big now. I guess it was an excuse to see how you were doing."

"As if you need an excuse. You did promise that you'd find me. Remember?"

"I think you promised to find me," I said, and then in an instinct I thought long gone, I reached up and touched his hair, ran my fingers through it.

"I remember all of it," he said.

"Me too." I nodded toward the coliseum. "Let's get you back to work."

"Yes," he said. "Let's. But, Kara, if you need a band—give me the date, I'll do the best I can to work it in."

"You'd do that?"

He nodded.

"You'd be a lifesaver."

"I do believe I've been that before. Why stop now?"

I took a quick breath; my eyebrows shot up. "Oh, my God, the day the boat tipped and hit me on the head . . . you pulled me out."

"Oh, how easily you forget the things I've done for you."

"Oh, please. . . ." I tilted my head back and rolled my eyes. "Must we now talk of all you've ever done for me?"

"No, we don't have that much time." He walked ahead of me and waved toward the coliseum. "The show must go on."

I caught up to him, and we strode in silence, and I understood that seeing Jack was nothing more than a nice reunion, visiting an old acquaintance. Leaving was inevitable; it loomed before us as it had that summer morning thirteen years ago. Life, like the river, had moved on, and so would we.

CHAPTER TWELVE

T he concert exceeded my expectations in every way. I'd believed that true beauty resided only within the tumultuous natural world outside my door, or within classical music and the human form, but this concert took me away on wings of something far beyond my experience.

Jack had dropped me off to the side where I could see half the stage. Isabelle came to me, grabbed a water bottle and drank it, narrowed her eyes at me. "You're not messing with Jack, are you?"

"Excuse me?"

"He's different, better than anyone you know."

I nodded. "I know . . . I knew him—"

"Before me, I know that. But you haven't known him after me." Isabelle's lip curled up on the left side.

"I wasn't going to say that. . . . I was going to say I knew him a long time ago. That's all. I'm not messing with anyone."

She nodded and returned to the stage, where her voice—rough and melodic—came through the echoing speakers as she backed up a song with Jimmy. I attempted to hear the words, but found I could only take them in a visceral manner, not understanding the exact meaning.

I lost myself in the music until we returned to their hotel. I curled up in the corner of the couch and watched, listened as the group talked about how the concert had gone, where they needed to make changes and how to switch the song list around.

I closed my eyes and allowed the conversation to soothe me like a lullaby, laughter punctuating each sentence. When quiet followed, I opened my eyes to see Jack staring at me. We were the only ones remaining in the room.

"Where did everyone go?" I stretched.

"It's two a.m.—they've gone to bed."

"It's two in the morning?" I shot to my feet, glanced around the room for my purse with a frantic twist of my head.

"You can have the bed, Kara. I'll sleep on the couch." Jack pointed to the rumpled all-white bed.

I shook my head. "I've got to go home."

He laughed, but with a sweet sound behind it—like a best friend laughs at your bad joke. "And exactly how do you plan to do that?"

I groaned. "There's no way I could drive an hour and a half right now. I don't even know where my car is. . . ." I plopped back down on the couch.

Jack sat down beside me and draped his arm around my shoulder. "Go—you take the bed."

"I couldn't do that to you," I said, and yawned. "Jack?"

"Yes?" He pulled me closer.

"Did you write all those songs?" I closed my eyes again, the smooth current pulling me under.

"Yes." His voice came soft, like cashmere thrown

over my shoulders.

"Hmmm," I think I said, then slid into the warm, plush place of his words, his shoulder.

The stars above me flared bright, exploding outward like large magnolia blossoms reaching toward earth. I lay on my back, reaching for them, laughing, calling out, "I saw them first."

Jack lay next to me, and the sand wrapped us together in a blanket as warm as seawater. He reached up, grabbed a starflower and rolled over, handed one to me.

I took it from him and touched his face. "I love you, Jack Sullivan. I just completely love you."

I glanced down to see the star he'd handed me, to hold it tight, but instead found a golden ring—a Claddagh ring with a diamond center flaring outward.

I gasped and reached for him, but found a handful of sand, grating, cold. I tried to sit up but couldn't; the earth held me flat. I cried out, "Jack," and my voice came hoarse, scraped raw.

Hands wrapped around my middle and the stars disappeared behind a fog so thick I believed it was made of wool—pure dark surrounded me and I was alone. I fought against the force around me, pulled away.

"Kara." Jack's voice came through the fog rolling over the stars.

"Jack." I reached up for him.

His hand grasped my shoulders; I jolted awake in the hotel room, holding on to Jack as though I were drowning. I released him, rubbed my face. "Oh . . . oh."

"Bad dream?" He touched my cheek.

I stared at him, almost expecting a star, a diamond star set in the middle of a gold ring of hands, heart, and crown. I shook my head, but was unable to shake off the emotion, the truth of the dream. I believed he was there still, with me, on the beach, with my confession.

I closed my eyes, certain he'd heard me. He pulled me toward him and I fell against him, and into sleep once again.

The morning came stark and bright as someone touched my face: Jack. The words I'd uttered in my dream hung above me like a flare, luminous in their import. I closed my eyes to avoid the open-heart emotions inside me.

"Good morning, sleepy head," he said, sleep in his own voice.

It was a dream, only a dream, I reminded myself. This was a hotel room and a couch. I smiled, sat up, and opened both eyes. "I'm so sorry I fell asleep here. I'll help pay for the room."

He laughed, looking down at me. "You've got to be kidding. You were adorable. One minute you were talking and laughing, the next you were curled and—"

I grimaced. "I do that. When I'm done, I'm done. I didn't disturb you, did I?"

"No. . . . I'd have let you sleep even longer, but we

have to pack the bus and play in Jacksonville tonight."

The blinking light of the clock across the room caught my eye. "It's ten o'clock?"

Jack sat down next to me on the couch. He wore a pair of tattered jeans and a black T-shirt, looking like a young boy.

I stretched. "It felt great to sleep so long. . . ."

"Then you must've needed it." He reached over to touch my arm, or maybe my face, but his hand wavered in the air, then fell in his lap.

"Not really . . . I've slept a lot lately. I was just so . . . comfortable."

"You were on a couch."

"No . . . comfortable in a different way." Then I realized how I must have looked: wrinkled clothes, messy hair, morning breath. I jumped up. "I'll be ready to go in a minute."

"You had a bad dream in the middle of the night . . . you remember?"

I closed my eyes, opened them. "It wasn't a *bad* dream. . . ."

"You were calling out like you were scared."

"I wasn't scared . . . I was—" I held up my hand. "Just a dream."

I stood, stretched, and went to the bathroom to stare at my well-rested self. Where were the purplish-green bags under my eyes? The listless look of fatigue? I grabbed a cloth and washed my face, then used a corner of it to brush my teeth with toothpaste from a crushed tube. I tried to fix my hair, but I needed a shower. My car? Where was my car? The world came rushing on at me like a released thunderstorm.

I came out of the bathroom, attempting to pull some of the tangles out of my hair. "My car."

"We'll drop you off." He grinned. "You are so damn cute."

"I need to get home. . . ."

"I know. Your cell phone has been ringing off the hook, by the way."

"Oh," I groaned. "How could I not have heard it?"

"You were . . . in a coma." He stretched. "I'm gonna take a quick shower and then we'll get out of here."

I lifted my cell from my purse, flipped open the cover. Eighteen missed calls. I glanced at Jack; my heart puffed up, then deflated. "They've probably sent out a search crew by now."

"Call and let them know you're okay—we'll leave in fifteen minutes."

I took the phone and walked out onto a miniature deck off the room, closed the French door behind me. I stared at the phone, trying to decide whom to call— and then dialed Charlotte's number first.

"Where the hell are you?" Her voice came through the line without a hello.

"Savannah."

"What?"

I laughed. "I'll explain later . . . when I get home in a couple hours. Just relax. Will you tell everyone I'm okay? I'll call you when I get home."

"You know Peyton is looking for you."

169

"I figured."

"Listen, Kara. Call me when you're in the car on the way home. I want to tell you something before you talk to Peyton."

"What is it?"

"Just call me from the road, okay? And how is Jack?"

"Good, he asked about you. And it's not what you think . . . I didn't spend the night with him. Or I did, but not like that. And—"

"Yes?"

"I'll call you when I get to my car."

"Good idea, Kara." She laughed. "I sure hope you had a great time . . . getting me all worried like that should most definitely have been worth it."

"Absolutely," I said, and glanced back into the room; Jack stood in front of his open suitcase with a towel wrapped around his waist. "I've got to go."

"Call me." Charlotte hung up without saying good-bye. I stood and stared out over the courtyard. Jasmine sprayed across the cobblestones and a gazebo across the back area; paving stones led through bushes and flowering plants I wished I could name. Jack came outside; his arms whispered around my waist. I started to turn.

"No," he said. "Let me say something without you talking."

I nodded and felt his chin atop my head. "I know you have to go home. I know you have an entirely full life with a wedding and family and a fantastic job.

170

And I have a tour. But please know how much it meant to me that you found me, that you came here."

I nodded, glad he'd asked me not to speak, because I couldn't have anyway.

Then he turned me around. "And if we can possibly play for your charity event, we will." He handed me a card with various numbers written on it.

"It's in a few weeks—second weekend in April."

He gave me a thumbs-up. "I think that's a free weekend, but let me check with the guys." He motioned toward the door with his head. "Let's go."

"Jack?"

"Yes?" He looked over his shoulder as he opened the door into the room.

"Thank you. That was the most fun I've had in as long as I can remember."

"Any time, Kara. Any time."

I wanted to grab that promise and hide it until I needed it.

The car thrummed with all my thoughts, everything I'd seen and done and said and heard over the last few hours. Not even a full day had passed and yet so much had happened. I reached for the phone to call Peyton; he'd be on his way home from Miami this morning. Then I remembered I'd promised Charlotte I'd call her first.

She beat me to the dialing; my cell phone rang. I yanked it from the console. "I'm here. I'm on my way home," I told her.

"Okay. . . ."

"This'll be fun—explaining where I was."

"Business, Kara. Business."

I blew out a long breath. Change of subject would be good. I couldn't speak of my last hours with Jack until I'd absorbed them in some way. "How was your date with that Tom guy? You've been out with him a few times now."

"Good, nice guy. Really. Hey, I want to ask you a question—and don't . . ."

"Go ahead, Charlotte. Don't preamble your question. I hate that."

"Did you know Peyton was engaged twice before?"

"No . . . ," I whispered, air rushing from my lungs. "No, I didn't. I don't think that is true."

"It is."

"How do you know?" My gut felt as though someone were squeezing me around my middle. I pulled over to the side of I-95, parked in the emergency lane. "How in the hell do you know this and I don't?"

"Well, when I was out with Tom, he mentioned how much better the guys on the tour like you than his other fiancées."

"That's it? Some offhand comment made by another golfer?"

"It wasn't an offhand comment. I asked him about them."

"And?" Now my head lay on top of the steering wheel; my heart fluttered like it wanted to stop completely.

"Just come on home and we'll talk . . . I don't want you driving into the Savannah River. I know how you drive when you're preoccupied."

"I've pulled over, and if you don't finish telling me what you know . . ."

"Okay, it's not that big a deal, I guess."

"Two other fiancées. That seems like a sort of big deal, Charlotte."

"Okay—I guess they didn't last long, which is probably why he hasn't said anything."

"You've got to be kidding."

"I'm sure Tom doesn't know Peyton very well."

"Finish, Charlotte."

"Tom said Peyton likes to have someone . . . there during his tournaments. It has always worked out well for him."

"Okay, who were they?"

"I have no idea. Really."

I shifted the car into drive and pulled back onto the highway. "Don't you think this is something he should've told me?"

"Of course I do."

"What else did Tom say?"

"That I am gorgeous and funny and warm and intelligent."

I laughed. "Liquor?"

"No, he's just an extremely intelligent and intuitive man. But, of course, I'm just not that into him."

"Of course not, because he's just so into you."

"The curse, I know." Charlotte made a clucking

noise. "Drive carefully. Call me when you get home. I want to hear every detail of your trip."

I hung up and focused on the road. Two other fiancées. How could I not know this? My mind twisted around trying to figure out who they could've been, and I realized I didn't know much about Peyton's life . . . before me.

When I pulled up into my driveway, he was pacing back and forth, his Jaguar in the driveway. I parked and took a deep breath, wishing there'd been time for a hot shower and a sustaining cup of coffee before I had to face him.

I parked my car and faced him in the driveway. "Where the hell have you been, Kara?"

"Savannah." I squinted at him in the sunlight. "I thought you were in Miami or I would've called."

"What were you doing in Savannah?"

"Well, I went to check out that band—Unknown Souls—and it ends up that the singer and songwriter are old friends of mine. I hung out with them for a while, and then it was too late to drive home, so I stayed at the Courtyard Savannah."

His face turned red, blotched. "Who are these guys?"

"Old friends who used to live next door."

"What? How come you never told me about them? When you were looking at that Web site, you could have told me you knew them."

"Like telling me about your two other fiancées?"

His lips formed a straight line; he closed, then opened his eyes and shook his head. "They weren't important to us in any way."

"Useful information, maybe? Useful so that I didn't have to feel like a fool when my best friend told me?"

"Charlotte?" He punched a fist into the other palm. "She's so freaking nosy, acts like she's your mother half the time."

"That's not fair, Peyton." My heart slowed, tears threatened. "You absolutely can't be mad at Charlotte for telling me something you should've told me at least a year ago. I can't believe no one else ever let me know . . . from the tour or anything."

"Because it's not important."

I attempted to push my hair back from my eyes. Our voices were raised now, too loud for a quiet Saturday. I glanced up at the house. Deirdre stood at the front door, Daddy behind her, and they could easily hear us. I waved at them, then looked back to Peyton and lowered my voice. "Would you like to tell me now who they were?"

"You don't know either of them. And it doesn't have anything to do with us." His facial features softened into those of the calm, beautiful man I knew and had promised to marry; the man with the hardened mouth and clenched teeth dissolved into the morning. He placed his arms around me and pulled me to him. My head fell against him where his shoulders curved to his chest. Something small and mean in me noticed that this was a completely different place than where my head rested on Jack, against the cleft below his throat.

"I love you, Kara. Those women were just the mistakes I had to make to get to you. Huge mistakes."

My heart softened. What woman wouldn't want to hear these words? I looked up at him, but something small had shifted. Maybe I was too tired, too frazzled to know. I hugged him back and kissed him. "I need a shower. Why don't you come over for dinner—family dinner tonight, okay?"

He stepped back from me. "Okay. But please don't ever disappear like that again."

I nodded toward the house. "We'll talk about it later. We appear to have an audience right now."

He kissed me again and walked toward his car, then turned to me. "I love you, Kara," he mouthed as he clicked the remote on his keys to unlock his car.

"You too," I whispered, and turned to the house. "You too."

When I reached the bottom step, Deirdre looked at me. "He's been engaged before?"

I looked behind her for Daddy; he was walking away down the front hall.

"Be careful, Kara," she said.

Anger rose in me like a tunnel of wind. "What do you mean, Deirdre? I am careful."

She shook her head and turned away from me. "You can lose his love just as easily as it came to you."

"What is that supposed to mean?"

"Exactly what I said."

I walked past her and up to my room. *You can lose his love.*

I sat on my bed, dropped my head into my hands, and covered my ears to shut out the one word that had followed me: "lose."

Deirdre set the table with the Wedgwood and Waterford. I lit candles set inside hurricane glasses, which served as centerpieces. Two of Brian's paintings hung on the far wall of the dining room: a palmetto backlit against the sunset and the tip of a sailboat rounding the bend of a tidal creek. The hummocks were pockmarked with fiddler crabs. Soft sweeps of sand showed where the water danced in its tidal retreat. Each brushstroke created a brilliant detail, capturing the furious beauty of the Lowcountry. I had seen lesser paintings in the galleries around South Carolina. I shook my head; Brian needed to paint more often, not sit in a law office with Daddy.

Deirdre entered the dining room. "Why are you standing there staring at the wall?"

"I'm looking at Brian's paintings."

She rolled her eyes. "He doesn't paint anymore."

I touched the edge of the frame. "How do you know?"

"Have you seen a new painting any time in the last six or seven years?" she asked.

"Have you been to his house?" I motioned toward the front door. "Have you bothered to visit him or see him or—"

"Don't you dare lecture me." Deirdre's teeth clamped down on each other; her jaw twitched.

I held up my hands. "I'm not lecturing you. I promise. . . . Thanks for cooking tonight."

Deirdre made a noise that sounded vaguely like the snort of a white-tailed deer startled in the woods, and walked back into the kitchen. It was her turn to cook, and I wandered gratefully through the dining room; I couldn't have focused on a menu tonight.

Brian had arrived an hour earlier and sat in the library with Daddy talking about some land he wanted the family trust to purchase off Fifth Street. I was tired in a way that went beyond the need for sleep; I craved respite from my thoughts, my confusion.

A knock sounded on the front door and I opened it to Peyton. "Hmmm . . . smells good in here." He nuzzled my neck.

"Deirdre is cooking her famous pot roast with vegetables. Daddy's favorite."

He walked in. His khakis were pressed with a sharp line down the front; his golf shirt's collar lay flat, as if it had been glued to his shoulders. His hair was thick, warm to look at, as if it might be giving off heat. He exuded the same aura as when I first met him—capable, truly capable of taking care of everything, of me.

"Where's your dad?" He glanced into the hallway.

I waved toward the library. "In there, with Brian."

He nodded and walked toward the library—just like family.

I entered the kitchen and helped Deirdre put the meal on serving platters. She held a full glass of red wine in one hand. She opened her mouth to speak, then closed her eyes and leaned against the counter.

"You okay?" I touched her arm.

"Yes. I'm fine." She didn't open her eyes.

I glanced over at the wine bottle; half the merlot was gone.

"Is there anything I can do?" I lifted the bowl of mashed potatoes, piled high and covered in melting butter.

"No." She opened her eyes, squinting at me. "You have too much to worry about in your own life without being worried about mine—or Bill's."

"Don't, Deirdre. Don't pick a fight with me when you're not mad at me. Take it out on him, not me. I've tried to talk to you about y'all's separation a hundred times. Even now I'm here to talk when you're ready."

She took a deep breath. "Not now."

I nodded. "Okay. . . ." I carried the potatoes into the dining room, set the bowl on the table and hollered for Daddy, Brian, and Peyton to come eat. They entered the dining room. Peyton came over to me, wrapped his arms around me.

"Deirdre, you need help in there?" I hollered toward the kitchen.

"Got it." She emerged with a pot roast balanced pre-cariously on an oversized cornflower-blue Wedgwood platter. The plate always made me remember Mama bringing the turkey to the table for Christmas dinner. In the memory she had an orb of light over her head, and although I was sure I had conjured that part up, I wasn't going to ask anyone if it was true. Sometimes it is just nice to hold a memory, even if it isn't exactly accurate.

Deirdre's steps were unsteady, her left hand grasping the side of the platter and her wineglass simultaneously.

"Whoa. . . ." I moved toward her. "Let me get that."

"No." She turned away. "I can take care of it myself." The platter tilted, and in slow motion the entire roast slipped from the plate and fell to the Oriental rug. I moved to grab the meat and ended up with gravy and mashed carrots between my fingers and down the front of my silk shirt.

"Kara Margarite Larson." Her words screeched across the room.

I jumped back, held up my sticky hands. "What? I was trying to help."

"You've made me drop the dinner." Tears came to her eyes. She slammed her wineglass down on the table; drops of red splashed onto her beige linen place mat.

Daddy stood up. "No big deal, here." He grabbed a large napkin, picked up the roast with it and placed the meat back on the platter.

Peyton's mouth hung open, his bourbon highball glass in midair.

Daddy took a knife, cut off the back portion of the roast and disappeared into the kitchen, then quickly returned. "Okay, good as new. The neighborhood dogs will have the perfect meal tonight, and we'll get the part that never touched the ground."

"I'll clean that up," I said, and went to the kitchen for a towel and carpet cleaner. When I came back into the dining room, everyone was sitting and a place mat covered the stain.

Daddy motioned for me to sit. "We'll clean it all later. Let's eat this delicious meal Deirdre has prepared for us."

After Brian had blessed the food and the awkward silence melted, conversation began again. Daddy asked Peyton who he was paired with for the pro-am. Brian wanted to know about the concert.

"It was great," I said. "You should've seen it." My gaze caught Peyton's.

"Tell *me* about it," he said, "I haven't heard that band in years."

"They're quite good. So, Brian, tell us how the malpractice suit is coming along."

He shrugged. "Just doing it to pay the bills . . . nothing near as interesting as hearing about the Sullivan boys. Don't change the subject."

"Really, it's not that interesting," I said. "Jimmy is still loud and funny and large—larger than life. Jack looks different—longer hair, beard. But not so different you wouldn't recognize him. They started this band about five years ago to raise money for a foster home in Texas. And . . . that's about it."

"What about sweet Mrs. Sullivan?" Deirdre's sarcastic tone cut through the room.

"She *was* sweet," I said.

"That's what I just said." Deirdre took a bite of her roast.

"That's not what you meant, though." I glanced at Daddy.

Brian touched my leg, his signal to let it go.

"Anyway," I said, "Jack really didn't say what she was doing. I guess I should've asked."

"Especially since you spent so much time with them." Peyton leaned back in his chair, lifted his eyebrows at me.

We all turned and stared at him, mouths open, but it was Daddy who spoke first. "So, Peyton, how was this last tournament? Did you move up in the rankings?"

He shook his head, lifted his glass. "Fell, actually. But I'll make up for it next week. You'll be there, right?" He nodded toward me.

"Of course."

Deirdre reached across me. "Kara, please pass the potatoes and finish your story."

"There's nothing more to tell." I took a bite of carrots.

"Well, I'm sure there is," Deirdre said. "What did the music sound like? What did Jack have to say about his past, where they've been? How much he loves you."

"What?" I gripped my fork tighter, tried to swallow.

"That boy has been in love with you since first grade. Surely that much hasn't changed." She looked at Peyton.

"A lot has changed." My teeth clenched, my jaw tightened.

"Well, if Peyton can have his little secrets about all his past almost-wives, I guess you can have yours."

Daddy stood now. "Deirdre, I believe you've had a wee bit too much of that red wine there. Why don't you excuse yourself and take a break from all this work you've done tonight?"

Deirdre stood, but she didn't move to leave. Then her hand flew over her mouth and she ran from the room. In the silence, as we all stared at each other, the sound of retching came from the kitchen.

"Nice," Brian said, and stood. He looked down at Peyton. "Well, I'm so glad you could join us for a nice family dinner. Want to go to the Oyster Shack with me, grab a beer?"

I wanted to bury my face in the tablecloth.

Peyton came to my side. "Brian, you stay, but Kara, I think I should leave now. Call me when things . . . settle down."

At the front door, I hugged him, kissed him. "Let me go talk to Deirdre. I'm sorry she was so brutal to you. She didn't mean it."

He grabbed my shoulders, looked into my eyes. "Yes, she did mean it, and I should've told you about my engagements a long, long time ago."

"Yes, but she didn't need to unload on you. I love you. I'll call you in a little bit."

The front door clicked shut, and with Peyton gone, Daddy's voice rose. "What in the living hell is going on here? What . . ."

Deirdre came back into the dining room, a wet

183

washcloth in her hand. "I'm sorry," I think she said, but her voice cracked, and she fell into the chair. "I'm so sorry. That was pretty reprehensible, wasn't it?"

I sat next to her, lay my arm around her shoulder. "What is going on with you?"

Daddy stood and began pacing the room. "This is what I was always afraid would happen. Your mother would not want to see this, see you fall apart like this."

Deirdre pushed my arm off her shoulder and stood. "How would you know what Mama would want? She is gone." Spittle landed on her bottom lip.

Daddy's face crumpled; he shook his head. "Because she told me exactly what she wanted for all of you—and this isn't it."

Deirdre's fists clenched and unclenched at her sides. "What do you mean? Mama told you what she wanted and you never told us?"

Daddy glanced around the room, his face white, closed in. "Don't you get disrespectful and judgmental with me, Deirdre Marie. Your mother was out of it toward the end, but she would not want you—or us—to fall apart like this."

"Daddy," I whispered, feeling something of great import moving toward us. "What did she say?"

He stared at each of us, one at a time, allowing his stare to rest on each of our faces before he spoke. "Your mother was a dreamer, a wisher, a wanter. Toward the end, she lost sight of the more realistic parts of life. She faded back and forth between dreams and reality." Pain crossed his face like a quick shadow,

184

moved, flickered and disappeared. He walked around the table, picked up crystal glasses, set them back down. "Your mama fought until the very end, trying experimental treatments . . . wanting to stay here . . . with our family."

"You never told us that," I said. "I thought she quit the meds because she . . . gave up, wanted to leave, that she couldn't stand it one more day." My voice came in a whisper, as though I were a scared child.

Daddy stared at me. "No." He placed one hand over his chest. "God, no, she stopped the traditional treatment because she knew it wasn't working, and she tried an experimental new drug—it didn't work either."

"I believed . . . she gave up, left us." I stifled a cry.

"Oh, dear God, did I let you believe that, Kara?" He stepped toward me.

I shook my head. "I don't know. My memories are all so mixed up." I slumped back into a chair.

Daddy spoke softly. "She loved all of you so much, she tried everything out there, every treatment, every tea, every medication. There is no way to explain what it was like to watch the only woman I had ever loved die, and I knew she was dying but I couldn't admit that I knew. It was hell."

"Why have we never talked about this?" I asked. No one spoke; I tried again. "Why haven't we ever talked?" I stood, spread my hands apart. "I believed she wanted to leave." I took a step toward Daddy. "What did she say?"

He glanced upward as if he could see through the ceiling, find Mama and ask her what she had said. Then he looked directly at me. "She said for me to tell all of you to please remember to follow the hints of your heart . . . to listen. Those were . . . her last words."

"What does that mean?" Deirdre's voice echoed across the room.

Brian came to her. "Just listen, sis. Just listen."

"She was so afraid that without her here, in the pain of losing her, all of you would shut your hearts," Daddy said.

The magnificent substance of his words cowered in the corner of the room, crouching and ready to move toward me when I would allow it. This under-standing—that Mama hadn't left us willingly, that all I'd believed of her death was wrong—stretched and advanced on my heart in lumbering motions. "Why didn't you ever tell us this?"

"You were so young," Daddy said. "Her wish was so . . . abstract." He stumbled on his words, and his eyes wandered as though he were lost. "Follow the hints of your heart. It only seemed to confuse the real issue—her death."

"But my God, Daddy, those were her last words," Deirdre cried. "She asked you to tell us that, she asked you to tell us, and you never did."

"What did she want from us?" Brian asked.

Daddy closed his eyes. "It's not that she wanted any-thing *from* you, just *for* you. She wanted you to both give and receive love—those were her words."

"Does it really matter what she wanted for us?" Deirdre spoke low now, as if her scream had left her with remnants of her voice. "She hasn't been here to make sure it happened. Does it really matter at all?" She spun on her heels, took her wineglass and stomped from the room. The sound of her childhood bedroom door slamming made us all jump, then stare at each other.

"I think I've had quite enough for tonight," Daddy said, then turned away from us and walked across the hall and into his library.

Brian came to my side and put his arm around me. "Mama's last words? All right then. What do you think that was all about?"

"I don't know," I said, and leaned against my brother's shoulder. A lifetime of misunderstanding wove its way through my thoughts. "Maybe it just means we need to be careful what we believe." I quoted Maeve and released a long, withheld breath.

After Brian and I finished the dishes and he went home, I stared across the lawn to the street. Night surrounded me, loneliness its companion. The desperate ache for Mama rose and I was nine years old, and abandoned. Brian had found solace among his friends and sports. Deirdre had disappeared into her cliques and never came home until the moon was high in the night sky. Daddy was so far gone into himself that his eyes had not focused on me in months. I was alone save for the Sullivans, save for Jack and our haven among the roots of the live oaks.

I squinted into the night, adjusting my eyesight to where the trees would be, although I could not see them. But I couldn't find the feeling—that one feeling of unfailing love. All this time, all this damn time, I'd believed that Mama left of her own free will, that she'd given up and left us.

I stood and ran back into the house, grabbed my keys and drove to Peyton's house.

His home, which would soon be our home, sat behind the eighteenth green of the Palmetto Pointe Golf Club. It had been the most coveted lot on the course, overlooking the river, live oaks with Spanish moss spread like custom-made draperies along the backyard toward the green, then to the gray-blue water beyond.

Peyton's front door was crafted of solid cherry. An intricate design of a golf club and ball were carved along the left side. I twisted the handle; it was unlocked. I entered the two-story foyer with the curved staircase and called his name.

He came to the top of the stairs and looked down at me, a smile on his face. "Hey, darling. Come on up, I'm watching films from the BellSouth Classic in Duluth last year."

I climbed the stairs, kissed him. "When you made that miraculous chip from the sand trap on the fifth?"

"Exactly . . . but I'm watching how I kept slicing my drive . . . analyzing . . . oh, forget it. I'm so glad you came." He picked me up, kissed me for a long time, then unbuttoned the top two buttons of my silk blouse and ran his finger over the front of my shirt. "You still have gravy on you."

I looked down. "I'm so sorry you had to witness that family meltdown."

"I want to hear all about what happened after I left . . . but not until I show you how glad I am that you came over tonight, just when I thought I wouldn't see you for at least three days." He picked me up and carried me to his bedroom at the far end of the hall.

I kicked lightly at him. "Put me down, you goofball. You're not supposed to carry me over the threshold until after the wedding."

"I'm not supposed to do this until after the wedding, either," he said, pulling me into his bedroom.

I closed my eyes and let myself absorb how much I loved this man I would marry.

Peyton's ceiling fan whipped around in circles, making a rhythmic clicking noise. We stared at it; he pulled me closer on his king-size bed. "I cannot wait until you are here every single night."

I snuggled up against his side, ran my hand over his bare chest. "Do we have to do this big wedding thing? Can't we just run away this weekend, get married and I'll move in?"

"Who knows where we'll live," he said.

"What do you mean? We'll live here, right?" And it

came to me—we had never discussed where we'd live.

"I don't know. I was thinking, maybe we could talk about moving to Ponte Vedra. That's where most of the players live."

"Yeah, but that's not where your mom lives, or Daddy or Brian or . . . Charlotte."

He put his hands on both sides of my face, kissed me. "You can't live in your hometown forever."

"Oh," I said. "But you'll be gone so often and I'll be there . . . alone." The word "alone" haunted me tonight.

"You'll get to know all the other players' wives and make tons of friends." He pulled me closer. "And we do not have to talk about this now. Those are decisions we can make later. Don't get upset—right now let's focus on the wedding, on us."

"Let's elope," I said. I sat up and drew my knees to my chest.

"You know we have to have the wedding. Could you imagine canceling it now?" He rolled over and propped his head on his palm, with his elbow denting the mattress. "The magazine crews and photographers that are coming . . . the planning. At this point it would be harder to cancel than just have it. All that hard work we've done."

I pushed at his elbow; he fell back on the pillow. "*We've* done? *Who's* done, mister?"

"All the work *you've* done, my sweet. You. You. You." He pulled me toward him again. "But you can move in now, I've already told you that."

"I couldn't . . . it would break Daddy's heart." I lay flat on my back, then glanced at the far wall, where a signed picture of Payne Stewart hung. "Did you ask your other fiancées to move in?"

Peyton sat up and swung his legs over the side of the bed. "Okay, let's talk about this and get it over with."

I sat up, pulling the bedspread up to my chin. "Go ahead. I'm listening."

"I love you. That should be enough. I didn't love them—I just thought I did. I said this before—they were the mistakes I had to make to get to you. I didn't understand what love was . . . is, until I met you." He turned to me and held his right hand in the air. "I swear to God."

"But why didn't you tell me about them?"

"I was so afraid of losing you . . . of making you upset enough to leave me. That is the one thing I couldn't take—you leaving."

"You didn't tell me because you didn't want me to leave?" I pulled a pillow tight to my chest, repeating the words to see if they tasted true.

"Yes." He leaned toward me, and there were tears in his eyes. "Exactly."

"You shouldn't hide things from me because you think they'll upset me. We can't have a life like that. Do you believe I am that damn fragile?"

"No, baby. No."

I slid down on the bed, curled into the pillows. "I just don't want secrets between us."

"No secrets," he said. "Just hurry up and live with me, take care of me. . . ." He lay down next to me and wrapped his arms around me.

"Take care of you?"

"Hmmm . . . ," he said. "I can't wait until I can come home to you every day, every night. When we can cook our own family dinners and decide where to live, where to go, when and how. When it's just . . . us."

In moments, his slow, even breaths let me know he'd fallen asleep. I twisted quietly from the bed, dressed, and drove home with his last words resonating in my mind: when it's just . . . us.

CHAPTER THIRTEEN

The gerbera daisies I'd brought couldn't mask the antiseptic smell in Maeve's room, which caused the knot in my stomach to tighten. I sat in the large club chair in the corner and stared at her. She sat in bed fully dressed, her hair twisted into a braided knot on top of her head. Her eyes were closed, but she didn't appear to be asleep.

Something curled and asleep, cold and stable, within the middle of me—somewhere near my heart—stretched and awakened every time Maeve told more of her story. I wanted this arousal, this open feeling, yet it brought with it an ache, as if the awakening and the aching were bound together and I must accept them as one. If I wanted to hear her story, feel these pangs and stretches of sleeping yearning, then I must accept the companionable hurt, which told me, in the quietest whisper, "Things are not as they should be."

A piece—a sad, hardened piece—of me stared at Maeve and did not want more of her story, more of this awakening, and more of the ache that hinted at a life gone amiss, of an unmet craving for unfailing love.

The one-winged angel was still on her dresser, next to her silver hairbrush. She opened her eyes, turned to me, and tilted her head. "Well, well now, you've come back, haven't you? I'd thought you'd forgotten me altogether."

"Never." My hands flew in the air; I placed them in my lap. "I've come a couple times and you haven't . . ."

"Aye, did you find him?" She grinned.

"Who?"

"Him. Jack. Now tell me."

I stood. "It was not the smartest thing for me to do." I picked up the angel, ran my hand over the place where the wing had broken off.

"I never did say it was smart. But the heart has reasons . . ."

"That reason knows nothing of." I finished the Blaise Pascal quote, and set the angel back on the dresser.

"You know the quote?"

"It has nothing to do with daily life." My foot tapped against the linoleum floor. "They are nice words written by a man hundreds of years ago who was not engaged and running after his first love for no apparent reason. I shouldn't have gone."

Maeve giggled like a young girl. "You shouldn't have gone? Ha, that means you did go. Tell me all about it."

I returned to the chair, sat with my hands still, my heart in a frenzied beating. "No, I want to hear what happened to Richard. Where did he go? Did you find him?" I leaned forward. "I really want to know if he is the man you married."

I wanted her to tell me this was a legend before she disappeared again into that place where I could not reach her; where her eyes were cloudy and her mouth moved with words I could not understand.

"No, tell me about this Jack."

"Okay." I released a breath that wanted to catch in the back of my throat. "I went to Savannah, saw his band play, talked to him, had a nice time of catch-up, got in a fight with my fiancé. The end."

"No, Kara, those are the facts. It's easy to believe in facts, my dear. To believe in the *story* you need faith. Tell me the story as you experienced it."

I did, and found I wanted to tell her. I explained how my wet shirt clung against my skin, how my heart paused in my chest when I recognized him, and how I was afraid it wouldn't start again before I had to speak. I told her how everything seemed to screech to a stop, how time spun out as if it had changed or moved or maybe just waited.

I attempted, as best words could, to explain the concert and how the music made me feel wider, larger, as if my heart had expanded, as if the aches of aloneness could be filled. Then I told her of my Mama's last wish that I'd never known about.

"It is unfolding now," she said, and tapped the braids on top of her head.

"What is?"

"Your story, your life and journey, Kara, which involves what came before you and what comes after you. The hints of who you are."

"What do you mean by that?" My chest constricted in an understanding I couldn't yet fully grasp.

"You are listening and feeling and seeking, all the while keeping a tight, very tight hold on your life's circumstances. Let go."

"What?"

She sat up straighter than I had ever seen her, swung her legs around the bed, and touched my fist curled in my lap. "Look at your hands, tight and closed. What are you holding on to? You are not allowing something even better to happen in you and to you because you're holding so hard to what you already have."

"No, I'm not." I looked down, then opened the fingers that I didn't even realize I'd made into a knot.

"I dressed myself this morning. Will you be getting me my shoes now?" she asked in an accent as beautiful as a song.

I nodded, shook my hand out. Holding on? To what? I opened the door to the right of her bed. Inside the

195

closet hung a thin, tattered afghan with *Verandah House* embroidered on it in script letters. I grabbed her white Keds from the bottom of the closet. I waited while she fit them on her feet. She grabbed the handrails and stood, waited a moment, then reached for my arm.

I held out my elbow, let her place her hand on my forearm, and dropped my other hand on top of hers. "Would you like to take a walk?" I asked.

"Of course."

"It's beautiful today," I said. "The kind of day that fools the tourists into believing we don't have no-see-ums or mosquitoes."

She laughed. "Now that would be fooling them, for sure. There are enough of them here in South Carolina to eat a small woman alive."

"Well, not today. Would you like to go out to the fountain?"

"Yes, why yes, I would."

I slipped her tattered afghan over her shoulders and we headed toward the French doors at the back of the recreation room. Her weight against my elbow was insubstantial.

Residents greeted Maeve as she walked through the room. "You're looking good today, Maeve," "Nice to see you up, Maeve." Several groups sat at tables. A man snored in his wheelchair, his head back and his mouth open. A group of schoolchildren in pressed plaid uniforms stood in straight lines in the lobby, where a chalkboard announced that children from the

Pointe Elementary School would be singing at ten a.m. in the recreation room. I pushed open the French doors to the outside. The air was as clean as a crystal glass, sparkling against the azure sky, as if the day could be poured into this vessel, drunk and enjoyed. The fountain gurgled in the side garden in an offbeat sound. We took our seats on a bench in front of it.

The gardens at Verandah House were lush and well tended: azaleas and dogwood were in bloom, a fulfillment of the promise of spring . . . and my wedding. I'd always wanted a spring wedding, since I was a little girl. The invitations were in the backseat of my car—four hundred envelopes addressed in calligraphy by hand. Soon they would go in the mail.

Maeve's voice startled me. "It takes me three months to find him, it does."

I turned my attention from the garden, from the invitations.

"I go to the police station and the Industrial Schools. I knock on the door of every state home I can reach by foot. I ask and beg for information, but can find none."

I held my breath, my fist knotted again. Maeve reached down, uncurled my fingers before she resumed speaking. "Then one day in early spring, I knock on the door of still another school."

"An Industrial School?" My chest expanded in the hope, in the need to know she had found him, that this motherless boy was found and loved, even if he wasn't real.

"In that time there are more children in Industrial

Schools in Ireland than in all of the United Kingdom put together." Then she nodded, descended into her story. "A young boy in a torn T-shirt and tattered tweed pants answers the door. It is a wooden door, taller than any I've ever seen, except in ancient castles. The knockers are iron and larger than me. I tell the boy who I am looking for. He glances around the foyer like a trapped animal expecting to be hit at any moment. His eyes are wild and full of tears. He says, 'Can you take me out of here, now, right now?' I am confused. Then a nun appears from the side.

"At this time in my life, my experiences with the nuns and priests is all positive. I live below St. Mary's on the Hill—the Dominican church. I live with a God of the water and earth, of love. Nuns mean comfort and beauty and an explanation of a God I cannot understand: the wild Irish God of St. Patrick and the Celtic language that is unexplainable. So when I see this nun appear, my instinct is not one of fear, but one of relief. I step inside the door."

Maeve closed her eyes, and I thought she was gone, but then she continued and I was there with her, in the Industrial School.

"The stone walls are cold to the touch, but high and grand. The furniture in the hall is dark and polished until you can see your face. Celtic hymns being sung come from the back of the hall, in a harmony so haunting I think my heart will burst. I feel no fear; there is no understanding of what I've stepped into, until the boy who answered the door begins to cry

198

harder. Then the realization comes to me in a slow crawl of dread: this place is not one of refuge."

Maeve stopped, looking directly at me. "Now, Kara. Here is where you must be careful. Not all things are as they appear to be. You must understand that this was the first time I had ever come to a place and time that appeared to be something it was not. I did not understand my visceral instinct. I was a thirteen-year-old child who had grown up in the Claddagh village." Tears filled her eyes. "Not all things are as they appear."

I shook my head to let her know I heard her, but I was afraid to speak, afraid to stop the flow of words. The sun sat warm on our shoulders, and tears threatened at the back of my eyes for this poor motherless boy, and this child-Maeve looking for him. Even if, as Caitlin had told me, this was not a true story, my heart ached for Maeve as she believed and remembered a pain that was real to her.

She brushed at a tear. "I look up at the nun—her habit so tightly wound around her head that her wrinkles are smooth. I tell her who I'm looking for, that he was taken when his parents died three months ago. The nun's face registers nothing and my pain deepens."

Maeve turned to me now. "Do you know this pain I mean, when you look and look and want and want and don't find?"

I nodded my head, which was heavy and full of unshed tears.

"You know," she said. "Already you know."

She took a deep breath. "Then the boy—the one who'd answered the door—runs from us. The nun reaches for him, grabs his ear. He lets out a yelp like a puppy. He flicks her hand away and runs through the hall. The nun looks down at me. 'Do your mam and da know where you are?' she asks.

"I still believe she will be the one to help me, but doubts creep in and I do something I have never done: I lie to a nun. I wait for the bolt of lightning, the earth to swallow me whole. But this is my mission—to find Richard. I tell her that my mam has sent me to find him, as he is our neighbor and should live with us and not in a state home. Then this nun stands, calls out in a voice that sends shivers down my spine. Another tall, thin nun appears and looks at me. 'This girl states she is looking for a Richard and that she has been sent by her mam to find him. Do you know such a child?'

"The other nun says 'no.' I hang my head and turn away. When I open the large doors, the tattered boy runs to me, reaches my side, looks up at me. 'Richard is here. He's here,' he tells me. The nuns grab him by the cuff of his collar, pull him away. The older nun leans down and looks into my face and tells me, 'This poor child lost his mind long ago. God bless his soul. He also thinks St. Patrick lives here.' I nod at her, but I am feeling it for the first time."

Maeve paused; I squeezed her hand. "Feeling what?"

"The Spirit talk to me."

"The spirit?" Maybe Maeve was too senile to tell this story.

"Our prayer, the prayer of St. Patrick. 'Christ with me, Christ before me, Christ behind me, Christ within me, Christ beneath me, Christ above me, Christ at my right, Christ at my left.'

"I'd heard these words since I was a child; I probably heard Mam's words echoing inside me. But it is there, in the Industrial School, that I finally feel it and know what it means as the Spirit whispers in my ear, *'He is here.'* And I see the nun's terrible lie spin and shimmer around me."

"Richard was there?" I asked.

"Yes, he is there and I feel it in every way as the door slams behind me. I stand outside that locked door and weep as I have never wept. My world closes around me as evil threatens my soul. I have never experienced it before, as even in Richard's parents' death I felt only sorrow and grief, not evil.

"This is a terrible revelation for a child—that evil exists beyond the bogeyman and the drunk father."

I nodded.

Maeve looked at me; tears filled her eyes, but did not fall. "Richard comes out a side door, bursts into the lane. We fall into each other's arms, weep and hold on to each other. He is thin, so frightfully skinny I think he will break beneath my weeping. His clothes are more tattered than the rags my mum uses to clean the hearth."

"Maeve, you saved his life," I said as quietly as if

we were in the lane, whispering to escape the nuns.

"But, Kara, it was for that moment only that I saved him."

"What do you mean?"

"I took him home to my family knowing that they would take him in."

"And of course they did." I lifted my hands.

She shook her head so furiously that hairpins scattered, her bun released and her braids fell to her shoulders. "Three nights later, while I was sleeping, they came and took him again."

"Who took him?"

"The Irish state. Mam and Da had called—afraid that Richard would bring peril to our family."

"Dear God, Maeve."

"You must understand the times, Kara. It wasn't as it is now—there was mysticism mixed with religion mixed with ideas of the revolution. The Irish Civil War had started that year—1922. Michael Collins was assassinated. There was much fear. My mam and da still adhered to some of the Brehon Laws. According to this law, marrying Richard would have meant a level five or six in the Brehon order. I was too young to marry, too young to know my own heart, they said. Da only wanted a level-one marriage for me. This meant my husband and I must be equal— with the same financial means and from the same class. These were confusing times, and Richard's mam and da had been involved in the Resistance. My mam was scared out of her mind that evil would come to us through Richard's family."

"What did you do?"

She looked at me, but her eyes were glazed, as though she wore thick contacts over her pupils. "It is the ache, you know?"

"The ache?"

"For him. For that time. For that adoration. But life is so much more than the ache you feel for the person or place. What you remember about that person, about that place has much more to do with what you felt then—an expansive time when you felt the most loved and believed you were loved."

"But Richard . . . where was he?"

"Of course I went again to find him, but he was truly gone now. My Richard O'Leary."

"O'Leary?"

Maeve's head rolled back onto the bench. "When you felt the most loved." She released a long, hollow breath. Her gaze wandered upward to the crystalline sky. Her body slumped forward. Her legs splayed open, forming a tent of her robe. My limbs went numb.

"Help over here," I screamed, and grabbed Maeve's body to keep it from falling to the ground.

White coats, hollering voices came running. They held Maeve, carried her to the building on a stretcher. I followed them. "What's wrong with her? What happened? Is she okay?" Questions flew out of me like birds released from a cage; frenetic, eager, not knowing which way to go.

A nurse turned and grabbed my arm. "Stop. We will come and get you when we know what's going on. Why did you take her outside?"

"She wanted to go." I bit the inside of my cheek to keep the tears from coming.

"Mrs. Mahoney is not supposed to be out of bed without a nurse."

"No one told me that."

"You volunteers are supposed to ask for permission to go anywhere with these residents."

"I'm sorry, so sorry. I wanted to help her, let her get some fresh air."

The nurse placed her hand on my arm. "We'll come get you when we know something. You can wait in the lobby."

I nodded, fear mixing with my thoughts like the mud and sand at the marsh edge—unable to separate one from the other. I sat in the lobby and stared at the taupe-colored walls and the poster announcing Tuesday night bingo. Scattered thoughts, which would not stick for more than a moment, twisted inside me: Christ behind me, Industrial Schools, mail the invitations, Xerox the forms for Friday, tattered clothing, Christ under me, pot roast with potatoes, hints of the heart, Deirdre's anger. Each thought begged for attention, and yet I sat in the lobby and observed them as passing strangers.

Finally I shook my hair out of its rubber band, walked to the front desk. "Any more information?" I asked the volunteer.

"On?" The woman in a shapeless tent dress looked up at me.

"Maeve Mahoney?"

The woman raised her eyebrows. "They didn't come tell you?"

"No." My throat constricted as if she'd leaned across the desk and grabbed my neck. "I guess I wouldn't be asking you if they had."

She grimaced. "They took her to Memorial Hospital an hour ago."

"How did I miss them?"

"They go out the back door so as not to frighten visitors and other residents."

I stepped toward the door with my heart beating differently—not faster, not slower, just more . . . sporadically, then I ran to my car to drive to Memorial Hospital.

CHAPTER FOURTEEN

Peyton sat across the restaurant table from me. My glass of wine sat untouched, my food growing cold as he stared at me.

"You've got to be kidding me, Kara. Have you lost your mind?"

"No." I shook my head. "I thought you'd think this was interesting, an adventure."

"Okay, let me get this straight. You want to add more work to your plate—give yourself one more thing to do."

205

I closed my eyes. He might be right—I didn't need one more thing to do. I grimaced. "I've just been thinking about it and I thought I'd tell you."

Peyton wiped his mouth with a linen napkin, then stood. "I'll be right back." He patted his waistband. "Mark is beeping me and I've been trying to get hold of him all day about this investment."

Peyton drew his cell phone from his side pocket and walked off. I nodded, picked up my fork, and pushed the uneaten food around on my plate. Maybe I shouldn't have brought up my newly born desire to go to photography school. When I got to Memorial Hospital that morning and was told Maeve was in a coma and I couldn't see her, my first regret had been that I had never taken a picture of her. The more I realized how much I wanted one, how much I relied on my camera to preserve my life's moments, the more I understood I wanted to learn about photography, about light and dark, about f-stops and film speeds.

I'd called the Savannah College of Art and discovered that one could major in photography, that there were over thirty-five different classes I could take on the subject. My college degree was in management and had nothing to do with art, with photography. I'd gone online and sat for over an hour reading the descriptions of each photo class, of the myriad techniques I could master. My heart had sped up and I felt that, for the first time since Daddy told me what Mama had said, I understood what she meant by feeling the hints of the heart. I'd sent away for an application without knowing any details, without determining whether I'd take evening or day classes. All I'd understood was that I needed to know more.

I wanted Peyton to be the first person I told, the first one to see and hear my new desire unfold. Now I only felt a bruise below my ribs, as if his negativity and disinterest had hit me from the inside like a dense punch.

He sauntered around the corner, sat down. "Sorry, darling."

"I understand." I dropped my fork onto the table.

"So." He took a sip of water. "How are the wedding plans coming along? Have you talked to Mom lately about the rehearsal dinner?"

"Peyton—" I took a deep breath. "I was trying to tell you about—"

"I know, I know—photography school. Are you sure this is a good time to be taking on another big project? Are you sure this is the right time to start something new? We've got a huge tournament, a wedding and a life to start. Going to SCAD would mean a long commute to Savannah. You have to look at all the factors here, Kara, be logical. Do you want to be going to school, working and raising a family?"

"What?" My right hand clenched into a fist below the table.

"Kara." He leaned forward, grabbed my left hand in his. "I want you to pursue your . . . hobbies. I really do. I'm just trying to be the voice of reason here. Maybe there is a better time to do this."

I nodded, but felt as though he had just sunk my

dreams with the anchor of reason. And he was probably right—I couldn't do one more thing right now
even if I wanted to, even if I was accepted into the
program.

"Let's be rational," he said. "If you're talking about
this to make me mad, to get back at me because of
what I didn't tell—"

"Speaking of—I do have a couple questions about
that."

He leaned back in his seat. "Go ahead, Kara. What
do you want to know? I thought we reached the end of
this last night."

"Who were they?"

His answers were robotic, empty. "Mia Garbinski
and Emily Williams."

"You're right. I don't know them." I lifted my wineglass, tilted it toward Peyton. "Go ahead."

"Nothing else to tell."

"Who broke off the engagements?"

"Me."

"Why?"

"My mother couldn't stand Mia and Emily was
clingy and needy, freaked out about everything I ever
did, everywhere I went."

"I'm not sure your mom likes me much, either."

He squeezed my hand. "I love you."

For the first time the words sounded hollow, empty
of anything but the outline of the letters. "You do?"

"How can you doubt that? Kara, I am so sorry about
all of this. Please let it go. I can't take it when you're

upset . . . but quitting your job, running off to take some art classes, will not get back at me."

"I am not quitting my job—I'm exploring my options. I just want you to understand something: I am not asking for your permission. I am telling you about it because you're about to be my husband. I don't know if I'll do it, I don't even know if I'd get in the program, but I really *want* to do it. I feel like it is . . ." I searched for the right word, then looked up to him. "A hint of who I'm supposed to be."

"What does that mean? That doesn't make any sense at all. Of course you're already who you're supposed to be." He held his hand out to me. "My sweet, adorable Kara."

My heart skittered across his words, like a flat rock thrown over the water, then sank. I closed my eyes, took a deep breath, then opened them, reached across the table for his out-held hand.

"Okay, let's talk about something else. Tell me a little bit about this investment."

Conversation smoothed into our regular cadence while I waited for the waters inside my heart to quiet. When he dropped me off at home, he kissed me. "We're okay, right?"

"Perfect," I said, and touched the side of his face.

I stood on the porch and watched Peyton's car disappear. Darkness came complete on that night. The stars and thin, waxing moon hid behind low clouds— as if someone had forgotten to turn on the night-light. I looked over to Jack's old house.

Could it have been only two days since I last saw him? It seemed as though a lifetime of events had happened since the concert—my discovery of Mama's dying wish, learning that Peyton had been engaged before, and Maeve falling into a coma. Time, like the river below Jack and me in Savannah, just kept moving. I didn't even know him anymore—I only knew what I remembered, what had happened between us a long way up the river, a distance not measured in miles, but in lost years.

I looked up to the night sky, then sat on a rocker and stared out to the road, to the neighbor's front lights. A motor thrummed at the end of the road, then stopped in front of my house. I squinted and leaned forward. A man stepped out, stood with his hands on his hips and stared at my home. I stood to walk inside, then turned back to glance again at the confident manner in which he stood, as though he knew how to keep the earth solidly beneath his feet. Jack.

I waved; he didn't wave back. He turned to the house next door—his old home. He couldn't see me in the dark night, but I saw him backlit against a streetlamp. I walked down the steps and moved toward his truck, came up beside him before he heard me.

He jumped as I stepped closer.

"Kara," he said, then laughed. "Never sneak up on a man like that."

"What are you doing?" I patted his truck.

"This is embarrassing, but I came to—see the old

house. I haven't really seen it since we moved, except for the other day when I drove past quickly."

I pointed toward his house. "It looks different, doesn't it? At least five families have lived there, and each one has changed something about it."

"You know," he said, "you haven't left and you remember better, I'm sure. But I've lived ten, twelve places since here, and I really had forgotten a lot of it, a lot of those times and days. Until I saw you." He turned back to me and touched the side of my face. I backed away in a slight movement.

"Sorry," he whispered. "I came in the dark so you wouldn't see me. Guess that plan didn't work."

"Why didn't you want me to see you?" I leaned against his truck.

"I didn't want you to think I was trying to mess with your life, since you're engaged and all that."

I laughed. "Now why would I think that?"

"Because I am," he said, and pinched the tip of my nose.

"You're what?"

"Wanting to mess with your life."

"Jack—"

"But I won't. I promise."

"You're not messing with my life."

He faced me with his left shoulder against the truck. "Do you remember the ring I gave you?"

I nodded.

"You really do?"

"Yes, I really do. In fact, I still have it."

In the light of the flickering gas lamp, his eyebrows rose. "You do?"

"I do. It's dented, but I have it."

"I bought that for your fifteenth birthday. I thought I'd give it to you down by the footbridge and ask you to go steady with me." He laughed. "Steady? No one says that anymore, do they?"

"No," I said.

"I bought it at the downtown jewelry store—McRorey's. Do you remember that place?"

"It's still there, still run by Mr. McRorey."

"Wow, how old is he now?"

"Jack—it's only been thirteen years . . . or so. He's in his sixties, I think."

"Thirteen years—seems like a lifetime. Well, he talked me into that ring when I was going to buy you a star pendant."

"For our game of who saw the first star. . . ."

"Well, Mr. McRorey told me the ring stood for love, loyalty, and friendship. And well, then—back then, I mean—I thought that's what we stood for."

"That is awful sweet."

"Or just awful, huh?" he asked.

"No. Just sweet."

"I don't know what happened to that boy." He sighed. "Why don't you just go on in"—he waved toward my house—"and forget you saw me. I really didn't mean to bother you. I just came to take a little walk down memory lane."

"You're not bothering me. I'm . . . ." I fought for the

right words and came up with something completely inadequate. "Glad to see you."

A clap of thunder met my lukewarm declaration. I jumped as rain pelted us in a sudden downpour. Jack grabbed my hand, pulled me toward the side of the lawn, toward our tree cavern of the past.

We ran toward the line of oaks. I laughed, immediately soaked. "I don't think we can squeeze in there anymore."

We ducked together under the branches. Jack pulled me to him. "Looks like we still fit."

I didn't know whether he meant that we fit together or that we fit under the tree. I scooted backward on my bottom. "Wow, I *do* still fit in here." I looked up at him. "I haven't come in here since you left."

"Really?"

"I waited." I picked a leaf off the lower root, feeling I could say anything, that the thoughts and emotions would stay here, under the tree, and not be carried outside with us.

"You waited for me?" He touched my bottom lip, held his finger there.

Everything in me stilled: thoughts, reactions, rationalizations all quieted. I touched his hand. "A long time. Then I finally had to stop. . . ."

He leaned toward me now, never moving his hand. "Am I too late? Did you wait too long?" Then his hand moved as his lips touched mine, found my mouth.

Thunder pounded our hideout; I jumped back. "Jack . . ."

"Wow, this place is so full of . . . so much."

"I know."

He pushed the wet hair off my face. "How could you still live here and not feel the past all the time? Your mama, my daddy, us?"

"Just because you stay in one place doesn't mean life doesn't go on as it went on for you—new experiences, new people. You don't have to leave to move on."

"But sitting here with you, under these roots, it's like time never moved, like—"

An unbidden tear escaped my eye; I wiped it away. "Don't, Jack. I'm confused enough. Don't do this. You're remembering what we had then, who I was then. Memory and love are elusive enough. I can't confuse what I remember with what is real."

"No," he said, and put both hands in my hair now. "I know the difference."

I turned away. "Please. I've had an awful night. Can we change the subject?" The rain pelted the trees, creating a symphony that I wanted to slip into like a silk nightgown.

"Okay," he said, his voice low and raspy, "change of subject coming up. How did you end up being an event planner for the golf tour?"

"I'm called a service manager. Daddy got me an internship during college and . . ."

"You just stayed?"

"Yes. It's a great job. . . . I have thought about changing, though."

"To do what?"

I held the words tightly; I couldn't bear to share my desire one more time and have it shot down, ridiculed. I shook my head. "I'm just thinking—that's all, just thinking."

"About?"

In the shadowed cave, I spoke. "I'm exploring . . . going to photography school."

"Now that, sweet Kara, is something I would expect you to be doing. You have always loved nature, loved capturing it in pictures. You should definitely—" He stopped, placed his hand over mine. "I'm sorry. I shouldn't give you my opinion. I don't know you well enough to . . ."

"But you do," I said. "You do know me well enough." I wanted to reach for Jack, hold him, but I pushed my hands under my bottom. "What ever happened to your dad?"

He shrugged. "I don't know. Mom kept us moving. He never caught up with us and she never told me. I've thought about trying to find him, but—why?"

"Because he's your dad."

"Who beat us, beat his wife and drank his way into oblivion. He's probably dead or in jail or . . . on the street."

"I guess I'd just want to know."

"That's because you love your dad."

"Well, then, how's your mom?"

"I think she's finally come to a peaceful place in her life. She lives in Virginia Beach in a small cottage behind some sand dunes."

"Please send her my love."

"I will."

The rain had stopped now; the thunderstorm disappeared as fast as it had come, as though it had only visited to force us back under our trees.

Then there was nothing left to do but touch his cheek, run my finger along his chin.

"One," I said in a whisper.

"One what?"

I shook my head. "Oh, just damn, Jack."

He smiled, crooked, sweet. "Kara."

"This is absolutely not in my plans," I said.

"Yeah, you weren't exactly dressed for an evening in the root caves."

I looked down at my off-white pants, my pink blouse. "Ruined."

"Yes, you're absolutely ruined." He grinned, reached for me again.

"Jack, I don't want to do it all . . . wrong. Mess things up. Please let me sort this out. I think we're mixing up the past with now, story with truth. . . ."

He closed his eyes, nodded.

We shimmied our way out of the trees, stood and looked at each other over the wet grass.

I hesitated, then spoke. "Would you like to come in for a drink?"

"I don't want to bother you or your family. But I do want you to know that if you still need a band for that benefit in a few weeks, we can do it. No problem."

"Really?" I hugged him. "That is just such awesome news. When I go to work tomorrow I won't get fired. The only thing I could find during this time of year— wedding and graduation season—was a string quartet. This is just so great." I reached my hand up to give Jack a high five, and he hit my hand, laughed with his head back.

"I'm glad I can make you so happy," he said. "Doesn't take much, does it?"

I reached for my engagement ring, twisted it around my finger. "Come on in, have a drink—celebrate that I will not have my butt chewed out tomorrow morning."

By the time we entered the house and I'd poured us each a glass of wine, Daddy came home. He stood in the doorway of the library, narrowed his eyes at both of us.

"Jack Sullivan?" Daddy took another step into the room.

Jack nodded. "Yes, sir." He held out his hand. "Good to see you."

Daddy shook his hand. "I can honestly say I never thought I'd see you in this house again."

Jack dropped his hand, placed his glass of wine on the side table. "I should probably be going now." He nodded at me. "Kara, we'll talk soon and I'll get the details for the concert." He moved toward the entranceway.

"No," I said, "don't leave." I glanced at my father. "That was so rude, Daddy. He just stopped by to say hello and bail me out of big trouble."

"Trouble?" Daddy raised his bushy eyebrows.

"Yes, I lost the band for the benefit and Jack's band is going to save my . . . job."

Daddy nodded at Jack. "Thank you." But his words were empty of anything but indifference. Then he gave me the look: the one I'd dreaded my entire childhood. His eyebrows moved together, then down. His mouth pursed forward, but he didn't speak. I felt like I was eleven years old and late for dinner, late for something—just late. When love is sparse in a house without a mama and with an angry sister, when approval has love as its sidestepping companion, disapproval is avoided at all costs.

Daddy approved of Peyton.

The thought caught me by surprise, like realizing the tide has come in and washed over your feet, swept away your beach towel and book. I wanted to rebel against this need inside of me, this desire to earn my daddy's approval.

Jack was almost out the door; I went to him, grabbed his arm. "Stay," I said.

Daddy made a noise that sounded like a grunt, and turned his face from me, then walked from the room. Jack and I watched him leave, then he came to me, touched my arm. "Are you sure?"

"Sit," I said, and made a motion toward the leather club chair.

Jack sat, lifted his glass of wine. "Wow, he still doesn't like me after all these years."

"I've never understood it, Jack, and I'm sorry." I sat in my chair.

"It's not that complicated. He knows, and always has, that I'm not good enough for you."

"That is not true."

"True or not, it is what he believes."

I sighed, leaned back. "Sometimes it just doesn't matter if it's true, does it?" A chill ran through me and a single name burst forward: O'Leary. I bit down on it; tucked it into my heart to look at later.

"You know what?" he said. "You look almost exactly the same. Especially when you're curled up in that chair. I almost expect to see a Nancy Drew novel on your lap, or cross-stitch on the table next to you."

"Talk about remembering odd details."

"Yeah, but not until now. I could never give you a life . . . like this. One that your daddy gives you, one your fiancé will give you."

"Don't say that . . . you make me sound so shallow, as if material comfort is all that matters to me."

He shook his head. "I don't think that's all that matters to you. It's just an observation. My life is nomadic at best. And look what you have here." He gestured with his hand. "I don't have the . . . means for this style of life. I travel, move around. I don't even have a place I call home."

"But you want one, right?"

"Yes, but not if it's filled with nonsense and busyness, not meaningful in any way."

"Are you saying my life—"

219

"No," he interrupted me. "I'm not saying that. I'm just saying that I need my life to be meaningful—I need to contribute somehow. And right now that means I have no place to call home."

"Jack . . ."

He held up his hand. "Just the facts." He tilted his head at me as footsteps echoed in the hallway. We glanced toward the doors. "I really think I need to be going," he said, and stood.

I nodded and rose with him, staring directly at his face. I moved toward him, touched his arm. "Thanks for . . . everything. Really. Are you sure this gig isn't a hardship on the band?"

"No. We'd love to do it." He took my hand and squeezed it.

I dropped my hand from his. "We probably can't afford you."

"Ah, hell, whatever your budget is, we'll do it."

"Why?"

"Because—it's you. And exposure is exposure."

I let out a whoop and threw my arms around his neck. Someone coughed; I turned to stare at Peyton. I released Jack. Peyton stood at the threshold of the library, his mouth straight, the muscles in his cheek clenching and unclenching.

I moved toward him. "Hi, honey," I said.

He nodded at me.

I reached his side. "This is Jack, Jack Sullivan. He used to live next door. He's the songwriter for the Unknown Souls. Anyway, he stopped by to tell me

220

they can play the tour benefit."

Peyton nodded again. He was beginning to look like an angry bobble-head statue.

Jack walked toward him, held out his hand. "Nice to meet you, Peyton. Congratulations on your engagement and on winning the BellSouth tournament. That chip out of the sand trap on five was magnificent."

Peyton smiled, held out his hand. "Thank you. Nice to meet you too. Thank you so much for being willing to play the benefit. Your band should draw a huge crowd."

Jack glanced toward the door. "Well, I best be going."

"Yes," Peyton said, "thanks for stopping by."

I opened my mouth, closed it. What could I say now?

Jack nodded at both of us and closed the door behind him. Peyton and I stood in the hallway. "What the hell was that about?" He backed away from me.

"Just what I said it was about."

"I come here to tell you I'm sorry, to try and find a way to talk to you about what happened at the restaurant, and I find you in the arms of another man. And why are you soaking wet?"

I looked down at my pants streaked with mud, my wet blouse. "Got caught in the thunderstorm. . . ."

"What did you do?" He touched my shirtsleeve. "Roll around in the mud?"

"Peyton, please . . . he stopped by . . ." I stuttered, stumbled on my words.

"A phone call wouldn't have sufficed?"

"He was looking at his old house. Look, why don't we just discuss us, what happened at the restaurant?"

"I'm not in the mood now." Peyton turned away from me.

"Please don't be this way. I want to find a way to talk all this out, be able to discuss what is important between us."

"No secrets, right, Kara? Isn't that what you asked for the other night? No secrets. Seems like you have some of your own."

"Jack is not a secret—he's an old neighbor."

Peyton sat down on the bottom step of the staircase, dropped his head in his hands. "Tonight, about the photography, I just meant you should give some thought to what you want to do, not run impulsively after it."

"Okay, I will. I will give it more thought. But we could talk about it." I touched his clenched fist. "Maybe now isn't a good time, but maybe you could listen to why I want to try."

He took my hand, stroked my palm. "I'm sorry, Kara. I'm just under a lot of pressure, and when you said you wanted to leave . . ."

"I didn't say I wanted to leave. I said I wanted to consider photography school, that I wanted to explore my options."

"I'm a schmuck," he said, and drew me toward him. I fell against his chest.

"Kara, I need to ask you one more question."

I drew back. "Okay."

"Where did you say you stayed in Savannah when you went to check out the band for the tournament?"

"The Courtyard Savannah. I told you that already."

"Then why don't they have you in the register?"

I pushed away from him. "You checked?"

"Obviously I needed to. No secrets? Shit." He stood, kicked the edge of the stairwell.

"I never lied. I told you I stayed there . . . I didn't say I had my own room."

He leaned down and put his hands on both my shoulders. "That, Kara, is no different from me not telling you I'd been engaged before. You spent the night in some guy's hotel room."

"On the couch."

"Oh, what a gentleman." He rolled his eyes. Peyton stood up straight and fought for control. I'd seen this struggle before, on the golf course. He stood taller, looked ahead, and his nostrils flared as he took a couple of deep breaths.

The next words that came out of my mouth were unbidden. "I'm not a bad shot."

"What?" He focused in on me.

"You're acting like you just had a bad shot on sixteen while you're two strokes behind."

"You're very perceptive, Kara, because that is exactly how I feel. Except right now I'm on eighteen and it's a golf course I've never played before and it's sudden death for the championship. Something is going on with you and you're just not acting like yourself. I think I need to go home before this descends into a fight we regret."

"I agree."

Peyton kissed me. "I love you. I really do. I'm sorry about this night. Let's wake up tomorrow and start all over, okay?"

"Good deal."

He walked out the door, and I sat back in the chair, picked up my glass and let the wine spill warmly all the way down to the knot in my stomach.

No, I wasn't acting like myself at all. At least not the self I'd grown accustomed to being over the past few years.

I reached for the words Mama had told Daddy. Listen to the hints of your heart. Should a wish from the past influence today? Should an old woman's story change the present? I didn't know, but I thought I was about to find out.

CHAPTER FIFTEEN

My head spun in a thousand directions, like a multicolored pinwheel in the wind, while I waited in the kitchen for Daddy to come get his coffee the next morning. I'd been up most of the night, tossing from the left to the right in my bed while trying to find a comfortable spot on my down pillow. Daddy walked in rubbing the stubble on his chin.

"Good morning," I said, attempting a smile.

He nodded at me, then glanced away. He grabbed his coffee mug, poured himself a cup.

A palpable tension shimmered between us, and I knew only one way to make it disappear, to diminish this loneliness—I needed to tell Daddy I was sorry for being disrespectful, that Jack meant nothing to me. I opened my mouth to try, but the words wouldn't come.

Sunlight streaked through the window at that moment, casting a sharp yellow glow on Daddy's face. His wrinkles were set deeper, his stubble now gray, and my heart reverberated with love.

He turned away from me, then walked out of the kitchen without saying a word. I called after him. "Daddy, don't be mad at me." I sounded like a child, like a desperate child.

He returned. "It is all well and good to listen to your heart, as your mother said, but you must also have integrity and character. Kara, my biggest fear was that if I ever told you all what your mother said before she died, it would do more harm than good."

"Don't let that be a fear, Daddy. That is not what that wish means to me. I think she just meant that I need to think about what I'm doing, about who I am." I took a long breath, and with the new day coming through the window, soft and full, I found words that I didn't even realize I'd hidden in the safer part of my heart. "I . . . have been afraid to think about what I really want because it might not be what other people want."

Daddy nodded.

"I feel like you gave me a gift—Mama's words before I get married."

He wrapped his hands around his mug and stared at me, but didn't speak.

I moved toward him. "Do you think you could ever love again?"

His face blanched, his hands gripping his mug tighter. "Kara Margarite, that would not be any of your business."

"She would want you to love again, Daddy. She would."

He turned around and walked from the room without speaking. My stomach knotted like a rope pulled tighter and tighter.

Daddy and Peyton: wanting and needing only the Kara they knew. A sob began to rise from the back of my throat, but I held it tight, let it dissolve before I moved, ran up the stairs to my room and grabbed several rolls of undeveloped film.

I stood in the Palmetto Pointe Photography Studio's darkroom with only the developing pictures beneath my fingers, beneath the fluid in the pan. Clarisse, who managed the studio, had taught me years ago how to develop my own pictures, and she rented me the space when I needed it. There were at least fifty photographs on the rolls of film. I watched the pictures appear one by one, taking my time, focusing only on the pictures, not on my fatigued and shadowed thoughts. I focused on the skill of developing, on creating the right light contrast for each photo.

I knew exactly how to fix the rift between Daddy and me, between Peyton and me. I could just say, "I'm sorry. I didn't mean to bring Jack Sullivan back into this house. I'm sorry. I didn't really mean I would leave and go to photography school." And I'd probably still say these things, smooth the rougher edges of our relationships with my words, but now I stared at the developing photos below the water.

One of my favorite things about seeing the pictures was that often I forgot what was on the film, what I'd taken pictures of. This roll held mostly landscapes of the Palmetto Pointe golf course and the river behind it at Peyton's house. I'd become enchanted with the way in which the sun—from the rising dawn to the fading evening—played with the river, tossed its light and shadows across the water, around the edges. The hummocks were exposed during low tide, then covered with the thick ribbon of blue-black water during high tide, with the spartina swaying behind the water in sage-gray contrast. I could taste the air when I'd taken this last shot right before the rain came.

Now a body formed on the photo paper beneath the water, its form taking shape as I watched: Peyton on the eighteenth green. I stared at his face, glancing down at the golf ball, at his body with his club in the air. He was such a familiar figure, part of a comfortable and known world. I knew this man: the way he walked, the way he raised his club or glanced up at me. I understood the words to say to him, where to touch him and how to make him smile.

I did love him. Then why was I having these doubts, these new . . . feelings for Jack, for another kind of life than the one I'd planned? It was a big question, the answer looming so far out on the horizon, beyond the sun, that I couldn't catch a glimpse of it. I stared at the photo as if it could tell me. His body came into full focus and I leaned down, watched it below the water until it started to overprocess. I had left the picture in too long; it was time to take it out, let it dry. But my fingers did not move to pick up the prongs, yank the picture from the solution. I stared and watched Peyton fade without disappearing.

The next few photos were more landscapes: river, sea, estuary. I hadn't realized I'd taken so many of the water—all kinds of water in every shade of light. Then Jack appeared with his lopsided grin, sitting at a restaurant table in Savannah. It was the last photo in the roll, the last picture I'd taken. I took a deep breath, leaned too close to the solution. When the light fell directly on his features, I lifted the photo from the water, hung it on the wire above my head and stepped back. Photographers often joked how the last photo was always the best, how it surprised them because they had only meant to take one more photo to finish the roll.

I remembered snapping the camera; but I also remembered that I'd focused on the entire table—all six of them sitting there with their empty plates and

228

beer mugs, with their arms around each other, smiling at the camera.

But this photo showed the band and singers in the background, fuzzy and clipped off at the edges. In this photo I'd focused only on Jack.

I piled my photos together as a buzzer went off; my time in the rented developing booth was over. I swung the revolving door around and stepped into the light, into a bright room with four long metal tables. I nodded at the next person in line and walked toward the tables, laid my photos out in a row.

Clarisse came up beside me. "Kara, your photos get better and better." She grabbed four of them from the row, lined them up against each other. "These are the exact same scene taken from four different angles. These are an amazing study of light and shadow." She looked up at me.

"Thank you," I said. "I was trying to catch that section of the river at different times of the day. It's right behind Peyton's house."

"You do know you have a gift, right?"

"A wedding gift?" I glanced toward her desk.

She laughed. "No, I meant you have a gift for photography. You have a natural eye for light and composition."

"I do?" My spirits lifted, rose above the room, where her compliment seemed to float.

"Surely you know that."

"No, I just love to do this."

"Usually the one thing we love to do most is a hint

of the thing we are most gifted at. Doesn't that make sense?"

"I never thought about it like . . . that." I gathered up the photos, put them in a pile.

A bell rang across the room, a signal that someone in a darkroom needed assistance. Clarisse touched my arm. "I mean it, Kara. I see a lot of photographers—professional and amateur—come through here, and you are one of the best."

"Thanks." I smiled at her, then patted the pile of photos. "I'll just take these and go. Put it on my bill."

Clarisse pointed to the top photo as she walked off. "Now look at that photograph—you knew exactly what to focus on, whose face held the most interest, and yet you didn't cut out the remainder of the scene. You are very good, Kara."

Clarisse disappeared into one of the developing rooms, and I stood in the main hall for a long time, just stood and stared at Jack's grinning face. Had I focused on him for art or heart? And was there a difference?

CHAPTER SIXTEEN

The ICU machines hummed around me like white noise. The atmosphere in the room was tense, fearful. My heart stuttered and breath caught below my throat as I sat and stared at Maeve.

A tube pulled at the side of her mouth and intermittently burst forth with sucking noises; another tube with two prongs fit snugly in her nose. An IV ran into her arm with a clear yellow fluid. Suddenly the mechanical box where the IV fluid hung began to beep and flash lights. I jumped up, waved at a nurse. "Something is wrong over here," I called out.

The nurse in pale green scrubs ran over. She was younger than me, with long brown curls pulled into a ponytail. She patted my arm. "The IV fluid just needs to be changed. Nothing to worry about. I'll be right back."

I sat down again and dropped my head into my hands. She returned and replaced the bag. I tapped her arm. "Is she going to come out of this coma?"

The nurse gave me one of those sympathetic looks they must teach in nursing school, but not medical school. Squint your eyebrows together, they must say, purse your lips and tilt your head. There you go, that's it—now you look like you care.

She sat next to me, placed her small hand on my knee. "Sometimes they do come out of it, sometimes they don't. Despite all of medical science's break-throughs, strokes are still a mystery. Patients surprise us all the time. It is up to her body whether she will come out of this."

"Can she hear me?"

"Some experts say that people in comas can hear us, and absorb the information. Others believe that to be bunk."

I laughed with my palm over my mouth. I'd never

heard anyone under fifty years old use the word "bunk." "Do *you* think she can hear me?"

"Yes, I do." The nurse stood, patted the arm rails of the bed. "Go ahead, talk to her. Even if she can't hear you, you'll feel better."

I nodded and watched her take long strides across the room to another beeping machine. I leaned down to Maeve. "Hi, Maeve, it's Kara."

I glanced around, feeling foolish, but no one paid any attention to me.

I took Maeve's hand. "I'm so sorry you're here in the hospital. I wish you could tell me your story, that we could take a walk at the edge of the sea you talk about. Maybe that's where you are right now. . . ."

I laid my head on the edge of the bedside table, turned to stare at Maeve with her oxygen tubes and IV fluids. Her face was faded, like an old sweater that had been bleached one too many times. Her eyes moved back and forth under her eyelids, and I wondered what she saw: Richard, the three brown sails dipping and swaying across the bay, or nothing at all—just blank and empty space where love and family once lived.

I left Memorial Hospital with a leaden weight on my chest, and drove to the post office to mail the wedding invitations. I dropped the box of ecru envelopes onto the counter. "I just need to mail these," I said to the round man in the blue U.S. Postal Service uniform.

"Wedding invitations?" He picked up an envelope from the box.

"Yes." I nodded. "They're already stamped."

He held his palm out flat, placed the envelope on it. "This here weighs more than the postage you have on it."

"What? I have a regular stamp." I pointed to the white dove stamps I'd spent half an hour picking out.

"Yes, but these are too heavy. You must have high-weight paper and response cards."

I groaned. "Now what?"

He turned his back to me, tossed the invitation on a scale, then glanced over his shoulder. "They need five more cents of postage on each one."

"What if I leave it off?"

"They'll all end up back in your mailbox." He pointed to the return address. "How many five-cent stamps you need?"

"Four hundred." I dropped my head into my palm.

He laughed. "Don't worry, I see this happen all the time." He motioned to a table in the corner. "Just take your box over there and I'll bring you the stamps."

"I don't have time for this."

He shrugged. "Then don't mail them."

I picked up the box, heard my name being called. I turned to see Sylvia Ellers waving from the back of the line.

I nodded at her, then turned back to the man and handed him my credit card. "Thanks for telling me. I'd hate to get all these back."

"Might save you some money on the food and drink at the reception." He smiled.

I was on the fourth page of stamps, peeling, sticking,

peeling, sticking, when Sylvia came up next to me. "Hello, Kara. What're doing?"

I held up a forefinger with a five-cent stamp stuck to it. "I didn't have enough postage on the invitations."

"Oh." She stood staring at me for a brief moment, then picked up a page of stamps and assisted me.

"Thanks," I said. "I had no idea they'd weigh too much."

"You're mailing them today?" She set a pile of envelopes to one side.

I nodded.

She opened her mouth, closed it.

I lifted my eyebrows at her. "You don't think I should mail them today?"

"No . . . I mean, yes. I just . . ."

"What?" I exhaled.

"You love my Peyton."

"Is that a question?" I stopped plucking stamps, stared at her.

"No. I just . . ."

"I love him, Sylvia. I do. I wouldn't wear this ring or—"

"I've just seen his heart broken too many times."

I leaned against the table, dropped a handful of stamped envelopes into the box. "Not by me."

She nodded, walked over to the nearest mailbox, and dropped a handful of invitations in the slot. "I've got to go—late for a manicure. See you . . . soon."

I smiled at my future mother-in-law. "Thanks for the help."

"It's the least I could do." She pushed open the door and walked out, allowing a flush of warm air to pirouette into the room.

I stood without moving for long moments and wondered whose invitations Sylvia had dropped in the box. If I didn't mail the remainder, who would receive their invitations, a result of Sylvia's show of belief in me? Panic, like thin fingers of icy mist, spread along my arms and legs. I didn't have any guarantees that this would all work out, that I was doing the right thing.

I filled the box with stamped envelopes and dropped them off with the postal worker, then watched as he tossed them into a large bin behind the counter.

"Invitations mailed," I said to him.

He nodded at me. "Yes."

"Thank you." I turned and walked out the door of the post office, headed toward home.

CHAPTER SEVENTEEN

Afternoon sunlight fell in the striped pattern of the plantation shutters onto the pine floorboards in my bedroom. I stood at my dresser staring at the dented Claddagh ring. Recent events seemed odd and coincidental, and yet I felt deceived by everyone.

Peyton had been engaged twice before; Maeve had made me believe that a legend was her real-life story;

Daddy never told me Mama had fought to live until the end, or that she'd left a dying wish for her children. Truth played hide-and-seek with me, shrouded in the dark corners of story and memory.

I slipped the ring on my finger, turned it around and around, then sank down on my bed, spread flat on my back, as though I were making snow angels in the sand with Jack beside me. I groaned. Back to Jack. I had to settle this, find some conclusion to that story, because it was an old one. I'd let Maeve's legend take me back to a story that didn't belong to me anymore. I had a new story . . . one that was not a myth or legend, but a real fiancé and a real life to build.

I stood and wiped my face. A soft knock came on my bedroom door. "Come in," I called.

Daddy stood at the threshold. "Are you okay, darling?"

I nodded as he came and sat on my vanity chair. Daddy had never, in all these years, done more than stand in my doorway. He looked oversized and overwhelming in my room, sitting at my makeup table. "Are you and Peyton okay?"

I nodded.

"Don't blow this, Kara."

"Don't blow what, Daddy?" The room would spin if I allowed it, but I focused tight on his face, his words.

"This engagement. This is all you've ever wanted, Kara."

"Is it?"

His elbow knocked my hair dryer to the floor in a

clattering noise he didn't notice. "I promised your mama I would make sure you girls grew up with integrity and character, that you married the right men. If you break this engagement, I'll have broken a promise."

"You'll feel that *you've* failed if I don't marry Peyton?"

He looked up at me. "Yes. I shouldn't have told you what she said during this vulnerable time in your life. I know she didn't mean you should see how you feel about Jack Sullivan before you get married."

"Oh, Daddy. I am not doing that because of what you told me. . . ."

He shook his head. "You cannot hurt others to pursue selfish, childish dreams. Just do the right thing."

"You've been telling me that my entire life. Well, maybe not my entire life, but at least since Mama died. What I remember you telling me is how to see the difference between a high or ebb tide, how to identify a blue crab from a ghost crab, the path of the migrating osprey or the impact of the full moon on the marsh." Tears choked my memories of my other daddy, the one before Mama died.

He dropped his hands to his sides, and in my small chair they almost touched the floor. "Oh, Kara. I did tell you to do the right thing back then. I did."

"Well, you might have, but it was mixed up in all the other great things you told me. What happened to that daddy? That man who knew the rhythm of the land around us, the one who laughed?"

"My role changed, Kara. I had to be both parents when she left."

"She didn't leave. She died." The truth grew larger, substantial as I spoke it.

He nodded. "And there were promises made."

I leaned forward on my knees, reached for his hand. "You teach me to do the right thing just by the way you live. You don't have to tell me all the time and you don't have to leave the fun parts out. Really you don't."

His eyes opened wider. "Oh, now you tell me." His laugh held little gaiety.

"Isn't there a way to combine what your heart wants and the right thing?" I asked.

He stood and looked around my room as though he couldn't believe he'd come in and sat. "I don't know, darling."

"Daddy, I promise this confusion I'm going through has nothing to do with you not teaching me character or integrity. It has everything to do with . . ." I stared off to the ceiling, heard Maeve's words. "With what I believe."

He squinted at me.

"What?" I asked.

"You asked me yesterday if I could love again."

"Sorry . . . I overstepped my bounds." I pressed my lips together.

"No . . . I just wanted you to know that I love you. I don't say it enough, do I?"

"You show it, Daddy. I promise."

As he walked out of the room, he looked over his shoulder. "Don't forget, you're the cook for the family dinner tonight."

I groaned and slumped in my chair. "Damn."

"This is quite possibly the worst family meal you've ever made." Deirdre pushed her plate away. "What was that?"

Brian lifted his fork and waved a piece of dry, burned pork chop. "Five star, if I do say so myself."

"Yeah, right," I said. "I'm so sorry, y'all. Really. I was at the hospital with Maeve and . . ."

Peyton leaned forward from his seat across the table from me. "How is she?" he asked.

I shrugged. "Still in a coma. . . . So anyway, how is everyone else doing?"

Conversation flowed about jobs and weather and other burned meals. Brian glanced at Peyton. "When is your next tournament?"

He looked across the table at me. "We leave tomorrow, noon, I think."

"Yes," I said, "you do." I touched Brian's arm. "It's in Dallas."

"Whoa, whoa," Peyton said. "What do you mean, *you* do."

"Well, Caroline is taking this tournament. I need to wrap up a lot of things with the Palmetto Pointe Open, and management wants her to take this one. I'm swamped."

"You won't be there?" Peyton set his fork down, lifted his napkin to wipe his mouth, although he hadn't eaten a bite.

I shook my head. "Sorry . . . I meant to tell you this morning . . . and I couldn't get ahold of you."

He glanced around the table. "Well, I better get home to pack. It was great seeing all of you."

"Can't you wait until after dinner?" I asked, then stood to walk over to his side of the table.

He shook his head, and I followed him out to the front porch, where he swung his keys in a circle around his forefinger. "So," he said and pouted his lips out, "you decided to wait and tell me you weren't coming in front of your family?"

"No. I tried to call you this morning, but I couldn't find you."

"And you didn't bother to try again."

"I'm sorry, Peyton."

He shook his head. "If you're just not into this marriage anymore, tell me."

"Marriage?"

"Yes . . . we're getting married, Kara."

"But we're not married yet." I stepped toward him, took his hand. "I'm sorry I'm not going to this tournament. Frieda wants me to stay and make sure every detail is done for the Pointe tournament. You won before you met me and you'll win without me there. And, yes, I do want to get married, please don't suggest that I don't, just because I'm not going to a tournament."

"You do want to get married?"

"What is that supposed to mean?" I stepped back, jerking my hand away from his.

"You haven't talked about the wedding at all lately."

"You want me to keep you updated on wedding plans? I thought you hated them. Okay then—I've had my dress altered for a final fitting, the flowers will have Swarovski crystals that look like rain, the invitations have been mailed, the bridesmaids' dresses are cream, and each bridesmaid has a different-colored satin ribbon around the waist with a crystal jewel—"

Peyton laughed, held up his hand, "Okay, enough. I get it."

"See? I knew you didn't want to hear it."

He pulled me close and kissed me. "Will you please stop by later tonight? I'm gonna go home and pack, get ready for this tournament, but will you come over later?"

I nodded, then kissed him again. "Yes, as soon as I clean up."

He walked to the car, and I watched him and smiled. It felt good, even right when he smiled at me, when I made him smile . . . when he loved me.

The night carried the scent of jasmine, floating in off the neighbor's yard. The dishes were done; Deirdre and Brian had gone home. I sat on the porch swing; I needed to drive to Peyton's and see him as I'd promised, but something kept me still and quiet . . .

241

waiting. The hum of a motor cut through the silence. I lifted my eyes to see Charlotte's car pull into the driveway.

"Hey, girlfriend." She climbed the porch steps. "I've come to take you out tonight." She held up her palm. "No arguments; follow me now."

I shook my finger at her. "I am not in the mood to go out."

"You, my dear, need some good old-fashioned fun, and I just told Tom I only wanted to be friends. So there you go—another one of Charlotte's broken relationships. We're going to Danny's Pub."

"I haven't been there in years."

"And it's high time we changed that."

"You scare me," I said, then followed her down the steps toward her car.

The pub was dark, but Charlotte and I had been sitting at the bar long enough for our eyes to become accustomed. I picked up my pink martini, took a long swallow. "When was the last time we were here?" I twirled my glass on the bar.

"Six years ago for your twenty-first birthday. You danced with the bartender behind the bar."

I groaned. "I did, didn't I? Why do you always remember my most embarrassing moments?"

"Because they're my favorites." She clinked her martini glass against mine, but I couldn't hear it over Hank Williams's voice coming out of the jukebox, the roar of the growing crowd.

242

I leaned toward her. "What in the hell does 'follow your heart' mean?"

She shrugged. "Like I know. Look at me—I break up with everyone who likes me. You, on the other hand, are engaged. Maybe you can tell me."

"I can tell you it's a bunch of crap. Seriously. Mama said, 'Listen to the hints of your heart.' People say it all the time—'follow your heart.' What are we supposed to do—take our heart out and walk around behind it—follow it down the sidewalk to the mall?" I slung back the martini. "Your feet will lead you to your heart. Ha!"

Charlotte picked the lemon rind off the side of her glass, twisted it like one of her curls between her fingers. "Maybe it just means you should know your heart, because if you know it, you might do what it says to do. I don't think it means you do whatever you damn well please. I don't think the heart speaks very loudly either—just tosses you hints and whispers. Or maybe I have no idea whatsoever."

"You have more idea than me, that's for sure. When I try and listen all I hear is what everyone else says to do, what I'm supposed to do: I can hear that loud and clear. Maybe it's the same thing. Maybe what I'm hearing is what I want."

"Maybe it is, Kara. But maybe it's not and maybe you need to find out before you're standing in the middle of the laundry room folding his underwear and wondering, 'How'd I get here?' Then again—you can't drop your life to run after someone who makes you feel twelve years old and adorable, either."

I groaned, motioned for the bartender. He came up. "Is that you, Kara Larson?"

I nodded. "Hey, Frank, haven't seen you in years."

"Yeah, you must not get out much."

"I do too," I said.

Charlotte shook her head back and forth. "She's way too busy to have fun."

"Thanks, pal." I hit Charlotte.

Frank laughed. "You want another martini?"

"Nope," I said. "A Guinness, please."

"Okay." He nodded at Charlotte. "You?"

"The same. If Kara is going down, I'm going down with her."

"Now there's a true friend," Frank said, and slung two glasses off the back bar, filled them at the Guinness tap.

As the music got louder, as the crowd thickened, Charlotte and I laughed and remembered. It seemed that talking about what was ahead was too hard, so we talked about what used to be, until Frank's face wavered before me and he swung me into a repeat performance of my twenty-first birthday. When he dipped me for the finale of our dance, I remembered something—I was supposed to stop by Peyton's and say good-bye before he left for his tournament.

CHAPTER EIGHTEEN

T he empty ballroom possessed the faintest odor of mildew, which I was acutely aware of in any room in which I was planning an event. No one wants to walk into a party and smell dampness, the kind that pervaded every dwelling here. I pulled out my notebook, jotted a note to spread real gardenia bushes down the sides of the room.

I glanced at my watch, paced the room in circles. Jack was late to meet me to go over the plans for the benefit concert. My heart did somersaults in my chest. I pulled out my phone to call Peyton.

"Hey, babe." The sound of his voice mixed with static came through the phone.

"Hey . . . I can't hear you very well."

"Sorry. I'm in the airport, not getting very good reception. Hey, Mom called—did you remember to invite the Miller family to the wedding? She says she forgot to ask you."

"I didn't invite them. Do I need to?"

"Yes, Mom says it would hurt their feelings—"

"Peyton, I swear, if I invited everyone whose feelings would be hurt, we'd be broke. I can only invite the families that—"

The connection severed; I stared at the phone. I clicked it shut and shoved it in my purse, then looked up at Jack standing in the doorway. A sphere of light from a wrought iron chandelier lit the edges of his curls.

I waved at him.

"Sorry to interrupt your conversation," he said, walking toward me. "I'm late. I couldn't find the damn place—didn't this used to be a park or something?"

I nodded. "Yep, owned by the infamous Darby family. He deeded it to the country club when he died. What an uproar." I grinned. "Sorry you missed it."

"Me too," he said.

"Okay, let's do this really quickly. I have a two o'clock appointment."

"Busy girl." He walked toward the stage, stepped up.

"That's where the band will play." I took the steps two at a time to keep up with him.

"I figured that part out." He turned to me, wrapped one arm around my shoulder. "Stage, band—they usually go together."

I pushed him away. "Smart ass."

His laugh echoed in the empty room, washed over me like an unexpected wave—just when I thought it was safe to go swimming again, a monster wall of water knocked me down. I turned away, knowing that the desire to have him pull me toward him, touch me, would show all over my face.

Old want; old story—only the ache of remembering when I had been adored, adorable and adored.

I pointed to the far side of the room. "The soundboard will be set up over there; the tables will be eight-person rounds arranged in an oval pattern." I pulled the papers from my folder, held them out.

"I don't need to see the table configuration. I just need to see the room, the acoustics. Will there be anything besides tables?"

"Yes," I said, felt my heart go back to its regular, businesslike rhythm. "Palm trees, gardenia bushes at the edges, centerpieces . . ." I stopped as he walked across the space, ran his hand over the cedar posts in the center of the room.

"Great acoustics in here. This will work out perfect. That's all I needed to see."

"Really?"

"Really," he said. He walked toward me and pointed to the grandfather clock in the far corner. "You have half an hour. Would you do me a huge favor?"

I nodded.

"Will you show me around town? I hate to admit I don't know how to get around anymore . . . but I'd love to see it."

"It's not that complicated." I pulled my file close to my chest. "Palmetto Pointe hasn't changed all that much. Main Street down the middle, numbered streets off to the sides. Bay Street running along the water. Come on, Jack, you can't be that confused." I suppressed a grin.

"Okay, now who's the smart ass?" He tapped my nose. "Come on, I just want to see it again—with you. Please."

I rolled my eyes and said, "Yes," with a rising spirit of laughter hiding just below my chest.

Words poured out of my mouth faster than the engine beneath Jack's truck hood as we drove down every street in town. I told him who lived where now, who'd married, who'd divorced. I explained which buildings had been torn down and which ones had been renovated.

"So," he said, turning a corner onto Bay Street. "How is the family taking it that the youngest is getting married?"

"Everyone loves Peyton . . . they're thrilled. They think it's the perfect . . ." I paused. "They're happy about it."

He nodded, stared straight ahead through the windshield. "What do *you* think?"

"The same, of course."

"Of course," he said.

We drove past the elementary school, then he stopped in the parking lot of Palmetto Pointe Middle School, got out of the car.

I followed him to the playground. "What are you doing?"

"I remember," he said.

"Remember what?"

He looked at me, and the old pain I last saw that summer morning he left returned to his face; he was fourteen, broken in spirit. "That morning."

"You'd forgotten?" I touched his cheek, jerked my hand away.

"Yes. At first on purpose, then even when I tried to remember, I couldn't. All I could see was the truck, and then you on the ground. Now I remember it all: Dad hitting you, Mom waking us and telling us to take anything we loved, throwing things in boxes, filling what we could into the back of a truck in the middle of the night, knowing we'd never see the house or our other stuff or your family again—ever."

My tears rose, but words did not. I wrapped my arms around Jack, buried my face against his chest and listened to his torn breath.

He released me, sat on a swing. "I don't need sympathy, Kara. I just remembered, that's all."

I swallowed hard and wiped furiously at my face. "I wasn't giving sympathy, just empathy. It was terrible for everyone."

"No, it wasn't. No one gave a shit that we were gone. One less problem in Palmetto Pointe."

"I gave a shit," I said, and sat on the swing next to him. "Doesn't that count?"

He pushed his feet against the ground to lift his swing into the air. He pushed higher and higher until he was flying so high I thought the swing would wrap itself around the pole and flip him over.

Then he stopped, planted his feet firmly on the ground. "That you cared was all that counted."

He stood and walked toward the parking lot, then stopped, looked at me, and waved his hand toward the middle school. "You know, this is probably as far as we'd have gone—even if I stayed. This is as far as we'd have gone."

I tucked a piece of hair behind my ear. "You mean you wouldn't have gone to high school? Damn, Jack, you were the best athlete in the school. You would've been the star in everything by tenth grade."

"No, I mean us. We wouldn't have made it past middle school. Too different, you know? All the things you would've wanted, the life I couldn't have given you."

My shoulders slumped. "Why am I taking this as an insult?"

"Don't. I'm a different kind of man than the kind you've chosen to spend your life with."

"And what kind of man are you, Jack?"

"A wandering soul who doesn't care how old the house is, who used to live in it, where the family silver came from, whether the wedding guests are from the right families. That kind of man."

"And you think I'm that kind of woman? You don't think I'm anything like the girl you knew?"

"That's not bad, Kara. It's not an insult, I swear to God, it's not. We all change with time. You are still beautiful and kind and—"

I held up my hand. "Stop."

"Just the facts," he said.

Damn. He didn't believe in who I was anymore—at all. I wasn't even sure I knew who I was anymore. And suddenly it seemed infinitely important that we both believed in this young Kara, beyond the facts of

250

my wedding, my job, my pressed linen suit.

"Okay," I said, "I don't blame you for thinking that I've changed so dramatically that I'm nothing like the girl you gave the Claddagh ring to. So, now take us up Bay Street to Fifth, take a left to the dead end."

"What?"

"Just listen to me."

"Okay, boss. Whatever you say. But aren't you late for an appointment?"

"The wedding shoes . . . they'll wait."

Jack drove us to the end of Fifth Street in less than five minutes. I jumped out of the car, pointed to the small, slanted house behind the bluff. "Brian's house," I said.

"Man, how is he?"

"Good. I'm sure he's at work right now. We're not here to see him, just his kayaks."

Jack squinted at me. "You're kidding, right?"

"You don't believe I'm still that girl, that I can't beat you in a kayak race along Silver Creek?"

Jack pointed to my suit. "You aren't exactly dressed for it."

"More than you are," I said and pulled off my heels and jacket and threw them in the open back of Jack's truck. "Wait here, I'll be right back."

I ran into my brother's house and put on a pair of tattered shorts and a T-shirt I had left there the last time I'd come to kayak.

I came out onto the porch, motioned toward the water. "Come on."

"You asked for it," he said.

We yanked two single-man kayaks out from under Brian's house, then pulled them over the boardwalk to the mud bank. I rolled my pants up and zipped a life jacket over my T-shirt.

"You're insane," Jack said. He pushed us both off into the creek. We settled into our kayaks and he came alongside me. "Okay, same rules. From here to Broad River, then back."

"You got it."

We began the back-and-forth paddling of our double-bladed oars, synchronizing our actions to the movement of the kayaks. Jack pushed two lengths ahead of me and I strained to catch up, but couldn't. When we rounded the bend to return, my kayak came next to his and we pulled into the bank simultaneously.

I collapsed backward on the bow. "You let me catch up."

"But I didn't let you win," he said, jumped out of the boat and pulled mine up on the bank.

I swung my legs around, stepped out of the kayak and let the mud squish beneath my toes. Sweat dripped down my chest; my shirt clung and my hair stuck to my face. I tasted the salt air and my own sweat in an intoxicating mixture.

"Come on," I said, "we'll steal some of Brian's Coronas and cool off on his porch."

In silence, Jack and I sat in the rocking chairs, cold beers in our hands at four o'clock on a workday. Guilt prodded at me; I glanced at him. "I wanted to beat you," I said.

He laughed. "I know. I just couldn't let you."

"I remember, once, you let me win the star game," I said.

"I did?"

"I know you did—it's how I knew you loved—" I stopped, placed my palm over my mouth.

Jack leaned close, wiped my hair off my face. "I sure did love you then."

I nodded, heard and understood the word "then." "I probably need to go back to work now."

"Like that?" He grinned and pointed to my disheveled condition.

"Maybe not," I said, stared out over the water, to the edges of the shore, and thought of Maeve.

Then we talked, Jack and I, about everything we could remember, and everything he'd wanted to forget.

When light dwindled to the farther corners of the creek and the frogs began their evening song, Brian came home. When he saw Jack he let out a holler and offered him a large hug.

"Man, I thought I'd never see you again. What's up?" Brian asked.

"Bailing your sister out of trouble, as usual." Jack lifted his beer to me.

"Oh?" Brian raised his eyebrows at me.

"His band is playing the tour benefit," I said. "That's all."

Brian pointed at me, then looked at Jack. "What in the hell have y'all been doing? You're a mess."

"Kayak race," I said, pulling my shirt out from my body.

"Who won?" Brian looked back and forth between us.

"Tie," I said.

"Yeah, right." Brian punched Jack's side. "Y'all stay here and let me get a beer. I'll be right back."

The three of us sat with cold Coronas and watched the remainder of the day descend into the edges of spartina and cord grass, lighting them like the tips of sparklers. Brian and Jack talked over each other, their words and laughter echoing across the porch.

I closed my eyes, leaned my head back on the rocking chair and disappeared into the warm haze of this place, of my brother and Jack Sullivan. I floated above them, beyond them, as their words blurred together in a benediction. Then it was quiet, the air still and hot like someone had wrapped a blanket around me. A thrumming noise echoed across the black night—my eyes jerked open.

Jack and Brian were gone—I was alone.

The warmth fell away from me like a waterfall. I jumped up, glanced around. They'd left me. Panic, the irrational sort that brings numb toes and tingling fingers, cold mist around the throat, overcame me. Abandoned. Alone: these words twisted across the porch like mist.

"Brian," I called out, but my feet didn't move.

"I'm right here." He came up the side steps. "You woke up."

"How long was I asleep?"

"A good hour," he said, then pointed toward the driveway. "Jack just left."

A place inside me, directly above my middle but below my heart, which had been filled since our encounter in the ballroom, emptied in one final rush of air.

I slumped down into the chair. "I can't believe I fell asleep like that."

"Sis?"

"Yeah?" I looked up.

"He said to give these to you." Brian handed me my shoes and jacket. "He didn't want to leave."

"What?"

"He knew he should leave—and he did."

I released a long breath. "All the things we should do. So many damn things we should do." I stood. "I need a ride to my car at the club."

"I think I can handle that," he said, and wrapped his arm around me.

CHAPTER NINETEEN

The two weeks before the tournament—advance weeks—were so completely full that there was no room for silence or for wondering about my life. Peyton was enthralled with the prospect of winning his hometown tournament. His anger at me that I hadn't gone to the last tournament with him dissipated in his desire to win the Palmetto Pointe Open.

I sat in Charlotte's passenger seat and stared out the windshield at the spring day—sunlight pierced through the air with cut-glass clarity. I slid my sunglasses over my eyes.

Charlotte turned down the radio. "Whatcha thinking about?"

"That I have no business going to meet this makeup artist when the tournament is this weekend."

"You're the one who made the appointment. Relax. You've trained Caroline well enough . . . it's all under control. Of course it is of the utmost importance that you decide which shades of makeup to wear on your wedding day. Whether to use brown or black mascara, whether to use silver or blue on your eyelids." Charlotte slapped the steering wheel and laughed. "I just crack myself up."

"Please just take me back to work, Charlotte. Even you think this is a joke."

"Old pal, I don't think it's a joke—I'm just trying to lighten the mood. You're very sullen today." She pouted her lips.

"I don't know what is wrong with me . . . let's talk about you. How's your latest article about influential women in Palmetto Pointe coming along?"

Charlotte blew out a long breath. "I've worked my butt off on this article and they keep telling me I need to change the angle. I really hope that other newspapers, the bigger ones, pick it up. Wouldn't it be nice to have my work . . . appreciated?"

"Of course it's appreciated."

"Yeah, now I'd just like it to spread beyond our humble town, you know? Maybe I just need to . . . move on."

"What are you talking about?"

Charlotte pulled the car into a spot in front of MaryAnne's Beauty Shop. "I'd love to get bigger jobs . . . bigger pay. I can't stay here my whole life."

"Why not? Why would you want to leave?"

"Don't you ever feel like there must be more? You know, more out there than all we've ever known?"

I leaned against the passenger-side door. "This doesn't sound like you at all. This isn't all we've ever known. We went off to college . . . traveled. Maybe this is just the best we've ever known. It doesn't have to be bigger or fancier to be better. It doesn't have to be new and shiny . . . it could just be the simplest and first thing you loved that is the best. Maybe, Charlotte, you can run all over this world looking for something better when it was here all along."

Charlotte smiled. "Whoa . . ." She held a palm up. "Who are you talking to?"

"What?"

"You," she said and opened her car door, "are talking to yourself."

I opened my own door, stepped out and slammed it shut, looked over the car top at Charlotte. "What do you mean?"

"You . . . you keep talking about finding the best thing, about how you're in a better and newer place with Peyton. Like you searched the whole wide world for the 'right' man and you found him. Like he's a prize you won in a damn cereal box. Like he's a car that's got all the right extras. I've never once heard you say you love him because he makes you weak in the knees, because he is kind and fun. I'm worried about you. I really am. I've watched you my whole life—always wanting to be loved and adored—which, by the way, has been infuriatingly easy for you."

"Stop, Charlotte. You're saying things you don't mean. I think." I paused. "I hope."

She leaned on top of her car and stared over at me. "I've loved you my whole life, Kara. And I've watched you change during the past year. If you love Peyton, marry him, for God's sake, just marry him. But stop talking about him like he's a prize. He's not. He's a man. Only a man."

Charlotte turned from me and I watched her walk toward the beauty shop. I followed with intense love for my best friend. I spoke behind her back. "You don't marry someone just because he makes you weak in the knees." But after I said it, a small thought wandered across my mind like a lost memory—*Be careful what you believe.*

When I'd settled into a chair, a white cloth wrapped around my neck, the makeup artist, Sally, leaned toward me. "Okay, now this is for a wedding, right?"

I nodded. "Yes, a wedding. I just need to decide on

colors, then buy the right shades. I'll do my own makeup that day."

"Who ya' marrying?" Sally pulled a box of eye shadow from a drawer. "Anyone from here?"

"Peyton Ellers," I said, and lifted my face as she swathed concealer on my skin.

"Oh, cool," she said. "I know him. He almost got engaged to my friend Rebecca. But she didn't want the sports-traveling kind of guy." Then she slapped her hand over her mouth, made a strangled noise. "Oh . . ."

I waved my hand as if I didn't care, but nausea forced its way upward. "Oh, I know about that."

Sally leaned back, removed her hand. "I am so sorry, that was so stupid. I'm always talking before I think. I'm such a moron. She said he was the nicest guy in the world. Really."

"He is." I smiled, then grasped the cell phone on my belt as if it were vibrating. I looked down. "Oh, Sally, I am so sorry. I've got to go now . . . can we reschedule this for next week?"

Charlotte had been twirling in circles in the styling chair next to me. She stopped, squinting at me.

Sally stood with a makeup brush in midair. "Oh, please don't tell me you're leaving because of what I said."

I touched her arm. "No, I really am swamped at work and they're beeping me. Thanks for your help. I'll be back," I lied.

Neither Charlotte nor I spoke for long moments on

the drive back to work. Then she looked sideways at me. "Do you want to grab something to eat before you go back?"

"No."

"Don't be mad at me, Kara. I'm sorry for what I said. You're confused and frustrated and sleepless. I know Peyton is a great guy, and maybe this is just prewedding jitters."

"It is," I said. "Just because I'm nervous about work and the wedding doesn't mean I don't think I'm doing the right thing."

Charlotte pulled up in front of my office. "Okay, tell me one reason you love Peyton."

"I'll tell you ten, a hundred." I pulled the visor mirror down, wiped off the makeup that Sally had plastered on my cheeks. "You want to hear them?"

"God, you're in a terrible mood."

"No. I'm. Not."

Charlotte held her hands up in the air. "Okay, go ahead."

"I loved Jack when I was fourteen years old—adolescent angst. Nothing more. Nothing less. I love Peyton because . . ." And then I couldn't find the answer, couldn't find the *why* until I stared at Charlotte, at my friend I'd known my entire life. "Because when I met Peyton, he reminded me of Jack."

"Well, I can tell you one thing, girlfriend—I don't know a lot about love, but I do know that no man wants to be loved because he reminds a woman of someone else."

"But then I came to love Peyton because he is . . . Peyton. Kind and good and funny, and he loves me. . . ."

"And?"

"And . . ."

"Everything you've ever wanted?" she asked.

Now tears came with my frustration. "Charlotte, what is so wrong, so damn wrong about marrying the man who is everything you've ever wanted?"

"Nothing at all."

"Between you and Maeve, I'm going to lose my mind. It's like a 'don't let Kara marry Peyton' conspiracy. I've got to go to work. I can't just walk around thinking about Maeve and Peyton and Jack. This is getting insane."

"Did he tell you about Rebecca?"

I started to open the car door, glanced over my shoulder. "What?"

"The girl Sally talked about while she tried to make you look like Tammy Faye Bakker?"

I laughed. "Guess I won't be returning like I promised. And, no, he hasn't told me about every single old girlfriend, just like I haven't told him about every single old boyfriend. Now go back to work on that article so you can leave this small town and make your way in the big world." I stepped out of the car and blew Charlotte a kiss, then walked toward the job that would fill the remainder of the day, erase the questions Charlotte had thrown at me.

CHAPTER TWENTY

T he tree bark scratched my back as I leaned against the live oak, attempting to shield myself from the torrential downpour. The rain had come to the tournament without warning: my fault according to Frieda. The umbrella-free crowd stood disheveled in the onslaught from what appeared to be a solid gray cloud mass hovering over the eighteenth green, and nowhere else.

My attempts at staying dry were futile. My hair was plastered to the side of my head, my peach silk shirt clung to my body.

Peyton and Phil Mickelson came over the hill to the cheers of the wet crowd. I'd left the party preparations in the main clubhouse ballroom to watch my fiancé. The Unknown Souls had been setting up on the stage, and I had watched in my white-and-peach pinstriped suit, until I'd finally handed the responsibility over to Caroline.

Peyton came over the hill; I shifted from one foot to the other, scooted farther back under the tree, where it would leave a smudge of bark and dirt on my suit. A gust of fresh wind, smelling of warm sea and a passing shrimp trawler, seeped under my wet clothes. I skimmed water off my face and focused on Peyton as he walked toward us. He lifted his head, scanned the crowd. I stepped from behind a branch and waved with two fingers.

The crowd was six or seven people deep along the sidelines behind the rope and down the entire length of the fairway. Dad, Deirdre, and Brian waved at me from the first row.

Phil lined up for a twenty-four-foot putt in the pouring rain. He squatted and squinted at the water, then stopped and tapped the ball. It rolled, then came to an abrupt halt in front of the hole, as if someone had held out a hand. The crowd released a collective groan; Phil grimaced.

If Peyton made this putt, an easy ten-footer on his home course, he'd win the tournament. I held my breath as he lined the ball up with assurance. I'd seen him do it a hundred times; recognized his stance when he knew he'd won something: an argument, a tournament, my heart.

He wiped the rain from his eyes and tapped the ball. It rolled toward the hole; the crowd held its breath. The ball hit a patch of standing water and veered to the right, circled the hole and stopped two inches away. The crowd groaned; a few released yelps. Peyton glanced up and looked directly at me. I formed my mouth into an expression of empathy: lips pouted, brows pulled together.

He exhaled and putted the ball in, picked it up and walked toward the golf official. It would now be a sudden-death playoff: playing the eighteenth hole again, where the winner of the hole would win the tournament.

As suddenly as it had arrived, the rain stopped and the sky opened up to a wide blue expanse. I lifted my face, pushed my hair back. I crouched under the tape and went to stand with my family. Daddy put an arm around me. "He'll pull this off now, Kara. You just watch."

I whispered, "I hope so."

Sunlight poured through the wet leaves, splintered off the water at the end of the green as though the light itself were wet. After a solid drive, Peyton stood in the fairway of the par-five hole and slammed the ball; it landed just off the green in the low rough—a beautifully executed shot for a possible eagle.

Phil stepped up and attempted the same shot, but his ball landed in the sand trap on the left side of the green. The crowd gasped.

I stepped forward, leaned over the rope. Peyton's mouth was pinched together, his eyebrows forced down, his jaw set.

He lined up and hit a chip shot. The ball dropped on the green and rolled toward the hole, then stopped five feet short. The crowd seemed to deflate; this was supposed to be the shot to win, the shot on the front page of tomorrow's sports section. Peyton could still drop his putt for a birdie.

One of two things could happen now: Phil could hit out of the sand and putt for a birdie and another sudden death, or he could hit a miracle shot from the sand trap to the hole—which is exactly what he did. The crowed cheered, not so much for who won, but for how he'd won. Either way, Peyton seemed to shrink, as though each cheer for his rival made him less.

I scooted under the tape, reached Peyton's side, and stood on my toes and kissed him. I whispered in his ear, "I love you. Good sportsmanship now, they're watching."

An uneven smile spread across his face, and he wrapped his arm around me, then walked us both toward the clubhouse, waving and offering thanks to his fans.

When we reached the men's locker room, Peyton released me, stared at me and opened his mouth to speak, but nothing came out.

"What?" I said.

A news crew lunged toward us, shoved a camera in Peyton's face. "Peyton—ESPN here, can you give us a statement? What do you think happened out there?"

"They're watching," I mumbled as I walked away, headed out to the back patio to watch the interview on the large-screen TV with the crowd. Peyton's face filled the screen. "It's a tough loss, but that shot Phil made from the trap was one of the best I've ever seen. He deserved to win with a shot like that."

A voice came from behind me. "I'm sorry—tough break."

I turned to Jack Sullivan, nodded at him. "Yeah, this stinks. He really wanted to win this one."

"You do belong here, Kara." Jack leaned back on his heels. His eyes hid behind sunglasses so I couldn't see the implications behind the words.

"What?" I stepped back.

"You've found your place, you know that. You've built a great life for yourself. You're surrounded by family and friends and people who love you—a lot. This is the life you should have, the life you were made for."

I nodded.

He touched my cheek, then withdrew his hand. "I've got to go help the band . . . see you around."

"Yeah," I said, "see you around."

Jack turned to walk away, but I didn't watch; I watched the TV screen, where Peyton smiled and answered questions. "They're watching," I said to the TV, to Peyton. "They're watching."

The room thrummed with the beat of the guitar and drums, to Jimmy's baritone voice. Tables were spread in an oval with a dance floor in the middle. Palm fronds stood in vases with sand and starfish spread around the center of each table. Twinkling lights spread at even quarter-inch intervals on potted palm trees flickered around the room. I'd picked out the exact same trees for my wedding reception, and I loved how they looked in the urns.

I walked from table to table greeting players, their wives and guests. I checked every last detail, including who received the vegetarian plate. Jimmy finished his song to loud applause. He grabbed the microphone and asked Phil Mickelson to come to the stage and say a few words about winning the Inaugural Palmetto Pointe Open.

Charlotte, Daddy, Brian, and Deirdre sat at a table in the far left corner. I wandered toward them, leaned down and hugged each one.

Charlotte stood. "Wow, darlin', you have so outdone yourself. This is absolutely amazing."

"Thanks."

Brian came next. "The band is unbelievable. You downplayed how good they are."

"They sound great in here, don't they?"

They all nodded. Deirdre lifted her hand, pointed to the stage with her wineglass. "You were right, I woulda recognized Jimmy." She shook her head. "Crazy memories."

"Yes, crazy." I pulled a stray leaf from the palm frond off their table, when Caroline walked up next to me, tapped my elbow.

"Kara, we have an issue with a steak that's too raw. Would you like me to talk to the patron or do you want to?"

I turned toward my family and Charlotte and rolled my eyes. "Y'all have so much fun that it counts for me too." I walked off with Caroline. "I'll send the caterer out. You can continue to walk the tables and check on people, make sure there's no other major crisis."

Caroline touched the shoulder of a young woman next to her. "Kara, I'd like you to meet my friend, Mia."

I nodded. "Hi, Mia. Nice to meet you, hope you enjoy the party."

"Thank you." She nodded her head of round, bulbous curls surrounding a cherub-dimpled face. "What an amazing party. The band is fab."

"Thanks." A slow tingle of recognition spread down my arms and chest, then reached my mind. Mia? Peyton.

Caroline and Mia wound through the crowd. I caught up to them, touched Caroline's elbow. "Excuse us, Mia. I need to talk to Caroline."

"No problem. I need to get back to my table." She nodded, glanced over her shoulder with a slight grimace.

"Caroline, who was that?"

"An old friend I talked into buying one of these tickets for charity." She shifted her weight back and forth on her stiletto heels.

"You knew she used to be engaged to Peyton, didn't you?"

"Yes. She's my best friend—I tried to tell you a couple times that my dearest friend used to date him, but it always seemed like the wrong time, and I didn't want to get fired . . . and—"

"Date him? She was engaged to him, Caroline."

"I know, but it wasn't for long, and . . . I'm sorry, I guess I shoulda said something."

"Yeah, that probably would've been a good idea. Anything you'd like to tell me now?"

"No." She shook her head.

268

I swiveled on my heels to walk away when a thought, like the poke of a sharp pin against my chest, came to me. I stopped, looked back to Caroline. "Does Peyton know you're friends with Mia?"

She grimaced. "Yes, my boyfriend and I went out with them a few times a couple years ago."

"Thank you, Caroline. Please check on table six. It looks as though they're trying to get our attention."

I glanced around the room for Peyton, and found him leaning against a pillar at the back of the room. I wound my way toward him. He pulled me close. "I love you, Kara. You know that."

I didn't answer, but I did allow his arm to rest over my shoulder.

We stood together and listened to Phil thank the crowd, then ask Peyton to come onstage and say a few words to his hometown fans. He grabbed my hand, led me toward the stage to thunderous applause.

When the tables had been cleared and the band had packed up and gone, I stood at the back of the room with the satisfaction of a job well done. We'd raised well over our monetary goal for the Tuberous Sclerosis Society. I sighed, picked up my satchel and headed for the back door. Peyton had left hours earlier with his golf buddies; I'd see him in the morning. I had a few questions to ask him, but now was definitely not the time.

The parking lot was empty save for the catering trucks, employee cars, and the Unknown Souls bus. I clicked the button on my key to unlock the car door, then turned to the sound of popping gravel. Jack stood against the band bus, his hands in his pockets, his head tilted. His chinos were wrinkled, his cotton button-down open at the top. A gas lamp flickered from the back door of the clubhouse, sending shadows across his face, his hair.

We stood like this for a long moment, neither of us moving, staring at each other across the dark night. Then he stepped into the bus and closed the door. I glanced up at the sky, at a single star shimmering above. "I won," I said out loud. "I saw it first."

CHAPTER TWENTY-ONE

I entered the foyer with the last of the grocery bags, shut the door behind me with my foot. I was moving toward the kitchen when I heard a knock, loud and insistent.

"I'm coming," I said, and dropped the bag onto the kitchen counter. Fatigue pulled at me like an anchor. I just wanted to unload these groceries and crawl into bed. The tournament and benefit had gone so well, and the following week had been hectic with wrap-up. I just wanted to crash.

I opened the door to Jack.

He stood on my porch in madras shorts and a white, wrinkled button-down with rolled-up sleeves. His tan arms glowed in the overhead gas lantern. Evening had settled into night and I couldn't see past him.

"Kara," he said.

"Hi, Jack," I said. "Did we forget to pay you or something?" I tapped the side of my forehead with my finger. "I'm so damn tired I can't remember. . . ." An unnamed emotion pushed against my chest wanting to get out.

He placed his hands on either side of my face. I froze; my heart stopped and waited. Then he leaned in and kissed me and the thought returned: one. I pulled away. "What are you doing?"

"I came to see you. . . . Follow me," he said, and motioned toward the yard.

I did.

We wound our way around the lawns to the end of the street, where an old footbridge hovered over the marsh. Night overtook us; only the sounds of the water flowing into the estuary filled the air. Then he stopped, pulled me toward him. "Okay, I've practiced this . . . so just listen."

"Okay," I whispered.

"Kara, I've loved you since I can remember loving at all. I didn't come find you last time, I let it go, but I won't let go this time. I can't."

"No." I dropped my face into my hands, but I still tasted his kiss—warm, sweet. Everything in me reached for him, but I wouldn't allow it. Hadn't I already learned the lesson? It was foolish to believe this was real—like Maeve's story—running after an old story, a legend or myth, when I had a real life, a true story already. "I can't do this, Jack. I'm engaged. I've promised another man to marry him—there is integrity in that."

"There is integrity in being who you really are."

"There's . . . a promise." I twisted to the edge of the footbridge. "You only love what you remember about me. You don't know me."

He touched my arm. "Just listen."

Mist surrounded us, as if it had been there all along, but it just now touched us. "Jack, this is too hard. You can't come here and tell me you love me when I—"

"When you what?"

"I have a whole life: I have a fiancé, I have plans and . . . I mailed the invitations."

"Change them."

"Change what?"

"Change your well-laid plans, Kara."

"I can't, Jack."

We stared at each other across the years that had once separated us.

"I did come back. I told you I would and I did," he said.

"I'm the one who found you, Jack, remember? You didn't come looking for me."

"Yes, I did. Right now. I am here right now. I did come find you."

"This isn't some cute Irish love legend."

"What are you talking about?"

"The reasons I found you were all about curiosity— about the past and first love. I got carried away with a story and it wasn't even *true.*" My voice cracked at the last word.

"I don't know what you're talking about, but the reasons don't matter, Kara." His face shone without any light falling on it. I longed to grab him, wrap my hands in his hair, surround myself with this confession and acceptance. But something held me back—something to do with the very loud voice in my head telling me not to foolishly run after selfish dreams and desires. Something to do with messing up my life by discarding my plans, abandoning my good character.

He repeated his words. "The reasons you found me don't matter—at all. All that matters is that we've found each other, that we are supposed to be together, that I adore you and love you and always have. I don't see how it could be any other way. Your life is so damn full that you can't even see or hear what matters . . . how much I adore you."

"That is not all that matters." My voice came higher and harder than any time I could remember since I was a child.

"What else matters, Kara? What your father thinks? What Deirdre thinks? What the residents of Palmetto Pointe think? What else matters?"

"Honoring a promise matters. I can't just go chasing after the next good feeling, the next best thing. This is real life, with real invitations mailed, real rings and real family."

"Where is the strong girl who stood up to my drunk father on a summer morning, the woman who came to find me in Savannah? The woman who always knows what she wants? The right thing? Is the right thing always pleasing everybody else, not being who you are? Fulfilling somebody else's idea of Kara Larson and who she should be instead of who you believe you are?"

"What gives you the right to say that?" A furious wind rose behind my words. "I am the Kara Larson I want to be. The Kara Larson I . . . am."

"Okay. If that is true . . . I'll leave. Now." He paused. "But I don't believe it's true. I see the hints of you in there: the girl who loves fiercely and not logically."

"Believe what you want," I said.

He turned away from me then, and I felt as though my body rose above me. I understood that as much as I hurt now, the pain would be worse later: wondering if I should have embraced him, loved him—it would be worse later than even now.

Strength, I needed strength. I faced the water to find it—but felt only a hollow emptiness that my promises could not fill. I turned to Jack, but his back was to me.

"Jack," I said, or thought I said as he walked across the bridge, away from me.

He spoke, but he didn't turn. "I'm looking for the reasons you came back into my life. I'm looking up, down, to the left, to the right, and I can find only one." He moved back around now, returned to me, touched the side of my face and kissed me. "The reason is because I love you. If there is one thing I will not do, it is force you to feel something that isn't there for me—to talk you into something you don't want."

Then he walked away, and I was alone again.

I don't know how long I stayed in the dark, but I believed that if I stayed long enough I could leave what had just happened inside the ink-blot night. But I couldn't, so I rose, went home, packed my suitcase.

Half an hour later, I stood on my brother's front porch, stared out to the water. Daddy didn't like Brian living here, a shack on Silver Creek surrounded by stores and bars. But it was Brian's one act of official rebellion—if it could even be called that.

I knocked on the door, and it opened as I lifted my hand a second time. Brian threw his arms around me. "Hey, Sis, whatcha doing here?"

I shrugged. "Running away. I was hoping I could stay here for a couple days."

Brian drew his hand through his long blond curls, pointed down to my suitcase. "Haven't run very far, huh?"

"I guess not, but it counts." I grinned and shrugged. "The first and last time I ran away, I went home that same night. Still got grounded because I was late for dinner—the unforgivable sin."

"That would be my sister. If you're gonna run away, at least do it in a safe and reasonable manner." He grinned and backed up, knowing that my pinch to the side of his arm was imminent.

Instead, I picked up my suitcase. "Can I come in or not?"

He swept his hand across the warped heart-of-pine

floors. "Of course. I guess I'll cancel my hot date tonight."

I followed him to the back of the house, where he took my suitcase and threw it on a bed in a cramped room. I stood in the doorway. "You sure you don't mind?"

"You can stay as long as you want. But you gotta tell me what's going on."

"I'm not sure, Brian. I just had this desperate need to get away. Far away. But, like you said, this is as far as I made it."

"Why didn't you go to Deirdre's?" He leaned against the doorjamb.

I rolled my eyes. "You have to ask?"

"Or Charlotte's, or your fiancé's?"

"Okay." I held up my palms in surrender. "If you don't want me here, just say so."

"No, you're more than welcome. Can I do anything?"

"I'd love a drink." I pushed him back with my hands, then gave his left biceps the deserved pinch from the front-door conversation.

He jumped back. "Kara Larson, you are so lucky I'm your brother."

And as his footsteps echoed down the hallway, I whispered, "Yes, I am."

I threw my suitcase on the guest bed pushed up against the wall, which doubled as a couch in Brian's half-used art studio. I touched the edges of a just-begun long-abandoned painting of sea oats. Were any

276

of us Larson children listening to the hints of our heart, or were we all hiding our desire in the back corner room?

I sighed and walked out onto the porch. The dark creek spread before Brian's porch like the silver-edged infinity I'd imagined my mama had slipped into all those years ago. The moon hid behind the house. I took a deep breath and settled into the rocking chair.

"Well," I said to my brother, imitating my dad's voice, "I just don't understand why you would live in such a place."

"I know, it's a dump." Brian sat down next to me, handed me a glass of scotch and ice.

"You are so lucky." I took a long swallow of the drink, let my head cloud over with its warmth. I wanted the questions to take on a fuzzy edge.

"I am lucky," Brian said, "and so are you. So tell me why you're here."

"You really don't have to listen to it, Brian. I just needed a place to crash and think things through."

He sat with me for a moment, and we absorbed the sound of the incoming tide we couldn't see in the darkness, flowing over the oyster shells with a wind-chime song. These tides had gone on before me, and would go on after me. They had gone on before Maeve and before Mama and before life.

"Brian—go on your date, I just need to be quiet anyway."

He hugged me before he left. "Wake me if you want to talk."

277

• • •

The dream is clouded; I make out the shapes of the landscape, but not the details. I am late for my wedding, and I can't find the correct turn off Magnolia Street to the church. I go up and down, up and down, walking on the sidewalks I've known my whole life, but they are different, shifted to the right or maybe the left and the turn is gone. I am starting to panic, running and ruining my hand-appliquéd water pearls on the silk stiletto heels. The turn is gone. I run back to the garden shop—the one where I bought the angel— and call for Mrs. Marshall, but she isn't there; she's gone to my wedding.

I startled, awakened with a cold panic.

Confusion drifted over me like dust settling on a windowsill. I couldn't pull past the wondering— where was I? Why? Where was Peyton and why was he mad at me? Why couldn't I find him?

I opened my eyes to an art easel in the corner of the room—Brian's house. I jumped from the bed and dressed, went outside to the rising morning to yank a rowboat from beneath the porch.

I launched the boat, leaned back to watch the sun rise over the cordgrass blowing sideways inside the wind; I trailed my fingers along the water. *Be careful what you believe . . .*

I spoke out loud, "I believe . . . ," and found a vacant space as empty as the discarded shells on the mud banks.

I tried again, lifting my face to the wind. "I

believed . . . ." And I realized that, this time, I spoke about the past—about what I *had* believed. "I believed that Mama left us willingly, I believed that I loved Peyton with a full heart, I believed Jack was gone forever." I took a deep breath, lifted my voice to the sky. "I believed I knew my heart, I believed Maeve's story. . . ."

The sun burst from the horizon in a streak of pink light and the world unfolded; it opened and spread its wings wide and broad, and for the briefest moment, I saw it all—all the questions. I didn't see any answers, but the questions, which had been rattling around in my brain like pieces of broken china I couldn't put back together, became as delineated as the coastline: What was my story? Why was I here? Should I marry Peyton, and did I love him as I should? What were my gifts and how should I use them? Did I love Jack or only the youth he represented—a time when I felt loved?

I drew back from these larger questions, attempted to fold the world back in around me like a blanket, so that it would surround me and comfort me. If I understood the questions, where were the answers?

Mama's words came to me: *In the hints of your heart.*

In all the times I'd tried to find her, remember her, listen for the whisper of her voice, I'd only found scraps of torn memory. Now her words I'd never actually heard washed over me.

Tears stung the backs of my eyelids. I wouldn't find

279

the answers in a swift moment of revelation like I had found the questions. Those questions came clear and certain, but the answers were not so easy. Would trying to find them result in a quest that would lead to my own destruction?

I sat back down in the boat, leaned against the bow, and stared across the curve of the estuary and creek where I'd floated. An energy that felt like electricity ran down my forearms before I realized why: the landscape was unfamiliar; it was not the right-to-left curve of the creek I knew.

I sat upright, inhaled through pursed lips. I jerked my head to the left and right. How long had I been floating in and out of the small dead ends and curves of the creek? I glanced at my wrist—I didn't have my watch. I hadn't told anyone where I was going.

I groaned. I'd broken every Lowcountry safety rule I knew. I pictured the headlines, how they'd find me days from now petrified in the baking sun, how a local girl should've known better. Then I laughed. Here I was lost in the circuitous marshes, and I was worried about what the headlines would say when they found me.

God, what had become of me? If life, as Maeve said, was a journey, then my journey was about to abruptly end in a comedic twist: lost in familiar territory—a tortuous metaphor for my life. I lifted the paddles and pulled against the water, squinting against the sun to see the horizon. I had either floated to the east and was looking at Oystertip or had floated south and was staring at Backbay Island. Either way, if I could get there, reach some landmark, I could find my way home.

So here I was, lost in a land I thought I knew. Sunlight licked the tops of the grasses, which meant I needed to head that way—west, not toward the sea to the east. As I rounded a corner of marsh I spied Palmetto Pointe Lighthouse. I exhaled: my landmark. I released the paddles and lay back on the seat. I really hadn't been lost at all, just confused in my wondering and wandering.

I lifted my head, trailed my hand over the top of the water. A smooth surface rolled underneath my hand. I held my breath as a baby dolphin whispered beneath my fingers, lifted her bottle nose toward them. I petted her and a sob formed in the back of my throat, at the base of my heart. Where was this baby's mama? A second pewter hump formed next to the dolphin, rose as if in answer to my question. I'm right here, right here.

I flipped off the side of the boat in an instinctive act—from a desire to be part of them, part of their family—diving through the sea with a mama, with a family that laughed and played. I joined them without fear until I broke through the water and watched the boat floating away from me.

In a remembrance of the days when Deirdre, Brian, and I swam with long, strong strokes through these waters, I reached the boat, turned to find the dolphins gone, having vanished beneath the dove-gray water.

I paddled slowly toward the lighthouse, then to the left toward Brian's home.

The weekend passed as I reached for answers along the waters of Silver Creek. I walked down the beach or stared out to the water and wondered about the edges of land tied together by the sea—about the edges of the stories tied together by time. Maeve's land, my land; Maeve's story, my story. And yet not her story at all—a legend.

I'd ignored my cell phone and had even forgotten that the next tournament was over until I saw Peyton standing at the bottom of Brian's front stairs, looking up at me as if he didn't recognize me, as if all the confusion inside had changed the outside of me. And maybe it had as I sat on the porch, still in my drawstring pajama bottoms and tank top, a cold cup of coffee cradled in my hands.

I jumped up; coffee splattered across my lap, the warped porch boards. A long way off a seagull cried, and then squawked, and I could almost believe it came from the far side of the water: Maeve's sea.

"Hi, honey." I wiped at the spill, walked toward the stairs. Peyton reached the landing before I stepped down.

He pulled me into a hug, but it was weak, like someone had watered down his affection: a lukewarm offering. "Hello, Kara."

I raised my eyebrows at his formal greeting. "Well . . . how did you do?" I spread my hands out wide in a question.

"Do you care?"

"Of course I care. Why are you asking me like that?"

"Well, I couldn't get ahold of you all weekend, and it's not like you're busy. . . ." He waved his hand across the porch.

I groaned. "I—"

He held up his hand, successfully stopping my excuse. "I don't want to hear it."

"Please tell me how you did in the tournament."

"I won." His face said otherwise.

"That is fantastic, but you don't look like you won."

He nodded. "You weren't there to support me."

"You obviously didn't need me, and I *was* supporting you—just not on the sidelines. You don't need me there every minute to win."

"You know, I heard about you at Danny's Pub. You never came over that night. You never came to say good-bye or good luck, then I hear you're dancing at the bar. . . ." He closed his eyes, twisted away from me.

An emotion resembling fear, but more like anxiety, filled my stomach. Something threatening loomed at the edges of the horizon behind Peyton, but I couldn't make out its shape or form. Then he spoke.

"Maybe this engagement is not such a good idea," he said.

"Oh?" Had I screwed this up like my daddy had warned? Had my own selfish behavior lost my engagement, my fiancé? Please, I thought, no more leaving in my life . . . no more leaving me.

He sat on the bottom step. "I need someone who will be there for me, and you don't seem to want that. I need . . ." His face was set; still beautiful, but set and vacant, like a photograph of Peyton, but not the man. "Damn, why does this keep happening?" He dropped his chin down to his chest, his fists clenched at his side. "Mom warned me this time—not again, Peyton, not again. But I told her it was different with you. . . ."

"Your mom?"

"This isn't because of Mom."

"Yeah, but it might be that you keep thinking you'll find that one girl who will make you whole, who will help you win and keep you in line—and your mom will love her." I stared over his head, not wanting to look at him to feel the leaving coming again and again and again, like the waves crashing in monotonous curls.

"Kara?"

I looked at him and the abandonment crashed on the shoreline, higher and higher until tears came with it. "What?"

"Do you love me?"

I continued to stare at him. This was the most important question anyone had ever asked me—and there I was at this turning point, where my future lay to the left or the right, where I had to understand that the path I took would be the one I'd travel for a very long time. There was no U-turn here at all.

"Do you?" He stood now, and then moved away. "I

guess your silence is my answer."

"No." I stood. "My silence is not your answer." I grabbed his arm. "I do love you, Peyton. Do I love you the way I should? Or, more important—the way you need? The way that will last a lifetime of marriage, children, old age?"

"I can't answer that for you, Kara." His jaw clenched, twitched.

"I think you already answered for me, Peyton. You don't believe or feel like I love you the way you need me to. Something about the kind of love I have for you is not enough—and maybe that isn't your fault. Maybe it is mine—the love not being enough for you. Maybe because I don't have enough or maybe you need too much . . . I don't know. But . . ."

"I keep ending up here." His hands splayed open. "With my hand out for an engagement ring I gave in sincerity. I don't get it," he said.

And there it was: I'd done the thing my family, my friends, and Palmetto Pointe could chew on for years—broken an engagement with the invitations already mailed. I sank to the chair, and then reached over, slipped the diamond off my left finger and held it out without looking up.

I felt him take it from me, then I heard his footsteps go down the stairs and stop, but I still didn't raise my head. So this was how my heart broke—this easily, with the handoff of a diamond ring.

"Kara?"

I lifted my eyes, but didn't speak.

"I'm sorry." His voice cracked.

I nodded. "Isn't there a way to talk this out, try to figure out where to go from here?" But even as I said it, I knew the answer. I didn't love him deep enough, wide enough, and he knew it; he knew something I was only starting to realize.

"Maybe I do need too much, Kara. Maybe I do need someone who can be what you're not willing to be."

I nodded; he was right. There was something wrong with the way I loved—it was not enough.

When he was gone, the tears came, but not in full; the sorrow was mixed with wondering what Daddy, Deirdre, Charlotte, and Mrs. Carrington would say and do.

I pulled my legs up under me and leaned back on the rocking chair. The screen door behind me slapped; I turned to Brian.

"Hey, bro. I didn't know you were home." I wiped my face, tried to sit up straighter.

"I just arrived a little while ago, but snuck in the back door when I saw Peyton."

"Oh . . ."

He glanced down at my hand, my empty finger. "Over?"

I nodded. "There is something wrong with me, Brian. Why can't I love enough to beg him to stay, to fight for him to stay? I'm sitting here—just sitting here like a fool."

"Maybe because you don't want it that badly, Kara.

It is sad, but maybe not sad enough."

I nodded. "No, it's pretty damn sad."

"Then get up and do something about it."

I looked at Brian and spoke the truth. "I don't *want* to."

"Oh?" Then he laughed.

"It's not funny."

He sat in the chair next to me, leaned forward. "I know it's not funny. I'm sorry."

"Time to face the family music," I said. "I've got to tell Daddy, Deirdre, Charlotte." I groaned. "All that work, the dress, the damn flowers, the invitations."

Brian reached his hand out, took mine in his. "You want me to tell them?"

"No, I have to do it myself. It seems there is a theme in my life—leaving."

"I'm not going anywhere," my brother said, and hugged me.

CHAPTER TWENTY-TWO

The following weeks were filled with the mandatory calls to be made, reservations to be canceled, deposits lost, and family quagmire to wade through.

After I left Brian's house that morning, I sat down in Daddy's office to tell him and Deirdre about the broken engagement.

"Peyton and I are not getting married." I took a long,

deep breath and looked at my father, then my sister in the eye.

Deirdre jumped up, threw her arms wide in exasperation, then looked to Daddy. "This is why you should've never told us what Mama said about following your heart—she's broken off an engagement to the best man she'll ever catch."

I laughed, the sound reaching my ears before I'd even realized I'd laughed out loud. "Catch? You think Peyton was a catch? For God's sake, Deirdre."

She turned back to me. "You never think rationally, Kara. You're always chasing after the next thing . . . always thinking there is something better around the corner. You have no idea what you've done."

"Deirdre." I stood, touched her arm. "He broke it off with me."

She stepped back, then held up her hand. "Oh."

"It was probably my fault," I said, "but he broke it off—he didn't think I loved him enough."

Deirdre sat in the leather wingback chair and looked up at me. "Did you?"

"Probably not."

Daddy stood now, came over, hugged me. "I have to admit—I wanted this marriage for you, Kara. I did. But I've got to trust you." He shook his head. "I just hope it wasn't because of anything I told you . . . or did."

"No, Daddy."

"I have to believe that you know what you're doing."

Deirdre snorted. "Dad, you know you'll lose all your deposits."

"Better than losing Kara to a man she doesn't love."

I spoke to Deirdre. "I'm not really sure why you're so angry."

"Is this about Jack?" she asked.

When she spoke his name, I allowed the same question I'd held at bay to enter my heart. "I'm not sure, Deirdre. I'm confused and lost about a lot of things."

"You are?" She walked toward me, and half of her face appeared as though her muscles could not decide whether to crumble in tears or clamp down in judgment. "You're confused and lost? You were about to marry the greatest guy you have probably ever met and you're confused?" Her voice rose higher and higher until I wanted to cover my ears.

I lifted my hand. "Yes, I'm confused. I know this has probably never happened to you."

She narrowed her eyes at me, leaned toward me. "You have no idea what confusion is all about, Kara Larson. No idea whatsoever." Then the muscles wanting to cry gave way, her face fell in on itself and she ran from the room, up the stairs. The slam of a door echoed down the stairs and into Daddy's office.

I turned to him. "What in the . . . ?"

He shrugged. "Kara, I'm at a loss here. I don't know how to help you. I don't know how to help Deirdre." He bit his lower lip in a gesture I'd never seen from him. "I need your mother right now."

I reached for him and hugged him. "So do I. I've got

so much to do to cancel all this, Daddy. Can we talk later?"

He turned back to me. "Yes, and let me know how I can help." He pointed to a large envelope on the side table. "By the way, that small package arrived for you this morning."

I walked over, opened it, and took a deep breath: it was the antique postcard of Galway Bay that I'd ordered on eBay. A hooker dominated the photo; it sailed sideways, cutting through water so blue it must have been hand colored. The water separated for the boat as it aimed directly for the side of the quay, and the docked boats, to the thatched-roof houses. The vessel was reaching, sailing, yearning for home: to dock. I imagined Maeve standing on that quay—waiting. Did she really want me to find this man who might not exist? I sighed and turned toward the stairs, took them two at a time to Deirdre's room.

I pushed her door open without knocking and entered the room with my hands on my hips. "Tell me what in the hell is going on with you."

She sat on the bed, curled over, staring in her hands. I walked to the bed. She stared at me. "What if we're not who she wanted us to be? What if we're a disappointment?" Deirdre choked on the words.

I sighed, sat on the edge of the mattress. "I don't think that her last words had anything to do with being who *she* wanted us to be, but with being who . . . we were meant to be."

Deirdre's face hardened again. "Don't you think that

after Daddy told you what Mama said, you got confused?"

"No, if anything, I got clearer."

She lifted her eyebrows. "Clearer? What do you mean?"

"You know how Mama said to listen for the hints? Well, I heard them in a story."

"A story? You are not making any sense at all."

"I think we all hear hints differently. The way I hear it, you won't. I think the main thing is, Mama didn't want us to shut off our hearts."

Deirdre just stared at me; her face quivered.

"Are you okay?" I asked.

"I can't stand to disappoint one more person in my life. Now I'm disappointing our dead mother because I've shut off my heart. I want to love . . . I swear I do."

She spoke as though I had left the room and she was talking to the Spanish moss hanging in front of her window, as if it could catch her words in its net and carry them safely away. "I've guarded my heart in every way I know how. I have lost my friends, lost my husband. I've guarded my heart with duty, with busyness, with anger. . . ."

She turned to me now. "Do you think we both just don't know how to love enough?"

"No," I said, "I don't believe that." I paused in thought. "Do you remember when you woke me up in the middle of the night, and took me to see the turtles hatch?"

"What?"

291

"Do you remember that?"

"No, I have no idea what you're talking about."

I took her hand. "I was young; five, maybe six. You came into my room in the middle of the night and held my hand, led me over the lawn, across the footbridge and down to the beach to watch the turtles hatch, then crawl toward the water. We cried together because those babies had to do that alone, all alone. No one ever knew we sneaked out—it was our secret."

Her chin rose slowly. "Yes, I remember. I knew Mama was sick then, and you didn't."

"Yes, I did."

"No, we hadn't told you yet. I was eleven and we hadn't told you."

"But I knew. I remember how I knew I would have to do the same thing . . . figure it all out without Mama."

"Oh, Kara." She dropped her face down. I went to her, wrapped my arms around her and allowed her to cry until the tears subsided, and the sunlight turned dusty pink in her room.

Charlotte and I stood in front of Mrs. Marshall's Garden and Antique Store, where I'd bought the broken angel weeks before. I hadn't visited Maeve in the hospital in the past few days—her family had come from Ireland, and they'd promised to call me to report any change in her condition.

I pushed open the doors; I needed to cancel the urns and palm trees I'd ordered for the reception. Charlotte

292

lent her levity and brevity to every task necessary. She kept me laughing when I wanted to cry, and quickly severed conversations I tended to drag out with apologies and explanations.

The aroma of green plants and soil filled the air. I inhaled, then called out for Mrs. Marshall. She stood from where she'd been reaching down behind the counter. "Well, hello, darling." She walked around the corner holding her cat, Azalea. "It is so weird that you stopped by today—I was set to call you in a little bit."

"Oh? Well, if it's about the palm trees . . ."

She shook her head. "No, those are all ordered and arranged."

I grimaced. "I need to cancel them."

"Oh, why?" Mrs. Marshall tapped her chest.

Charlotte petted the cat. "We don't like palm trees anymore. We want large live oaks, real ones at least a hundred years old."

I laughed, shook my head. "You know better than to listen to Charlotte. There just isn't going to be a wedding."

"Oh, dear." She hugged me. "I do know these are the days you could use your mama. If there is anything I can do, please let me know."

I nodded. "No, I have to do everything."

"Ah, just like her. But you don't need to, dear. There are so many people who love you in this town . . . we're all here to help."

"Oh, I'm sure I've disappointed all of you." I reached over and rubbed behind Azalea's ears.

293

"Disappointed them? No, Kara. We love you."

I smiled and bit back tears. "Well, why were you about to call me?"

"You know that broken-winged angel you took?"

I nodded. "I love that angel."

"You are not going to believe this . . . the match came in to me from a junker in Georgia, and this angel has both wings."

"Oh, wow."

She nodded. "Isn't that just amazing? It seems the angels came from a garden in an old home in Savannah. They had markings on the bottom that stated they were a pair, and my junker remembered that he had given me the other one—incredible."

I wanted to speak, but I couldn't.

"A complete angel, she's not broken anywhere," Mrs. Marshall said.

"Can I see her?" I whispered.

Mrs. Marshall waved her hand. "Follow me."

We wound our way among the orchids and ferns, around the clay and concrete pots, until we reached the storage room. "Here," she said, and lifted the small concrete angel.

I took it from her, held it between my hands. "She's perfect." I looked up at Mrs. Marshall. "How do you think one of them got broken, and the other stayed whole?"

"It is the same as life. Some things break us and others keep us together."

"How much is she?"

"I have a feeling you need her more than I need the money." She touched my arm.

"I don't know how to thank you. This is the miracle I needed right now."

"That's how it works, my dear. That's what miracles are for—when you need them the most."

I drove too fast toward the hospital, my nerve endings thrumming like the air before a storm. I ran through the front doors, up the escalator to room 214 in the extended care unit.

The door was shut; I knocked lightly. Caitlin's face poked out of the crack, tear trails on her face. My heart sank; my hands almost slipped from the angel.

"Kara," she said, and opened the door fully.

I nodded. "Is Maeve . . . ?"

Caitlin nodded. "She woke up this morning. My mother's brother, Maeve's son Seamus, was just about to call you."

My hands gripped the angel. "Should I come back?"

She stepped out into the hall. "Let me tell you what the doctor said, then you can go in."

We stood in a corner by the window at the end of the hall. "She's awake, but they say she doesn't have long at all. Her stroke didn't affect her speech, but has caused decreased blood supply in the rest of her organs. The doctor says they often see patients become completely alert just before . . . before they die."

I shook my head. "No."

"I'm just telling you what they said, not what I

believe. I think she's waiting for my mother to come see her. . . ."

"She hasn't come?"

"She will . . . my brother is bringing her now."

I glanced toward the door; an older man stood in the hallway, his head tilted toward us. His white hair was like a shock of bleached straw on top of his head. His nose was red, bulbous, and his grin spread wide and kind.

"That's my Uncle Seamus from Ireland." Caitlin waved toward him.

I walked over to him and held out my hand. "Hi, I'm Kara Larson."

He shook my hand. "Mam has asked for you." Seamus took Caitlin's elbow. "Let's let Kara say hello to Mam while we go get some badly needed coffee."

As they walked down the hall, I pushed open the door to the hospital room. A soft swishing sound— like an angel's wing—filled the room as the door closed behind me.

Maeve sat up in bed, her hands folded on her chest, her gaze on me.

"Maeve," I said as I sat next to her. "It's me, Kara."

"As if I wouldn't be knowing who you are." Her Irish accent was as soft as mist.

"I'm so glad you're awake. You scared me, you know?"

She smiled. "Well now, it wasn't exactly on purpose, aye?"

I lifted the angel. "Look what I found."

"Oh, my. Oh, my. How did you get the wing on there?"

"It's a new angel . . . the match for the other."

Her eyes filled with tears. "What a miracle."

"That is exactly what I said." I placed the angel on her bedside table.

"Did you come here to show it to me?"

"Yes. I thought it might help you wake up, but here you are already awake. I also brought this." I held up the postcard. "I know they couldn't bring your oil painting from Verandah House . . . and I thought this might be something you'd like." I handed the postcard to her.

She held it up; a single tear fell from her eye. "This is where he returned, right there—at the edge of the sea in one of those boats. Three brown sails."

My fear that Caitlin's words were correct, that there wasn't much time, filled me with the urgent need to know why Maeve had told me this legend. "Maeve, may I ask you a question?"

"Anything, dear. There isn't much I haven't told you."

"Why did you tell me that myth about Richard Joyce? Why did you pretend it was your story?"

"It was my story, child."

I sighed. "Caitlin told me it was the legend of the Claddagh ring. She told me it has been a favorite story of yours for your entire life."

"It has been my favorite story, but that doesn't mean it isn't the truth."

"But it wasn't true, it didn't happen to you."

"Kara, my dear child, all good stories hold truth whether they are true or not. This time, though, everything I told was my story. Mine has a different ending than the legend. I didn't wait for Richard. When he came back, when he returned from the far side of the sea, I was married to Sean Mahoney. It was too late for me. But Richard's love waited."

Her words took my breath away. An important truth awakened within that space. "And you wanted to change the ending to my story. You wanted me to wait."

Maeve stared at me with such clarity and brilliance in her gaze, I held my breath. "Kara, listen now. I wanted you to wonder how you would change your life if you knew he was coming back for you."

I released my held breath. "What?"

"Did you not hear me? I wanted you to wonder how you would change your life if you knew he was coming back for you. Would you fill your life with all you have now if you knew, really knew he'd return?"

I had no answer to this question—one I had never dared ask myself. What, if anything, would I change if I knew he'd come for me?

I closed my eyes, but Maeve's voice continued. "I never thought of this, I just merely believed that he was gone. I believed he would never return, and so I filled my life with other people. I wanted to give you the chance to at least think about it, no matter what you decided.

298

"When you're old, you too will see and know things you do not know now. I saw myself in you. I am old. I saw your pain and I did what I've done my whole life—I told you a story. How this story works in you is how it was meant to work in you. The same story has a different meaning for and effect on each person—this story was yours."

"Do you wish you'd waited, Maeve, or gone off to find him?" I placed my hand on top of hers.

"Yes, I do. But I lived a full and beautiful life, Kara. No regrets, only a passing on of wisdom. But I believed he was gone. You think it is so different because you live here in this time, in this place, because I'm from the far side of the sea. But we are attached by the water between us. It is the same tide and moon, the same sea, love, fear, losing, and death. Love does not change with time. The love that fills us and empties us, that clips our wings so that we must decide whether to learn to fly after that. To love or to fear." Maeve squeezed my hand, belying the weakness in her face and body.

"Love," I said.

"I waited. I'd stand on the edge of the water while children played on the Big Grass, while the men fixed their nets. It was a terrible time in the village then— they were tearing down houses, building new and better ones. The young men had left for World War One. Some had come home, but many had died, and others had emigrated. I stood at the edges of the quay and waited for his hooker to return. Then they, my parents and the people of the village, told me to stop living in a dream, that he would never come, that he'd married and had children and lived in Scotland. They told me they'd learned this from his relatives in Connemara. I believed them.

"I finally married the boy from down the lane, the one my parents had chosen for me since birth—a descendant of the Claddagh kings. He was a good man and the right man for me and my family. I loved him in faithfulness that lasted through seven children and numerous grandchildren. A love that may not have been born of passion, but that endured nonetheless. But, Kara." She leaned forward. "Richard came back for me."

A free-fall feeling overcame me; I wanted to grab on to something to keep from descending into this truth—he came back and she hadn't waited.

"He came back." Maeve's expression became placid as the morning sea. "It was in August during the Blessing of the Bay." She looked back at me now, but somehow seemed to be still there, in Claddagh at the bay. "Someday you must go . . . you must go see the Blessing of the Bay. It is the most magical, beautiful event you will witness beyond marriage or baptism. It marks the beginning of herring season. The altar boys and choir flow down from St. Mary's on the Hill. Oh, Kara, they ring the bell and the boats form a grand circle. The priest reads from St. John—you know the story, about the Sea of Galilee, when the apostles cast their nets on the right side of the ship. Then all of creation is called upon, from angels to the fish, to give glory to God. We sing and pray."

Tears fell unguarded down her face. "Then a single hooker comes from 'round the bend of the quay. My body understands long before my mind does. I tremble when I see the brown sails; my limbs are weak, my heart races. I grab to my two babies, hold tight to them, believing my body is telling me to fear what comes. But it isn't fear—it is an overwhelming knowing that the waiting has ended—but wrongly. So wrongly. All I believed of my own decisions fades into a vast uncertain place of unbelief. I hope you never understand what it is to know that all you believed is wrong—sorely wrong."

"Was it him?" I asked, already knowing the answer.

She nodded. "Yes. He came during the Blessing of the Bay. He hadn't come before because he'd been warned that if he returned to Ireland, he would be killed in retaliation for what his family did in the Easter Rising. But he came back . . . for me. He'd been living in Scotland with relatives; he'd been at the other edge of the sea. But it was too late . . . too late."

Maeve turned away, then back to me. "He came back and I was married, with two babies. I struggled with a heart full of such grief I could barely move; I was weighed down with the knowledge that I hadn't waited for this man, that I'd believed the lies, that I hadn't had faith in him.

"In Claddagh there is no such thing as divorce. The battle that waged inside my heart was fiercer than the storm that came months later."

"Storm?" I leaned forward.

"Child, you're always trying to jump ahead. Just listen. Finally he begged me to see him; he slipped me a letter on the Big Grass during an afternoon festival. The note contained a W. B. Yeats poem called 'Where My Books Go.'" She stared off and recited the poem.

All the words that I utter
And all the words that I write
Must spread out their wings untiring
And never rest in their flight
Till they come to where your sad, sad heart is,
And sing to you in the night,
Beyond where the waters are moving,
Storm darkened or starry bright.

Maeve looked at me. "I will not tell you the rest of his words—they are mine to hold close."

"That is the most beautiful poem I've ever heard . . . I would've run to him . . . run," I said.

"For two months I struggled with my heart, with my reason—until I decided I'd meet him the next evening. He lived in Connemara, up the coast, with relatives. The Blessing of the Bay was in August—it was now October when I agreed to meet him. And what happened next, what happened that night was my doing because I was intent on betraying my family, my name, my honor."

"What happened next?"

"It was October, 1927. He had left the village and waited for me to respond, waited for me to meet him. Above all, he was a fisherman and needed to be in a city with a port, with fishing boats. The night before I was to leave to meet him, with the pitiful excuse of shopping in Connemara, a terrible storm arose. Our Claddagh men were out fishing in the night, in this storm, on the *TrueLight*—one of the remaining hookers." She stopped, closed her eyes.

"You don't have to finish if this . . . hurts," I said.

"Oh, child." She opened her eyes. "I must. I have never spoken these words until now and I must."

I nodded.

"It is called the Cleggan Bay Disaster. Forty-four men lose their lives when the storm hits our coast without warning. All night long the storm rages around our village, our bay and up and down the coast. All the wives whose husbands are on the *True-Light* huddle together. We pray and mourn what we believe is the inevitable—the loss of our husbands to the sea.

"It is there, on that night, in the darkness of the storm, in the fear, that I make a decision. I walk out to the dock above the quay and lift my face to the storm. I hold my hands out, offer my own life if it will not take my husband, the father of my children, into this night, into darkness and mourning. I am selfish, mortally selfish, and am willing to take leave if Sean will live, if his children can have their da.

"But the storm doesn't take me. Rain pelts me with

its stinging reminder of my own greedy needs. I lay on the dock, flat and cold, and I hear the Spirit again—the same as the day in the Industrial School—say, *'Is this the woman you want to be? Running off with another man? Is this who you want to be?'*

"And I know that is not the woman I want to be. I rage at the storm, at the wind and rain, and promise I will not run hard after Richard, that I will stay if the winds will cease.

"The storm settles then, calm and still like it is holding its raging breath. But I do not move; I stay flat on the dock, waiting for the news of my husband's death, which will be my own fault for the evil I was planning the next day."

"This is so . . . sad," I said. "My heart is breaking—"

"No. The *TrueLight* survived that night—another story entirely. Sean found me on that dock, and when I fell into his arms, I did not leave them again. Ever."

"What happened to Richard?"

"I don't know."

Chills ran down my arm, across my body. "You never heard from him or about him again?"

"No. I mourned him as if he were dead, and from that moment on went forward in my life. I chose to be the woman I was meant to be, regardless of who I was with. But I never found out what happened to Richard—when I didn't come, where did he go, what did he do? Did it break his heart beyond repair or did he move on with his life? I do not know any of this."

"The Industrial Schools . . . you devoted yourself to making them better?"

"That was my memorial to Richard."

A tear ran down my face; I wiped it away.

"Now, no crying," Maeve said. "I've only told you this story of mine because I needed to tell it. All that remains of him is our story, and his spirit out there beyond the moving waters in Yeats's poem. Your reason will understand this story on one level, your spirit will understand it on another . . . and you must understand both. All of our lives we must choose between what others define us to be and who we were meant to be, but this struggle is not a safeguard from sorrow. I believed my parents—believed in who they said I was and who they said I should marry. But I wish I had the chance to choose otherwise, before it was too late. But it is not too late for you. Base your choices on what you believe, on who you truly are."

"So, your story's true?"

"It is my last story. And it is fully my story, Kara. This time—it is mine."

"You asked me to find him."

"I was not free to ask this until Sean was gone. My precious husband died two years ago, and I have only now allowed the thought to enter about what finally happened to Richard, where he went, who he became."

Her hand loosened in mine, her eyes closed, and she faded to a place far away—perhaps to where sailboats dance on an ancient sea.

Caitlin entered the room, patted my shoulder. "Did you have a nice visit?"

"Yes. . . ." I stood. "She's asleep now. I'll let the family be alone with her. Do you promise to call if there's any change?"

She nodded. "Of course."

I stood in the hallway for the longest time, the second hand ticking above me on the hospital clock. She had told me the truth, round and full as she knew it.

The County Library research room smelled of old books, paper and mildew. I crouched over the computer I'd been staring at for hours, attempting to search old articles and lists from Ireland in 1927—the last year Maeve saw Richard. The librarian had gone to look for a book she thought she had about the Connemara area in the 1920s. I'd worked my way through years of articles and lists and come up empty-handed.

I possessed a desperate need to find this man for Maeve; she had changed my life, opened my eyes to wisdom only Mama could've passed on to me. I wanted, needed, to do something for her. I leaned back in the chair, rubbed at my eyes.

The librarian tapped me on the shoulder; I looked up to her.

"I found this old book." She handed me a book entitled *The Cleggan Bay Disaster* by Marie Feeney. "I'd ordered it for a school child doing a report—and completely forgotten about it."

I held the book between my hands, nodded at the librarian and thanked her. This book wasn't what I needed—I already knew about the storm. My eyes ached from staring at the screen; I picked up the book and flipped through the pages. My breath paused as my eyes skimmed to a list of the dead on the ships of Cleggan Bay. Richard O'Leary—born 1908, died 1927.

There he was listed: a real man with a real story. He was among the presumed dead fishermen who had gone out that terrible night in October, 1927.

I checked out the book, drove home and dropped into a chair in the study to read about the wives that had held their holy medals while praying, crying out for their loves ones, "Oh God who walked the waters once, bring them safely home." Maeve's true love had died the night she had decided not to run hard after him, not to leave her life for him.

My tears came with the knowledge and the sorrow: her story and sadness were true.

I don't know how long I sat curled in that chair, how long I mourned for Maeve, for Richard. It was Deirdre's face I finally saw when I looked up. She stood in the doorway with Bill.

"Kara." She ran toward me. "Are you okay? Is Daddy . . . is everything . . ."

I wiped at my face and stood. "I'm fine . . . really." I tried to smile. "I was just reading an old book. . . ." I glanced at Bill, at Deirdre. "What are you two doing tonight?"

Deirdre smiled, but her face was pale, drained. "We came to . . . well . . ."

"Thank you," Bill said, and stepped forward.

"For what, William Garner Barrett the Fourth?"

He laughed, slapped his leg. "For——"

Deirdre interrupted, "For helping me to—go to him, try and work this out, because I truly do love him, adore him."

"I helped?"

She nodded. "You did." She touched Bill's arm. "Can I talk to her for a minute?" He nodded and walked toward the kitchen. "I mean it, Kara. I want to thank you. It will be a long, long road we have to get down—but I refuse to shut myself off from one more piece of life."

"What made you decide to go to him . . . to try?"

"Your story about the turtles. . . ." Her voice choked and she turned away. "Your story."

When I returned to the hospital in the morning, the hush surrounding Maeve's room was ominous. I knocked on the door; Seamus opened it and came into the hall.

"She's resting now," he said, and wiped at his red face. "It has been a very long night."

"Can I just see her for one minute? That's all I need," I said, "one minute."

He squinted at me. "It's important?" His hair stuck up at odd angles; his wrinkled shirt was buttoned one button off.

"Very," I said.

He opened the door, escorted me in. The room was empty of other family members. "Where is everyone?" I asked.

"They all went home to shower, shave . . . . I'll leave you alone, but it can only be for a few minutes. She must rest."

I nodded. "I know."

Seamus closed the door behind him, and I sat next to Maeve. I leaned close to her face. "Maeve, it's me, Kara."

"Hmmm," she said, but didn't open her eyes.

"I found him." My words caught in a withheld sob.

She opened her eyes and stared at me with the clarity of a younger woman. "You found him?"

"Yes, Maeve. He is real."

"Of course he is. Did you ever believe otherwise?"

"Yes, I believed otherwise. I did. I loved the story and the sweetness of it, but I didn't believe. . . . I do now."

"You must not need proof to believe."

"I know that now; I know. I should have believed all along—and deep down I did, I was just afraid to believe."

"Don't be. . . ."

"I am telling you, Maeve, because on the day I met you, you asked me to find him. I will never be able to thank you adequately for all you've given to me, for all you've taught me, but I can grant you that wish to know what happened to him."

"And?"

"He died the same night you lay on the dock waiting for your husband, the night you vowed not to run after him, not to abandon your life for him. He was on one of the fishing boats out of Connemara; he died in the Cleggan Bay Disaster. You didn't know this? You never saw the list?"

"No, I never tried to find him and I never . . . knew all those who died that terrible night." She sighed. "He died; I lived." A tear rolled down her thin face. "My heart is full now, Kara. Full."

She closed her eyes and released my hand as her son, Seamus, walked in the room.

CHAPTER TWENTY-THREE

Sleep flirted with the corners of my consciousness, but would not fully come to me. I finally rose from my bed at four in the morning, then walked over the lawn of our home to the footbridge where Jack had professed his love. I sat, swung my legs below me, and leaned into the railings, into the dark.

Maeve was gone now, had been for a month. Something in me believed Mama had met her and thanked her. Maeve's family had told me that in her will she'd requested that her ashes be spread over the waves during the Blessing of the Bay this coming August. They'd held a memorial service in Ireland the week she died, yet they were waiting until August to put her to rest in Galway Bay. They explained to me that she'd made this request because her husband was a descendant of the Claddagh kings who had led the blessing every year. But I knew the real reason and held it close to my heart.

I'd filled out the application for photography school. I was still waiting to hear if I'd been accepted. Charlotte had held me like a life jacket through the storm of these past few weeks of canceling the wedding, facing those who disagreed with me. She knew my decision was not about choosing between two men, but about who I was meant to be. She had held my hand, listened to me cry. But she could not take the burden of my own thoughts away from me.

I lay flat on my back, staring up at a moon that would be full in one more night; it billowed above me like a dented pillow. I closed my eyes and slipped into the darkness of my own thoughts. If Maeve's story was true, was everything else she told me also true?

The lessons she'd taught were priceless, worth more than the engagement ring I'd given up, more than my job's salary or the wedding dress now wrapped in plastic.

With the sun still below the horizon, I decided I would write down Maeve's lessons, compile them for those who would never hear her wisdom. I listed them in my mind: directives about my feet leading me to my heart, about how our lives and stories are connected, about how family expectations influence what we believe, and who we love.

My eyes flew open at a sudden realization about two of the lessons I had listened to but not deeply understood until this very moment: first, that I must be careful what I believe because it defines who I am; and second, that I ache for the time when I was most loved.

I jumped to my feet and stared at the sky, where the moon descended below my sight. I twisted around. The sun began to rise in a crescendo, the edges of the clouds taking on color. My heart lifted.

If the ache inside me came from remembering the time I felt most loved, then why did I not feel the ache when I was with Jack?

Light broke from the horizon, consuming the edges of water with fire.

Would I fill my life with the things I had now if I knew he would come back for me? He *had* come back for me and I stood there—alone at the water's edge.

The answer rose with the sun: it wasn't that I couldn't love enough, I just couldn't love Peyton enough. It was with Jack that I was the most loved and that I loved the most. If I had loved anyone else, it was only because he reminded me of Jack.

The faith I'd had in Peyton, and in the life we would have together, had everything to do with what I felt I was *supposed* to do to diminish my yearning for something else. But the belief I had now—that I wanted to go to photography school, and I loved Jack—came with no guarantees, had no promised happy ending. I could no longer fill my life with busy-ness, with meaningless noise in a meager attempt to soothe my heart with cheap substitutes.

I ran home at the start of that new day, at the start of my own story.

I drove my car with the pure exhilaration of doing the very thing I most desired—running hard after love, after Jack. The Unknown Souls were performing at a concert outside Charleston at the Bay Side Amphitheater.

Scalpers stood on the outskirts of the outdoor amphitheater. Cars were parked at odd angles; couples dragged coolers and wine bottles, heading for the concert. The bowl-shaped amphitheater had flip-down seats toward the front, a wide lawn in the back spread with colorful blankets.

Twenty minutes of haggling later, after I'd just paid five times the usual price for a seat on the back lawn with the bay beyond, I entered the amphitheater and moved toward the stage, where those with better tickets sat at tables covered in white cloths and flick-ering candles, catered food spread between the china settings.

A warm breeze blew; sailboats, motor boats, and trawlers bobbed at anchor. I reached the bottom steps, where a man in a blue uniform held up his hand. "Ticket."

I handed him my stub; he shook his head. "Ma'am, this is for the back lawn." He waved toward the crowded grassy area in the rear of the theater.

"I can't see from the back lawn."

He laughed. "You got a good view of the bay from there, though."

My shoulders sank. "I know. I just need to talk to the opening band. I'm friends with them and I need to talk to someone."

"Sure you are," he said, and smiled.

"Really . . . can you go tell them I'm out here or something? Can I get a message to Jack Sullivan?"

"Is it an emergency?" He tilted his head toward me, his hat over his eyes.

"Absolutely. Most definitely an emergency . . ."

He laughed. "Okay. What's the message? I'll try and get it back to him."

"Tell Jack that Kara is out on the back lawn. . . ."

"That's the emergency?"

"Well, yes." I shuffled back and forth, wanting to grab one of the wine bottles off the table in front of me.

I nodded. "Please. He'll understand."

"I'll try. Now go on." He waved toward the back lawn. I moved to the grass at the far right side and sat on a patch of moist soil. I hadn't brought a thing with me; two hours from home without a bag, a blanket, or a plan.

I'd said things to Jack that I hadn't meant—words motivated by fear. Now it was time to say the true things; but what if he didn't want to hear them? What if. . . .

The band walked onstage. Jimmy grabbed the microphone. "Hello, Charleston."

Some cheered. Others ignored the opening act and went on with the business of opening their catered dinners and jabbing corkscrews in their wine bottles. Then the guitars started and the Unknown Souls began to sing; the crowd hushed, stopped their activity. The haunting sounds filled the theater.

I drew my knees up and leaned against the stone wall behind me. *Come find me, Jack. Come find me, please.*

Five songs into their set, Jimmy said into the microphone, "Okay, Charleston, we're gonna try a new song for y'all. My bro Jack Sullivan wrote this one. It's called 'Looking for the Reasons.' I hope you enjoy it—I think it is the best of our original songs. Oh, the angst of true love, ay?"

The crowd cheered. I held my breath; my legs went weak. The words Jack said to me on the footbridge, words I'd listened to but not truly heard, came through my heart now.

The flute started the song in a melody so other-worldly I could believe angels played an instrument that man had not yet invented.

My heart opened wider than I believed possible as the first words flowed to the back lawn.

Beneath the moonlight
At the edge of the sea
Where love feels like a simple thing

I find my need

The dreams return
The hearts still burns

Beneath the moonlight
At the edge of the sea
I look for the reasons
You returned to me

The dreams return
The hearts still burn

The chorus came next—a chorus about looking for the reasons—with an added guitar and piano; Jimmy's voice was deep and resonant with the want that now whispered like wings against my body.

I'm looking for the reasons, looking deep and wide.
I'm looking for the reasons that you've come into my life.

He sang of loving and knowing at the edge of the sea, of loving and losing in that meeting place. Jack's words in Jimmy's voice combined with Maeve's story until I stood, and wondered if Jack had found the reasons.

After a lingering flute solo, Jimmy sang the final words. "The reasons have only to do with love. Only love."

The crowd went wild; I clapped so hard my palms stung. I know the audience cheered for Jimmy's deep, lush voice singing with the haunting melody, but I rejoiced at the words, the lyrics of a man who still believed.

I glanced down at the stage; the band gave way for the main act. Jack came out, glanced into the audience, squinted and raised his hand over his eyes. I waved frantically in a futile attempt to make him see me all the way in the back row against the stone wall. He jumped off the stage, wound his way among the tables to the left of the theater—opposite from where I stood.

I pushed my way through the crowd to the other side of the stage. "Excuse me, excuse me. . . ." I kept my eyes on Jack, knocking over coolers, beer bottles, chicken salad on paper plates as I hurried toward him.

Then he looked up, and saw me. A smile so wide and accepting spread across his face. His strides were long, deliberate as he stepped over blankets, between people. He reached me at the back right side at the last row of chairs; I ran into his open arms, buried my head against his chest. "Jack, I love you."

He lifted my chin, placed his palms on either side of my face and drew me to him. He kissed me as I'd dreamed of since that first realization of love beyond family. The kind of kiss I'd wanted and needed all my life; a kiss filled with truth.

Then he pulled back from me, smiled again, and I touched his face. "I'm sorry about what I said, I'm sorry for being such an idiot," I said.

He shook his head. "No apologies. You're here."

"If I ever thought I loved anyone else, it was only because he reminded me of you."

He threw his head back and laughed. "My beautiful Kara—you know exactly what to say to make a man weak, doncha?" He picked me up, swung me around, then kissed me again.

"Do I?" I looked out over the amphitheater to the bay and almost swore I saw three brown sails, a sloped boat coming around the bend.

He nodded, then touched my face as the lead singer began to sing behind us: "I get weak in the knees, and I lose my breath. . . ."

Jack grabbed my hand and pulled me toward the side stage. "Follow me."

"Always," I said, and did.

Center Point Publishing
600 Brooks Road ● PO Box 1
Thorndike ME 04986-0001 USA

(207) 568-3717

US & Canada:
1 800 929-9108